"I need to protect my daughters."

Ross looked at Juliet in disbelief. "You think I'd hurt them?"

"Not intentionally. But I can't take any chances on them getting attached to someone who is only a transitory father figure."

"Is that how you see me?"

"You're a man who's used to coming and going as he pleases with no family ties, no responsibilities. Am I supposed to let my children get attached to a drifter?" She knew the minute the words left her lips she had made a mistake.

Ross reached inside his pocket and pulled out her house key. "And here I thought you had given me this as a sign of yor trust." He tossed the key onto the table.

"I didn't mean it the way it sounded. I know you're not a drifter."

He shrugged away from her outstretched hand and turned to leave. "The sad part is, you don't know me at all."

ABOUT THE AUTHOR

Award-winning author Pamela Bauer always wanted to do a story about mothers and daughters, since she has seen this very special relationship from both sides of the coin. The material she gathered and the feelings she wanted to explore were too diverse for a single book, and the result was a trilogy of stories about the Osborne family, of which *On Cloud Nine* is the second. Look for the final instalment in February.

Pam and her husband, Gerr, make their home in Minnesota—the setting for the trilogy—with their two children, Amy, fifteen and Aaron, twelve.

Books by Pamela Bauer

HARLEQUIN SUPERROMANCE

236—HALFWAY TO HEAVEN
288—HIS AND HERS
330—WALKING ON SUNSHINE
378—THE HONEY TRAP
406—MEMORIES
481—SEVENTH HEAVEN

Don't miss any of our special offers. Write to us at the following address for information on our newest releases.

Harlequin Reader Service
P.O. Box 1397, Buffalo, NY 14240
Canadian address: P.O. Box 603,
Fort Erie, Ont. L2A 5X3

On Cloud Nine

PAMELA BAUER

Harlequin Books

TORONTO • NEW YORK • LONDON
AMSTERDAM • PARIS • SYDNEY • HAMBURG
STOCKHOLM • ATHENS • TOKYO • MILAN

Published January 1992

ISBN 0-373-70484-4

ON CLOUD NINE

PROLOGUE

"WHY DOES GRANDMA look like she's gonna cry?" six-year-old Sara Harper asked close to her mother's ear. "Doesn't she want to get married?"

"Of course she does. She's just happy, that's all." Juliet Harper's answer was whisper soft.

Sara frowned. "But if she's happy, why isn't she smiling?"

"Because sometimes people cry when they're too happy to smile," Juliet told her, swallowing back the lump in her own throat as she listened to her mother shakily recite her wedding vows. "Now, shush!"

Everyone was happy. Kate and Donovan's wedding had been lovely, and as the small gathering of friends and relatives filtered from the pews to bestow their best wishes and congratulations on the newlyweds, Kate's three daughters looked on affectionately.

"Which one of you is going to be next?" seventy-eight-year-old Frances Binstead asked as she joined her granddaughters in the back of the church.

"I think two weddings in one year is enough for this family," Meridee Osborne answered, giving her grandmother's hand a tender squeeze.

Frances dismissed her comments with a harrumph. "Don't you know that good things come in threes? First there was my wedding, then your mother's." She wagged a slightly gnarled finger in the air. "Mark my words. One of you girls will be next . . . and it'll be soon."

All three sisters exchanged wary glances.

"It won't be me. I'm still a little kid," Brenda stated with an exaggerated innocence, a statement that was a contradiction to the skimpy black velvet dress she was wearing.

"Yes, which is why I'm moving into Mom's house to take care of her," Juliet added, putting a protective arm around her sister's shoulder. "And I'm afraid, Gran, that with Brenda and my own two girls to watch over, there'll be no time for romance for me." Both Brenda and Juliet looked at Meridee, who immediately held up her hands defensively.

"Oh, no! Don't look at me!" she protested.

"Maybe all three of you will get married," Gran said on a hopeful note, her eyes widening at the thought. "You could have a triple wedding. Wouldn't that be fun?"

All three sisters burst out laughing.

"Oh, Gran, you are a hopeless romantic, but we love you dearly," Meridee said, embracing her grandmother in a hug. "That's a pretty tall order."

Frances simply smiled smugly and said, "We'll see."

CHAPTER ONE

"DO YOU THINK this year you could bring the pumpkin pies instead of the mints and nuts?" Juliet Harper asked her sister as she sat at the kitchen table with cookbooks and recipe cards spread out in front of her.

"You know I don't bake." Meridee Osborne laughed sardonically. "I don't even own a rolling pin. Isn't there something else I could bring...like a jar of pickles or olives or something?"

"Meridee, I need help with preparing dinner—not with grocery shopping." Juliet raised her eyes as if appealing to the powers that be and gently shook her head. "You're twenty-eight. Isn't it about time you learned how to cook?"

"I know how to cook," Meridee protested indignantly, folding her arms across her chest. "It's just that I don't have the time to be putzing around baking. If you want me to be responsible for the pies, I'll pick them up at the pie shop. That'll save time for both of us."

"You want to *buy* the pies?" Juliet's lip curled in distaste.

"And what's wrong with that? Granted, they might not taste as good as Mom's, but they are good, Juliet. And since neither of us has the time to make two pumpkin pies from scratch, I think it's our only alternative...unless you want to ask Gran to make them."

Juliet shook her auburn head. "She's already making dinner rolls. I'll just have to make them myself," she said with a sigh of defeat.

"Don't be silly. Between working, taking classes at the university and raising two children, when are you going to find time to bake pies? At midnight?"

"But I want this Thanksgiving dinner to be just like the ones Mom always has."

"That's a great idea, but you simply don't have the time to make everything from scratch the way she does," Meridee stated in her usual down-to-earth tone of voice.

Juliet leaned back in her chair and sighed for the second time. "I suppose you're right." She tossed her pencil onto the table and watched it roll to one side. "I guess I should just accept the fact that it's not going to taste as good as it would if Mom were cooking."

Meridee patted her hand. "It's going to taste great. You're a wonderful cook—just like Mom."

Juliet forced herself to smile, then got up to fill her empty cup with coffee. "I still can't believe she's not going to be here. Do you realize this is the first Thanksgiving she hasn't spent in this house since before you were born?" She looked about the kitchen of the home that had been in the Osborne family for the past twenty-nine years. "I never thought I'd see the day when she'd miss a family holiday like Thanksgiving."

"What did you expect her to do? Cut short her honeymoon so she could cook a turkey for us?" Meridee stared at her through her large square-framed glasses.

"Of course not!" Juliet replied, ignoring the tiny voice saying that on more than one occasion she had wished just that. "But this is our family home, and it's going to seem strange without Mom sitting at the head of the dining-room table."

"Even if she were here, she probably wouldn't have Thanksgiving dinner in this house, Jules," Meridee told her, pushing back the strands of short blond hair that had fallen over her forehead. "She's making her home with Donovan now. Any entertaining she does will be there."

Juliet pondered the statement for several moments. She had known that her mother's marriage was going to bring changes to the family, but she hadn't even considered the possibility that family gatherings would be anywhere but this big old Victorian house.

"Well, I guess it doesn't matter. As long as Brenda and I are living here, it'll always feel like our family home to me," she said with more conviction than she was feeling. "And this year, Thanksgiving is my responsibility."

Meridee cocked her head. "Maybe we should dine out."

Juliet frowned. "You want to eat out on Thanksgiving Day?"

"Why not? Lots of restaurants offer special buffets, and just think of all the work it would save you."

"But it wouldn't be Thanksgiving if we ate out," Juliet declared firmly.

"Why wouldn't it?"

Juliet shot her a look of disbelief. "Only you would ask a question like that. Where is your holiday spirit? On the soles of your feet?"

"Aw, come on, Juliet. Just because I suggest eating out on Thanksgiving doesn't make me Scrooge!"

"Thanksgiving is families coming home to the smell of turkey roasting in the oven and freshly baked pies. It's tables set with china and crystal that have been in our family for years," Juliet said wistfully. "It just wouldn't be the same if we ate out. Besides, there wouldn't be any leftovers."

"Not true. I heard there's a restaurant in St. Paul where you can have a turkey carved right at your table. Then afterward they wrap up the leftovers and you take them home."

"No." Juliet shook her head vehemently. "Holidays should be celebrated rituals. Eating in a restaurant is not a ritual and it's not special."

"How do you know it wouldn't be special if you've never tried it?" Meridee argued.

"I did try it. Have you forgotten that my ex-husband dragged me off to California the first year we were married so we could spend Thanksgiving with his parents? It was awful. Their idea of tradition was dining at some exclusive restaurant, then attending the theater. I knew then that I wanted my children to have the kind of Thanksgiving we've always shared...with our family gathered around the big oak table in our dining room, passing on memories...creating new ones."

"All right, all right." Meridee raised her hands in surrender. "We won't break tradition. I suppose if we have to subject ourselves to Gran's 'Why aren't you married?' inquisition, we're better off in the comfort of familiar surroundings."

"Does that mean you're not bringing Richard to dinner?"

She shook her head. "He decided to spend the holiday skiing in Colorado. It'll just be me and Vanna."

"Vanna?" Juliet wrinkled her nose. "You're not really going to bring a dog to dinner?"

"She's more loyal than a man, that's for sure." Seeing the disapproval on her sister's face, she added, "But if you'd rather I didn't bring her..." she trailed off, feigning wounded feelings.

Juliet chose to ignore her ploy for sympathy. "I've got nothing against pets, Meridee, but it really would be easier for me if you left her at home."

"Say no more." Meridee raised a palm defensively. "Now, tell me. Do you have a date for the holiday?"

"Good grief, no," Juliet said soberly. "There's no one I want to invite, which means Gran's going to be doing her number on both of us again." She sighed. "Maybe we could hire men to be our dates...a couple of clean-cut, articulate types who would be sure to pass the Wally Cleaver test."

It was a long-standing joke among the Osborne sisters that their grandmother subjected every one of their dates to a scrutiny they had dubbed the Wally Cleaver test. If a young man were to meet their grandmother's standards, he needed to be someone as squeaky clean as Wally Cleaver, with a well-groomed head of hair, neat, conservative clothing, and a "yes, sir" and "yes, ma'am" manner of addressing his elders.

"I wonder if I'm growing immune to Gran's inquisition," Meridee mused. "Somehow the thought of spending the holiday listening to Gran ramble on about how someday my Prince Charming will magically appear is less frightening than risking being bored into unconsciousness by an unwanted date."

"Speaking of Prince Charming, Brenda claims to have found one," Juliet announced over the rim of her cup.

Meridee sprang forward. "Not that guy with the purple streak down the side of his head?"

"You mean the punk philosopher? No, supposedly he was only tutoring her in Aristotle and Plato and she had no interest in him romantically."

"Thank goodness," Meridee said with a sigh of relief.

"However, I think this Ross character is a different story," Juliet said warily. "He's from her theater arts class."

"An aspiring actor?" Meridee lifted one eyebrow.

"Among other things," Juliet answered dryly. "According to Brenda, he can do just about anything. Last summer he played Prince Charming in a traveling production of *Snow White*."

"Oh, then he really *is* a Prince Charming, eh? Does this mean he's good-looking, talented and stuck on himself?" Meridee asked cynically.

Juliet shrugged. "I haven't met him, but Brenda assured me he doesn't dye, sculpt or braid his hair, and—" she paused as she reached for a cookie and took a bite "—he wears socks."

"That ought to please Gran. Remember the look on her face when Brenda brought that guy home who was all dressed up but wasn't wearing any socks with his loafers?"

Juliet took another sip of her coffee, then said, "Brenda's convinced that as long as this Ross doesn't wear his black leather pants, he'll even pass the Wally Cleaver test."

"Black leather pants?" Meridee groaned. "And she thinks Gran will like him?"

"She thinks we are *all* going to be captivated by him, and she can't wait for us to meet him."

Meridee grimaced. "Does this mean he's coming for Thanksgiving dinner?"

"She's invited him, but apparently he hasn't given her a definite answer. I thought maybe he'd be going home for the long weekend, but apparently he has no family to go home to."

"An orphan who can pass the Wally Cleaver test?" Meridee lifted both eyebrows. "He's going to have to do some pretty impressive stuff."

"For Brenda's sake, I hope he can. I'm afraid she's fallen for him in a big way."

"Then we'll just have to do our best to see that he fits in—black leather pants and all."

"Maybe we'd better hope he just shows up. Otherwise there'll be three of us in line for Gran's inquisition."

UNTIL A WHITE delivery truck dropped off a package on her front doorstep, Juliet didn't give much more thought to Brenda's boyfriend. She was too busy polishing silverware, waxing furniture and fussing with food to worry about whether her nineteen-year-old sister's heartthrob would show up at their dinner table on Thanksgiving Day.

But on Wednesday afternoon, while elbow-deep in mashed cranberries, Juliet received word that Ross Stafford was indeed planning to be a guest at their Thanksgiving feast. From one of the local florists came a centerpiece so lovely Juliet was a bit taken aback when she tore open the packaging. On the enclosure were the words, *Thank you for including me in your holiday plans. Ross Stafford.*

It was not the kind of floral arrangement she would have expected from any of the boys Brenda had dated in the past. A mixture of chrysanthemums and tiger lilies, it was the perfect decoration for their holiday table. It also gave Juliet hope that Brenda's boyfriend might be a pleasant surprise. In her mind he was already an all-right kid—black leather or no black leather.

Juliet spent most of her day off in the kitchen, and after bathing Sara and two-year-old Annie and putting them to bed, she found herself once more returning to the familiar surroundings. She was at the sink scrubbing fresh vegetables when Brenda arrived at home.

"You're late. I thought you were going to help me with the cleaning." She gave her sister a cursory glance.

"I'm sorry, but I had to stay and work on my theater sets," Brenda explained, dumping her books onto the table.

"I don't suppose this Ross Stafford had to stay, too," Juliet commented dryly.

"Ross wasn't the reason I stayed, Juliet." Brenda's tone was defensive. "Besides, he was only there for a short time after class. He works nights."

"I hope it's a good job. The bouquet of flowers that came this afternoon must have set him back a pretty penny."

"He sent me flowers?" Brenda exclaimed excitedly, not bothering to wait for confirmation before disappearing from the room.

"They're on the dining-room table and they were addressed to me," Juliet called out as her sister's tiny figure raced past her, but she doubted whether Brenda heard.

When she reappeared, there was a wide grin on her face. "What a sweet guy! Aren't they the most gorgeous flowers you've ever seen? How come you didn't let me open them?"

"Because they were addressed to me," Juliet pointed out.

"Oh." The smile slipped from her face. "That must be why he asked me who was cooking dinner."

"It was a very nice gesture on his part."

"That's because he *is* nice." There was a dreamy, faraway look on Brenda's face. "Most of the guys I know are really fussy about their cars. None of them would let me borrow one, that's for sure."

"You borrowed his car?"

Brenda nodded. "His van. I had to. The theater department was throwing out this wonderful backdrop, and I wanted to bring it home for Sara and Annie to play with." She snatched a piece of raw cauliflower from under Juliet's nose and popped it into her mouth. "Wait until you see it. It'll be perfect for puppet shows."

Juliet peeked out the kitchen window and felt a wave of uneasiness at the sight of a vehicle that looked as though it could just as easily be used for sleeping as for hauling stage props around town. There were curtains on all but the front windows.

"Could you hold the door open for me while I try to muscle it inside?" Brenda asked.

Juliet wiped her hands on her apron and went to wait at the door for her sister, who bounced down the back steps, her long blond hair streaming down her back. When she saw the size of the piece of plywood Brenda was pulling out of the rear of the van, she stuck her head out the door.

"If you wait a minute, I'll slip my jacket on and help you."

"It's all right. I can get it," Brenda answered, hoisting the plywood over her shoulder. But in spite of her confidence, she was barely five feet tall and weighed less than ninety-five pounds and had trouble maneuvering the cumbersome stage set. Juliet was about to go for her jacket when she saw her sister stumble on the walk. With a yelp, Brenda dropped the plywood.

"I twisted my ankle," she cried out, hopping on one foot as Juliet rushed out to lend support. When Brenda attempted to step down on her right foot, she gasped in pain, grabbing onto her sister's shoulder.

"Lean on me. I'll help you inside," Juliet instructed, ushering her hobbling sister up the steps and into the house. As soon as Brenda was settled onto a wooden chair, she dropped down beside her to inspect her ankle. "Can you move it?"

"Yes, but it hurts really bad," she cried, gingerly removing her shoe. "What if I broke it?"

"Brenda, you didn't break it," Juliet stated calmly.

"How would you know? You're not a nurse!" she retorted.

"No, but I've had enough first-aid training to recognize a sprain." Juliet gently examined the ankle with her fingers. "It's starting to swell. I'd better get you a cold compress."

"Hurry," Brenda moaned. "It's killing me."

Juliet quickly soaked a towel in cold water, then carefully wrapped it around Brenda's bare ankle. "We'll leave that on for about twenty minutes, then we'll wrap it in an elastic bandage."

After several minutes of moaning and groaning, Brenda looked down at her foot and attempted to move it. "I don't think I'm going to be able to walk on it," she said apprehensively.

"Probably not for a while," Juliet agreed soberly. "I think Mom still has that old pair of crutches in the basement . . . those ones we used to play with when we were kids."

"I don't want crutches," Brenda whined. "Wouldn't you know it had to be my right foot, too. What if I can't drive?"

"Luckily it's Thanksgiving break and you won't have to."

"But I have to return Ross's van to him tonight!"

"Well, you can't," Juliet told her in no uncertain terms, returning her attention to the vegetables in the sink. "Not with your foot the size of a watermelon."

Brenda gingerly peeked under the cold compress. "Maybe the swelling will go down by the time Ross needs to be picked up."

"Brenda, you're not being realistic if you think you're going to be able to drive a car with your foot in that condition. For one thing, you won't be able to get your shoe back on."

"I can probably fit a slipper over it." She tried to stand, but immediately fell back onto the chair, her face twisting in pain as she attempted to put pressure on the sprained ankle.

Seeing her efforts, Juliet came back over and rewrapped the compress. "You can't do it, Brenda."

"I have to. Ross is expecting me."

"You'll have to call him and tell him what's happened. Maybe he can get someone to give him a ride over here to get the van."

"You don't understand!" Brenda cried, impatiently pushing back her long hair. "He only let me use it because I promised I'd return it to him before he got off work tonight. I can't just call him and tell him he has to figure out another way of getting home because I can't return his van."

"I don't see that you have any other choice," Juliet stated pragmatically.

Her sister sat quietly for several moments with her head in her hands before lifting her blue eyes appealingly. "Couldn't you take the van back for me?"

"Brenda! I have people coming for dinner tomorrow. Do you realize what I have to do tonight?"

"It would only take half an hour. And I can help you now that I'm home."

Juliet raised a skeptical eyebrow.

"Oh, please, Juliet. It's the only way I won't feel like a total idiot when he comes to dinner tomorrow."

Juliet exhaled in exasperation. "Where is this place he works at?"

"It's the White Wolf."

"You mean that jazz club in the warehouse district?" There was more than a hint of reproach in her voice. "Brenda, that's a bar."

"It's a nightclub, and lots of university students go there."

"Not underage ones—unless they have fake IDs." Juliet shot her sister a suspicious look. "What do you think Mom would say if she knew you were going to clubs like the White Wolf?"

Brenda covered her eyes with her fingers and grimaced. "Jules, I don't need a lecture."

"I think you do. It's not safe for a young woman to be driving through that part of the city at night alone."

"Does that mean you're not going to do it?" she squeaked in dismay. "Come on, Jules. Have a heart. Think of how I'm going to feel if I don't get the van returned tonight."

Brenda looked so distressed, Juliet found herself softening. "Oh, all right. I'll do it. But I'm not going to wait until after midnight." She untied the apron from around her waist and tossed it onto the counter.

Brenda glanced at the wall clock. "If you leave now, you'll probably get there during his break."

"What does he do—tend bar or bus dishes?" she asked, slipping on her loafers.

"He plays the saxophone."

"He plays the saxophone at the White Wolf?" Juliet repeated in disbelief. "I thought you said he was an actor."

"He is, but he's also a musician. I told you he played the sax."

"Yes, but I thought you meant in the marching band at the university." Uneasiness was settling in every nerve of her body.

"Ross is really talented, Juliet. Wait until you hear him play." Again the dreamy look was on Brenda's face. "It's magic, I swear."

The uneasiness had chosen its spot and had settled like a lump of dough in Juliet's stomach. "How will I know who he is? Do you have a picture of him?"

"Uh-uh, but you won't have trouble finding him. There's only one sax player in the band and he's gor-

geous. He has dark hair and there's this one hunk that
sort of hangs over one eye. You can't miss him."

"We'll see." Juliet carried the cutting board and the
raw vegetables over to the table and plopped them
down in front of her sister. "Here. If I'm going to
subject myself to the White Wolf, you can at least cut
up the vegetables for me."

ALTHOUGH JULIET had heard rumors about the pop-
ularity of the White Wolf, she had never been inside
the nightclub, and she knew little about the kind of
people the club attracted. Her uneasiness intensified
as she drove through the dark and deserted warehouse district on the edge of downtown Minneapolis.
When she reached the bright lights of a recently renovated block of buildings that was now home to various nightclubs and restaurants, traffic came to a stop
as cars queued up to get into parking lots already
overflowing with vehicles. Juliet glanced toward the
White Wolf and saw a line of well-dressed people
standing out in the cold waiting to get inside.

Until this moment, she had given no thought as to
whether she had dressed appropriately. Suddenly she
was painfully aware that she was wearing jeans that
should have been in the ragbag, well-worn leather
loafers that had splashes of dye on them and a navy-
blue coat that had definitely seen better days.

Thinking there had to be an entrance for employees, Juliet drove around the corner and found an alley
behind the renovated building. Double-checking to
make sure the doors were locked, she slowly eased the
van across the cobblestones until she came to an entrance where a single white light bulb illuminated the
words The White Wolf. Leaving the van in one of the

reserved parking spots, she climbed the steps, only to discover the door was locked.

Noticing a round button on the brick casing, she impatiently jammed her finger against it. Within seconds, the door was opened by someone who looked like a professional wrestler—the bouncer, no doubt.

"I'm looking for Ross Stafford. I have his van," she told him.

The man, whose arms were as thick as her thighs, mumbled, "Oh, yeah," and stepped aside, waiting for Juliet to enter. "Just go down here and take a right," he told her, nodding toward a dimly lit hallway saturated with stale smoke. "Don't take a left or you'll end up in the kitchen."

Juliet thought about asking him to give Ross the keys, but he disappeared into a small room and shut the door. As she walked down the hallway, the music became louder, and when she finally stepped into the actual nightclub, she felt a moment of panic. Between the thick haze of smoke and the glare of bright lights, it was nearly impossible to see more than three feet in front of her. The club appeared to be filled to capacity, and there were no vacant spots at the tables on the tiered floor surrounding the stage. As her eyes adjusted to the spotlights, she followed their beams to where they spotlighted the men on stage.

There were six men on the raised platform, but it was the one standing up front who caught and held her attention. When Brenda had said Ross Stafford wore black leather, Juliet had pictured a young man on a motorcycle with scraggly long hair, a couple of tattoos and a few chains. She couldn't have been more mistaken. This man's hair was not unkempt, but was pulled back in a small ponytail. She doubted there would be any snakes tattooed on the firm biceps beneath the leather jacket. And he was not young—at least not as young as Brenda had led her to believe he was. Experience was written all over him.

He was, as her sister had told her, gorgeous, but his allure didn't lie in his appearance alone. The sound coming out of his saxophone was indeed magic. Giving a solo performance, he moved his body in time with the music as though he barely controlled all the passion that was pouring forth from the brass instrument. Although he stood at an angle, only partially facing the crowd, Juliet could see that the reason he held the audience rapt with his performance was because he played with such emotion.

It was no wonder Brenda was so taken with him, Juliet thought. Even she felt mesmerized by the man standing on center stage creating such enchantingly beautiful music—music that reached out and grabbed her soul. She felt attracted to him, as though he were communicating with her through his music. Each note seemed to float gently through the air in such a sensual manner that Juliet's pulse was teeter-tottering by the end of the song. The sound of the thunderous applause broke the spell, and she remembered why she was there.

As the applause died down, the bass player announced that the group was going to take a short break. Within minutes, the musicians set their instruments aside and stepped down from the stage. Juliet watched as the drummer and the trumpet player exited through the door she had come in a few minutes ago. She was about to intercept Ross Stafford's progress when she noticed a slinky-looking blonde in a skimpy red dress walk up to him, place her arm possessively around his waist and smile seductively.

He laughed, whispered something in her ear, then reluctantly released her fingers from around his waist. Even though he didn't kiss her, Juliet could tell by the way they looked at each other that they knew each other intimately.

As Ross turned away from the blonde, he noticed Juliet watching him. Taking a deep breath, she met his gaze and signaled to him with a wave of her fingers. He came directly toward her, and Juliet was soon face-to-face with the sexiest-looking man she had ever seen in her life.

CHAPTER TWO

FOR A MOMENT Juliet was taken aback by the face gazing into hers. Even the dark stubble shadowing Ross Stafford's jaw couldn't diminish his rugged good looks, and she felt a primitive stirring in places she'd rather not feel anything at all. Up on the stage he had looked taller than he really was, and she was surprised to find he didn't tower over her. He was slender, yet there was a feeling of strength about him that managed to intimidate her.

"Ross Stafford?" she finally uttered, annoyed with the way her body was reacting to his presence.

"You're looking at him," he answered, his eyes making a slow, roving study of her, a curious gleam in their brown depths. "What can I do for you?"

The way he was staring at her caused her to stammer nervously when she spoke. "I...I'm Juliet Harper...Brenda Osborne's sister."

"You're Brenda's big sister?" The sleepy dark eyes widened as they studied her from head to toe, and she wondered if he was mentally comparing the two of them. When she heard his next words, she knew that's exactly what he had been doing. "Yeah, I guess I can see the resemblance," he said, his eyes raking over her figure appreciatively, lingering on the red curls that had escaped the confines of her French braid. "I expected you to be older and..." He paused, grinning in a way Juliet could only describe as wickedly sexy, before saying, "much larger."

Larger? Juliet wondered just what Brenda had said about her. It was true that of the three Osborne sisters, Brenda was the petite one, but by no means were she and Meridee built like football players. After all, she was only five foot four, and even though she was the mother of two children and had filled out a bit, she was still a size seven.

When a rhythm-and-blues guitarist began to warm up on the stage, Ross bent closer to her and said, "Look, it's going to get noisy here. Why don't you come with me?" He didn't wait for her to agree, but placed a hand on her elbow and ushered her through the door.

He led her to a small room lined with acoustical tile that was empty except for a couple of molded plastic chairs and a music stand. When the door closed on the tiny cubicle, all background noises disappeared, and they were alone in a room lit with bright fluorescent lights. Instead of sitting on one of the chairs, Juliet remained standing near the door.

"I'm a little surprised to see you here," he said, fixing her with the kind of gaze that, had they been in a singles bar, she could have easily interpreted as a come-on.

She felt her face grow warm under his scrutiny. She wanted to look away from the piercing brown eyes that were as rich as dark chocolate and just about as tempting, but much to her annoyance, she found there was little else to focus on. The skin-hugging black leather made his body off-limits, and unless she wanted to stare at the floor, she had no choice but to look at his face.

"I brought back your van," she told him, her eyes following her hand's progress as she removed the keys from her pocket and offered them to Ross. When he inadvertently grazed her fingers, she nervously retreated a step and shoved both of her hands into her pockets. "Brenda would have come, but she twisted her ankle earlier this evening and she wasn't able to drive."

"Is she going to be all right?"

This time Juliet deliberately avoided meeting his eyes, not wanting to see what emotion was there. Men like Ross Stafford could eat little girls like Brenda for breakfast, she thought cynically, annoyed with him for having any kind of relationship with her sister.

"She'll be fine," she answered, her voice deliberately cool.

In contrast, his voice was warm and almost as silky-smooth as the notes that had flowed from his sax. "I'm glad to hear that." He jiggled the keys in his palm and said, "Thanks for returning the van."

The way his eyes were raking over her with such undisguised interest, she felt the need to put things on a more appropriate level. "I only came because Brenda said you needed it tonight."

He shrugged. "I could have picked it up tomorrow. At least this way we have the chance to meet before I show up for dinner at your place." He ran a hand over his chin. "You know, you don't look anything at all like I had imagined."

Again the wickedly sexy smile appeared, and there was no mistaking the flirtatious tone. Juliet was tempted to ask him what he had been expecting her to look like, but she knew the answer would be connected to Brenda. After all, Ross Stafford was Brenda's date for tomorrow, a thought she found very disturbing.

She contemplated saying, "Now that I've met you, I really don't think it's a good idea for you to come to dinner." She chewed on her lower lip as she debated whether she should interfere in Brenda's love life, but the idea was dismissed as quickly as it had been conceived. It would be a big mistake for her to say anything. What she didn't need was to have Thanksgiving spoiled because her younger sister was angry at her for uninviting her boyfriend.

Instead, she said, "I've got to go."

"Is someone waiting for you?"

"No, I'm going to take a cab."

"You don't need to take a cab. I'll drive you home," he offered, slipping an arm around her to reach for the door.

Juliet caught the faint aroma of alcohol and edged away from him. As the door swung open, the background noises of the nightclub intruded once more.

"Just give me a minute to let the other guys know and I'll be right back." Ross started to leave, but she stopped him.

"No...please. Don't. I...I'd rather take a cab."

When he saw the look on her face, his smile disappeared, as did some of the charm he had been sending her way. For a moment he looked as though he were going to argue with her, but then he said, "Why don't you tell Brenda not to worry about finishing her renderings this weekend. It won't matter if they're a few days late."

"Her renderings?" She gave him a quizzical look.

"Her assignment. It's due next Monday, but if she's had an accident..." He left the words dangling between them.

"I don't think her ankle will keep her from getting her homework completed," Juliet answered stiffly, resenting the fact that not only was he too old for Brenda, but he seemed to think he had the right to tell her what to do. The last person she wanted Brenda to be taking advice from was a man who looked as though he slept away his days and cruised the nightclub circuit at night.

He shrugged nonchalantly. "I can talk to her about it tomorrow."

The comment made her wonder just how much influence Ross Stafford had in her sister's life. Any influence would be too much, she thought soberly. Yet she really couldn't blame her sister for being attracted to him. Even she was reacting in a totally physical way to the charm he seemed to emanate simply by breathing. She needed to get away from him.

"I'd better go," she said, turning away from his penetrating gaze. She could feel his dark eyes following her as she walked past him, but she refused to look at him.

"See you tomorrow, Juliet."

"Good night," she said, trying not to frown. She didn't want him at their Thanksgiving celebration. He was exactly the kind of man she didn't like—too good-looking, too self-assured and altogether too potently male. But he was coming to dinner, and as uncomfortable as the thought was, Juliet had no choice but to accept it. She'd just have to treat him like one of her grandfather's friends. She'd pretend he was seventy-five and bald.

"HE'S HERE," Meridee announced, poking her head into the Osborne kitchen, where Juliet was basting a golden-brown turkey.

"Who?" she asked innocently, looking up from the stove.

"Brenda's guy. Aren't you going to come out and say hello?"

"Do I have to or can I plead that my hands are tied up with the bird?" she asked with a smart-aleck grin.

"I really think you should come see what he looks like." Meridee stepped into the kitchen, deliberately keeping her voice low. "He's yummy."

Juliet grimaced at her sister's choice of adjectives. "I already saw what he looks like, and personally I don't think 'yummy' is quite right," she drawled sarcastically, reaching for two quilted pot holders.

"How about delicious?" Meridee posed cheekily.

"Try dangerous." Juliet lifted the roaster back into the oven, closing the door with a bang.

Meridee chuckled. "Yeah, he's probably that, too. It's no wonder Brenda's gaga over him."

"Well, she *shouldn't* be gaga over him. He's too old for her."

"He looks about thirty." Meridee snatched an olive from the relish tray on the counter.

"It's not his age I'm referring to. He's been around . . . and more than once," she said dryly, remembering the blonde she had seen hanging all over him last night.

"He's never been married."

"He doesn't exactly look like the marrying kind, does he?" Juliet raised one eyebrow skeptically.

"Well, all I can say is, lucky Brenda. Of the three of us, she's the only one with a scrumptious-looking date."

"Would you stop talking about him as though he were dessert?" Juliet snapped irritably.

Meridee gave her sister a curious look. "Why are you so grumpy? The house looks great, it smells wonderful in here and we're on schedule."

Juliet sighed. "I'll just feel better once everything's on the table and we can sit down to eat."

"Do you need me to help with anything?"

"No, you go out and entertain Mr. Stafford," she answered.

"You really don't like him, do you?" Meridee tried to snatch another olive, and Juliet pulled the relish tray out of her reach.

"It's not a question of not liking him. He just isn't going to fit in with our family celebration."

"I think you're wrong about that. He's only been here fifteen minutes, and already Gran seems quite taken with him. She's blushing and giggling every time he looks her way."

"Gran likes him?" Juliet's eyes widened. "What about the ponytail?"

"His hair's a little long but there's no pony. Even if there were, I think Gran would overlook it. She's treating him as though he could be Prince Charming."

"If he's Prince Charming, then Madonna's Snow White," Juliet retorted.

Meridee laughed. "Okay, maybe he's a street version—but he's still charming. So, are you coming out to say hello or are you going to make some sort of grand entrance carrying the turkey into the dining room?''

Juliet nervously ran her hands across the front of her apron. Ever since she had left the White Wolf last night she had been dreading the moment she would have to see Ross Stafford again. In fact, she had thought of little else. Never before had she had such a physical reaction to a man, and the thought of him sitting in the living room was enough to push her heart up into her throat.

Taking a deep breath, she straightened her spine and marched through the swinging door, telling herself she would ignore her feelings for Ross Stafford. As soon as she saw him, however, she knew that one thing she would never be able to be where he was concerned was indifferent.

Although the man sitting between her grandmother and her sister hardly resembled the jazz club musician she had met last night, he was every bit as attractive. For one thing, all traces of dark stubble were gone, his face cleanly shaven. Instead of being tied back in a ponytail, his hair was slicked back, and the one errant lock was smoothed into place. And no skin-hugging black leather clung to his lean frame. Instead, he was dressed in a double-breasted gray suit with a pale pink shirt and a bold-patterned tie few men would have dared to wear.

When he saw Juliet approaching, he rose to his feet. The same sleepy dark eyes that had flirted with her last night sent a shiver of pleasure skittering through her as they met hers with a familiar gleam.

He may have different clothes, but he's the same man, Juliet thought. She swallowed with difficulty before extending her hand and saying, "Welcome to the Osborne Thanksgiving celebration."

His hand was warm in hers, and much to her surprise, there was something oddly reassuring about the way it felt. "It was kind of you to include me in your holiday dinner," he said smoothly, his eyes never wavering from hers.

She was the one who finally broke the eye contact as well as the handshake. "It's good to see you again, Ross," she said politely. "Thank you for sending the flowers. They're beautiful." She gestured toward the dining room, where the floral centerpiece graced the table.

Ross was still staring at her as she turned to speak to her grandmother. The entire time she was in the living room, she felt as though his eyes never left her face, and it was with great relief that she heard the stove's timer and excused herself to check on the dinner.

While the rest of the family enjoyed appetizers and wine, Juliet was content to hide in the kitchen. She didn't like Ross Stafford. She didn't want him dating her sister, she didn't want him sitting at their dining-room table sharing their dinner and she certainly didn't want him in her kitchen, which is where he showed up a short while later.

"I came to get some mineral water for your grandmother," he said as he strolled into the kitchen. Noticing that Juliet was in the process of mashing the potatoes, he said, "If you tell me where it is, I can get it."

"Right-hand side of the refrigerator, lower shelf. She likes a twist of lime, too." She set down the potato masher and pulled open a drawer filled with cutlery.

Ross found both the mineral water and the lime. As he stepped closer to her, the faint aroma of after-shave wafted lazily about him. He smelled good—too good as far as Juliet was concerned.

"You grew," he said, moving closer to her. "Last night you only came up to here on me." He held his palm even with his nose, a grin on his handsome face.

"I'm wearing heels," she said flatly, trying not to let his closeness affect her, but it wasn't easy. Ross Stafford exuded sex appeal, plain and simple. Last night she had thought it had something to do with being in the nightclub and hearing his music. Today she knew differently.

When she would have taken the lime from him to slice it, he reached for the knife in her hand and said, "I can do it. You go back to your potatoes."

Instead of handing him the knife, she set it down on the counter, then moved to the opposite end where her half-mashed potatoes sat waiting. "The glasses are in the upper cupboard to your right," she told him, her eyes riveted on the potatoes.

Ross studied her profile for several moments before moving, not quite certain why he should be so surprised by her appearance today. Last night at the White Wolf he had thought she wasn't exactly the fat and frumpy woman Brenda had led him to expect. Today he could see just how pretty she was.

Dressed in a teal-blue angora sweater dress that clung enchantingly to her slender curves, she hardly looked as if she belonged in the kitchen mashing potatoes. Her red hair spilled over onto her shoulders in soft, gentle waves, framing her heart-shaped face with its small straight nose. Last night it had been an interesting face. Today it was more than interesting; it was captivating.

Judging by the looks she was giving him, the last thing she wanted was for him to find her captivating. Although her demeanor had been nothing but polite since he had arrived, he knew that was purely a result of social upbringing. She didn't want him around. It was there in her eyes—eyes that he had expected to be green but were actually the brightest blue he had ever seen.

Last night he had been a bit amused by her aloof attitude toward him. Today he didn't think it was funny at all. Did she think he was beneath her social standards? Is that why she was treating him with such cool disdain?

"Brenda tells me you're taking weekend classes at the university," he commented, filling a tall glass with mineral water.

"Yes, I am."

He waited for her to elaborate, but she said nothing else.

"What are you studying?"

"Nutrition and dietetics."

Again, he waited for her to go into a little more detail, but she didn't. Nor did she glance over at him or indicate any interest in the fact that he was trying to make polite conversation with her.

"You want to be a dietitian?"

"Yes."

"You must like to cook."

"I don't dislike it."

From the way she was grinding the masher into the potatoes, he questioned that. It was obvious she was tense about something—or someone—and it didn't take an Einstein to figure out it was his presence that was tightening those perfectly shaped lips.

He supposed he should ignore her not-so-subtle animosity. He had never cared much for redheads—at least not since the eighth grade when he had made a fool of himself over Margaret Danley. She was the ninth-grade cheerleader who had sat in front of him on the bus on the way to school, deliberately dangling her flaming red tresses over the back of the seat, hoping to get his attention.

Margaret Danley was the most beautiful girl who had ever flirted with him. Actually, she was the only girl who had ever flirted with him at that stage of his adolescence. She had flirted and teased and taunted him until he had mustered up the courage to invite her to the all-school dance, an invitation she had accepted. But before the night of the dance arrived, she had transferred her affections to a football player whose voice wasn't alternating between soprano and bass.

Juliet's hair wasn't flaming red, but more of a burnished copper that reminded him of the leaves of sugar maples in autumn. And for the first time since he was thirteen years old he found himself wondering what it would be like to bury his fingers in luxurious red tresses. Unfortunately, the look on Juliet's face was not unlike Margaret Danley's when she had waltzed past him with her quarterback boyfriend on her arm.

Maybe it was because of Margaret that he spoke as he did. "Look, if you didn't want me to come to dinner today, you could have said something to me last night. I wouldn't have intruded on your family gathering."

Juliet's arm froze, and there was an abnormal absence of sound in the kitchen. A red flush started at the base of her neck and spread up her face to the roots of her hair. She looked over at him and was about to speak when Brenda came hobbling through the swinging door.

"Grandpa George wants to know if you'd like him to carve the turkey." She glanced curiously from Ross to her sister.

"That . . . that would be nice," Juliet stammered, turning away from her sister's probing gaze to open the refrigerator.

As she rearranged bottles and jars in search of nothing in particular, she heard Brenda say to Ross, "I see you found the mineral water. Gran is waiting patiently for you to return so you can finish your story."

Juliet wanted to ask, "What story?" but kept her nose buried in the refrigerator until Brenda said, "Juliet, Meridee wants to know if you need any help."

With a bowl of coleslaw in her hands, she emerged from the refrigerator and said, "Tell her yes."

"What about me? Is there anything I can do?" Brenda asked.

"I think Meridee and I can manage. You shouldn't be hobbling around on that ankle, anyway."

"Here. Maybe you should lean on me," Ross suggested, offering Brenda his arm for support. He was rewarded with a gaze of adoration that Juliet found rather annoying.

As her sister clung to his coat sleeve and batted her eyelashes, Juliet turned away in disgust. If there was one thing she didn't want to have to witness it was her younger sister fawning over a man like Ross Stafford.

Unfortunately, she had no choice, for Brenda was seldom out of arm's reach of her guest for the remainder of the day. And it wasn't only Brenda who was making him the object of her devotion. Much to Juliet's chagrin, Meridee's and Gran's eyes seldom left his face, and even Sara and Annie smiled and giggled whenever he glanced in their direction. Ross Stafford was the life of their Thanksgiving party, only for Juliet it wasn't much of a party.

She wanted to blame her malcontent on the fact that her mother was gone, but she knew that what bothered her more than her mother's absence was Ross Stafford's presence. She didn't know how to deal with the almost animalistic feelings he aroused in her. If it had been possible, she would have excused herself after dinner and never returned to the group gathered in the living room.

Whenever her eyes met Ross's, she felt a pang of guilt. Never would her mother have made a guest feel unwelcome in her home, no matter how much she disliked him. After their confrontation in the kitchen, Juliet knew she should say something to him. If there was one thing she had learned from her mother, it was the art of being a gracious hostess. Yet the apology she wanted to utter stuck in her throat like peanut butter on the roof of her mouth. The best she could manage was to put on a false smile and join in the singing as Brenda urged Ross to entertain them at the piano.

It was something her father had always done on holidays—sat down at the aging, slightly off-key upright piano to play traditional favorites so that everyone could sing along. Maybe that's why Juliet found it disturbing when Ross placed his long fingers on the yellowed ivory keys. It didn't seem right that another man was playing music on that piano on this holiday.

But play it he did. And beautifully. Obviously his musical talent wasn't limited to the saxophone. Everyone sang along as he played popular music that ranged from folk songs to show tunes.

Everything Ross did that Thanksgiving Day seemed to please the members of the Osborne family—everyone except Juliet, that is. No one seemed to notice that the sparkle in her eye was missing or that her smile was forced. They were all too engrossed with Ross.

By the end of the day her head was throbbing and she was tired of being pleasant. Her grandparents announced it was time to go home, and Juliet silently heaved a sigh of relief as Ross expressed the same sentiment.

Then Brenda said, "You don't have to leave just because Grandma and Grandpa are going."

"No, by all means, don't leave on our account," Frances said, flapping her bony hands as if they were wings.

Even Meridee begged him to stay, and Juliet wondered why none of them could see that although Ross Stafford was a marvelous storyteller and a brilliant musician, he wasn't even close to Wally Cleaver.

"I've had a great time, but I really think I should be going," he said, despite the groans of protest coming from the females in the house.

Juliet felt her tense muscles start to relax. Finally he was leaving. Coats were retrieved from the closet and goodbyes and thank-yous were exchanged.

In the short time Ross had been there, he had formed some sort of bond with her family. Her grandmother even offered him her cheek. So did

Meridee and Brenda, as Sara and Annie clamored to kiss him goodbye. Juliet stood quietly to one side, watching the Stafford charisma in action.

When it was her turn to say goodbye, she stuck out her hand. "It was nice having you with us, Ross. I'm so glad you could make it." She pasted her best social smile in place.

He didn't try to kiss her cheek, but accepted the handshake, although something in his eyes told Juliet he knew exactly what she was feeling.

"Thank you for allowing me to crash your family gathering. I can't remember the last time I had such a wonderful meal," he said.

Juliet blushed, much to her annoyance, which only made Ross's eyes sparkle, and she wondered if he was remembering their encounter in the kitchen.

Then her grandmother shoved her arm through his and said, "Now, Ross, I want you to promise me you'll think of us as your adopted family. You're welcome to join us for dinner whenever you're feeling in need of some home cooking."

Juliet held her breath as her grandmother rambled on about the importance of families gathering together for Sunday dinner.

"Maybe you'll be able to have dinner with us some Sunday," the white-haired lady suggested. "Brenda's mother usually does the cooking, but..."

Juliet couldn't believe her ears! Agitation made her tune out the rest of the conversation until she saw Ross place his hand on the doorknob.

"Thanks again," he said as he opened the door.

When he had stepped outside, Frances turned to Juliet and said, "It's so nice to know that Brenda has such a marvelous teacher."

"Teacher?" Juliet repeated, a puzzled frown on her face.

No one seemed to hear, for despite the cold air rushing in, everyone was crowding into the open doorway to wave at Ross as he walked out to his van.

Curious, Juliet tapped on her grandmother's shoulder. "Did you say teacher, Gran?"

Her attention on the departing male figure, Frances absently nodded. "Umm-hmm."

"What kind of teacher?" Juliet demanded, wondering if he was giving Brenda music or acting lessons.

"A university teacher, dear," her grandmother replied, finally turning to look at her. "He teaches Brenda's theater arts class. I thought you knew that."

Juliet didn't know. How could she? Brenda had said he was from her theater arts class, not teaching it.

"He's such a nice man, isn't he?" Frances said happily.

"Just peachy," Juliet mumbled.

Frances clicked her tongue. "You young people. Always talking about men as though they were something to eat."

CHAPTER THREE

BY THE TIME JULIET had cleaned up the scattered remains of their holiday dinner, she wanted nothing better than to slide her exhausted body between the covers of her four-poster. She was about to do just that when Brenda came into her room looking like a cat who had found the cream.

"I thought you went to bed," Juliet commented, folding back the thick down comforter and fluffing her pillows.

"I did, but I'm having trouble falling asleep. Too much holiday spirit, I guess." She sank down onto Juliet's bed and sighed contentedly. "It was such a nice Thanksgiving. Your dinner was a success."

Juliet kicked off her slippers and climbed into the bed, propping her back against the pillows. "The gravy was a little lumpy, but overall I guess it went pretty well."

"Oh, it really did. Mom would have been proud of you. I wish she could have been here. I think she would have liked Ross, don't you?"

For Juliet, the sound of Ross's name was equivalent to hearing chalk squeak on a blackboard. "Why didn't you tell me he was your teacher?" she demanded, trying not to sound as cranky as she was feeling.

Brenda gave her an innocent look. "I thought you knew. He's the TA in my theater class. And am I ever glad I have *him*. Some of those other instructors are horrible." She stretched in a catlike fashion, then fell back against the covers, propping herself up on one elbow. "This really was one of the best Thanksgivings we've ever had. Wasn't it neat the way Ross fit right in with our family?"

Juliet was too tired to pretend she shared Brenda's opinion. "Personally I don't think the Ross Staffords of this world fit in with anyone's family," she said coldly.

Brenda sat up, her eyes losing some of their sparkle. "What are you talking about? You saw how he got along with Grandma and Grandpa. And Meridee made him feel right at home. Even Sara and Annie were fighting to sit on his lap."

"That's because he's a good actor."

"And what's that supposed to mean?"

Juliet saw the prelude to battle on her sister's face and immediately regretted mentioning Ross Stafford at all. She heaved a long, tired sigh, then said, "Nothing. Just forget I said anything."

"No, I'm not going to forget," Brenda insisted stubbornly, her back stiffening. "You were giving Ross funny looks all day long and I want to know why."

"I wasn't giving him funny looks."

"Yes, you were. You don't like him, do you?"

"If you're asking me if I approve of him as a date for you, the answer's no," Juliet replied candidly. "For goodness' sake, Brenda, he's your teacher. University instructors aren't supposed to date their students."

Brenda chuckled sarcastically. "Maybe if you're some stuffy old professor who's already married, but believe me, Juliet, nearly every TA on campus is dating a student. Administration simply turns a blind eye, that's all."

Juliet made a sound of disgust. "And that's supposed to make it acceptable?"

"I don't see why you're making such a fuss about it when three weeks from now the quarter will be over and it won't be an issue."

"There's the matter of your grade."

"You think my grade depends on whether or not I sleep with Ross?" Brenda gave her a look of disbelief. "That's disgusting!"

Which was precisely what Juliet thought. She didn't even want to consider the possibility that her younger sister could be doing anything intimate with a man like Ross. "Don't you think he's a little old for you?"

"Old? He's only thirty."

"Much too old for someone who's only nineteen."

"So what? Dad was ten years older than Mom, or have you forgotten?"

"That was different. Dad wasn't a congressman then, but he *was* an established lawyer with a reputable law firm when Mom met him, not some struggling actor who moves from city to city in search of work."

"Just because he hasn't put down roots in one particular spot doesn't make him disreputable, Juliet. And he's not a struggling actor moving from city to city. He's a Ph.D. candidate working on his thesis in theater arts. He designs sets, and someday he'll probably be famous."

"Yes, and someday my prince will come," Juliet muttered under her breath. "Brenda, guys like him are here today, gone tomorrow."

"Dad always taught us not to judge people by what they are, but who they are."

"That's true, but if I were you, I wouldn't pin any hopes on Ross Stafford."

"Why? Because he's studying theater arts instead of law?"

"Because he's all wrong for you."

"Wrong for me?" she repeated. "He's not wrong for me, and I'd appreciate it if you stayed out of my personal life," Brenda said haughtily, rising from the bed. "If I had wanted someone watching me like a hawk, I would have moved in with Mom and Donovan."

"I'm *not* watching you like a hawk," Juliet protested, sitting forward. "I just don't want to see you get hurt."

"I'm not going to get hurt. I'm not a child, Juliet, and I really think that if we're going to live together peacefully, you're going to have to accept that. Both you and Meridee want to treat me like the little girl in this family. I may be younger than you, but I'm not twelve years old anymore."

Juliet wanted to say, "Maybe not, but what you know about men could easily fit onto the head of a pin." Instead she held her tongue. It puzzled her how someone as smart as Brenda could be so naive when it came to the opposite sex. Judging by the funky way she dressed, people would think she was savvy about romance, but the truth was, Brenda in some ways was as innocent as a twelve-year-old. And Juliet didn't want Ross Stafford to be the one to change that.

"Don't be in such a hurry to grow up," she advised her sister. "Your teenage years should be fun and carefree."

"Ha! If you and Meridee had your way, I'd be at some convent instead of the university," Brenda retorted, spreading her hands in a gesture of frustration.

"That's not true. It's just that we both know how important it is for a woman to get her education...."

"If you're going to start in on your Value of Education speech, I'm going to bed," Brenda interrupted her. She limped toward the door.

Juliet sighed. This was not how she wanted to end their conversation, yet she simply didn't have the energy to continue. "Just promise me you won't do anything foolish when it comes to Ross Stafford."

Brenda paused at the door to say, "*Me* do something foolish?" She shot her a look of total incredulity. "It seems to me that *you're* the one who has a history of foolish behavior when it comes to men."

Juliet sank back against the pillows as the arrow went straight to its target. She didn't need her younger sister to remind her that she was the only one in the family to get divorced or that she had a tendency to be attracted to what her mother and her sisters described as losers. Talk about a smart woman making foolish choices...

But that was in the past. No more would she make the mistake of falling for the wrong man. If her mistakes had taught her anything, it was that crumbs were *not* better than no bread at all. And some gut instinct was telling her that Ross Stafford was definitely not a whole slice of bread.

As she tried to fall asleep, she kept seeing him in black leather and hearing him say, "If you didn't want me to come to dinner today, all you had to do was say so."

She punched her pillow and buried her face in its fluffy softness, commanding her mind to think of anything but Brenda's boyfriend. Still, his image taunted her, as did Brenda's innocent face as it gazed into his in adoration.

He *was* all wrong for her sister. And she hated the way Brenda made her feel like a wicked stepsister just because she was trying to give her some sisterly advice. Maybe her track record wasn't the greatest when it came to picking men, but that was why she was able to look at this playboy and see him for what he was.

She groaned in frustration and tugged the covers up over her head. "Quit thinking about him, Juliet," she commanded herself aloud. "Why are you wasting time on him? If you're going to lie here awake, you should be reviewing the U.S. dietary guidelines." But as she fell asleep, she was still seeing Ross Stafford's face.

FOR THE PAST TWO YEARS, Juliet had been a part-time student at the university, attending classes either in the evenings or on weekends and working full-time as a secretary for an insurance company during the day. Until her mother's marriage to Police Commissioner Donovan Cade, it had been the only option available to her.

Now she found that, beginning in January, she was going to be able to return to school on a full-time basis and work only part-time, thanks to her mother's generosity. Reluctant to sell the family home, Kate had suggested Juliet give up her apartment and move in with Brenda. The arrangement would save Juliet the expense of rent payments and give Kate peace of mind, as she was uneasy with Brenda living alone in the big old Victorian house.

Although Juliet still had five weeks to go before she quit her job, she got a taste of what it meant to be a full-time student at the university on the Monday after Thanksgiving. That was the day she had to register for the winter quarter.

Having taken the morning off from work, she was frustrated to find that the horror stories she had heard regarding registration were true. There were queues to see an adviser, queues to get registration override permits, queues to turn in registration materials and queues to obtain fee statements.

Because all her classes were on the St. Paul campus and the theater arts department was on the Minneapolis campus, the last person she expected to run into that day was Ross Stafford. But then, she hadn't expected she'd have to take the inter-campus bus over to Williamson Hall in Minneapolis and stand in yet another queue in order to have her picture taken for a student ID card.

It was while she was waiting in that queue that she saw Ross. He was in the bookstore directly across the hall from where she waited in line. Through the large plate-glass windows, she could see him browsing through the stacks of textbooks. He had on a brown leather jacket and washed-out denim jeans, his hair once again pulled back into a small ponytail. He looked more like a student than a teacher, and as he looked up from the stacks of books, she quickly turned her back to him, hoping he wouldn't notice her.

She sighed in relief when at last she was able to slip inside the small office. But then, after reaching the counter and posing for her picture, she was forced to wait in still another line for the photo to be processed. When the clerk finally handed her the credit-card-size ID with its black-and-white photo, she groaned.

"Good grief, this is awful."

She hadn't realized she had spoken the words aloud until a voice next to her said, "Don't feel bad. Everyone looks like an escaped convict on those things."

Juliet nearly dropped the piece of plastic when she realized the voice belonged to Ross. He was standing right beside her, leaning up against the counter, an attractive grin on his face.

"Ross...hi," she murmured, trying not to be affected by his proximity. After a brief glance at him, she focused her attention on the card. "I didn't think there could be anything worse than a driver's-license photo, but I guess I was wrong."

He leaned closer to get a better look at the photo, and she would have backed away had there been any room to move.

"Actually yours is quite good compared to most of the ones I've seen," he told her.

Juliet shot him a dubious look that he correctly interpreted.

"All right, so it looks like a mug shot," he conceded. "At least they put the picture on the *back* of the card. You're going to find that when you use it, most people just look at the student number on the front."

As the desk clerk called out, "Next," Juliet shoved the offensive photo ID into her purse and stepped away from the counter, squeezing between the two lines of students still waiting for their cards.

Ross followed her. "I'm glad I ran into you," he told her as they stepped out into the wide corridor of Williamson Hall. "I've been meaning to call you and thank you for dinner."

"You're welcome," she said politely. "We enjoyed having you."

"Well, I enjoyed being there with all of you," he said, wishing she'd look at him instead of avoiding his eyes. "I didn't expect to see you on this campus."

"I'm surprised you were able to spot me in that mess." She looked back over her shoulder to the crowded office.

He could see by the expression on her face that she wasn't happy that he had spotted her. She was giving him the same "don't look at me" expression she had given him on Thanksgiving, and any pleasure he had felt at seeing her again quickly dissolved. "Actually it was your hair. I noticed it the minute I stepped out of the bookstore."

His words brought a delicate blush to her cheeks, and he immediately regretted them until she said rather cheekily, "Now you know why they make fire engines red."

She was buttoning up her coat and getting ready to go back out into the cold. Ross wouldn't have been surprised if she left without saying another word to him.

When she dropped a leather glove, he bent down to pick it up. "I happen to like red," he told her as he handed it to her.

Her blush deepened and she quickly averted her gaze, reaching into her coat pocket for a folded piece of paper. As she opened it, he could see that it was a map of the campus.

"What are you trying to find?" he asked.

"The bus stop. I have to go back to St. Paul and finish registering," she answered, studying the map as she spoke. "I'm starting day school next quarter."

"You're going to be a full-time student?"

She nodded. "I thought I had stood in every line there could possibly be to stand in, but I guess I missed one."

"From my experience with registration queues, I'd say that at this time of day, your chances of getting through any of the lines in less than an hour are rather slim."

She groaned. "Don't say that. I only took a half day off work, and I told my boss I'd be in by noon."

He glanced at the gold watch on his wrist, then gave her a sympathetic look. "It's after eleven-thirty."

He had an idea that being off schedule was more disturbing to her than standing in the lines. Her next words were uttered with barely controlled frustration.

"I can't believe it takes an entire day to register for a few classes!"

"It's only because this is your first time registering for day school. It'll be easier next time," he assured her.

"The way I feel right now, I don't think I'll care if there *is* a next time." She shoved the crinkled map back into her pocket and looked around in disgust.

He placed his hand on her arm and said, "Why don't I show you where the bus stops?" When she would have protested, he added, "It's right outside the door. It will only take a minute."

To his surprise, she didn't object, but allowed him to escort her across the concrete plaza to the street corner where a maroon-and-gold bus was pulling up to the curb.

"It looks like you've timed it just right," he told her as the doors opened and students began filing off the bus.

"Thanks for your help," she said with an awkward smile.

"My pleasure. It's the least I can do for someone who fed me such a feast on Thanksgiving." He gave her a brilliant smile that made her glance uneasily at the bus, where students were now getting on.

"I guess I'd better go if I want to get a seat."

He nodded and watched her walk away. Just before she stepped on board he called out, "It was nice seeing you, Juliet."

Her only response was to force another small, polite smile to her lips before climbing the steps. He watched her take a seat near the front. Although she wasn't next to the window, she could easily have glanced in his direction. She didn't. Much to his annoyance, she sat looking straight ahead as if he didn't even exist.

The bus didn't leave right away, but sat with its motor idling, the doors open. Not once did Juliet look in his direction. Finally the driver closed the doors. Just as the bus was about to pull away from the curb, Ross rushed over and rapped on the glass. The doors slid open and he hopped on board, taking the seat across the aisle from Juliet, who was looking at him as though he had just landed from outer space.

"Ross, what are you doing?" she asked, a look of confusion on her face.

"I'm riding the bus."

"Why?"

"Because I want to."

"But this bus is going to St. Paul!"

"I know. That's why I'm on it."

They were drawing the attention of other passengers, and he could see by the way she was fidgeting with her gloves that she was uncomfortable.

"Why are you going to St. Paul?" she asked, trying to keep her voice inconspicuously low.

He didn't answer right away, but stared at her pensively before finally saying, "To help you through registration."

Again she blushed, and had the bus not pulled away from the curb, he thought she might very well have gotten off.

"Ah...excuse me," the girl sitting on the other side of Juliet interrupted their exchange. "Do you want me to switch places with you?" She looked at Ross appealingly.

He immediately stood up. "That would be great. Are you sure you don't mind?"

"Oh, no. Not at all," she said, flashing him a big smile as she hoisted her backpack over her shoulder.

Ross thought Juliet looked as though she wished a whale would swallow him whole.

"Maybe you should just slide over," he said to her as the three of them jockeyed for position.

She did as she was told, but Ross was certain it was only because she didn't want to make a scene.

"You don't have to do this. I'm perfectly capable of registering." There was more than a hint of irritability in her tone.

"I know you are," he said smugly.

"Then what are you doing on this bus?"

Ross was beginning to ask himself that very question. Juliet was obviously uncomfortable with his presence. She always had been, ever since the first night he saw her at the White Wolf. This was the third time he had seen her, yet not once had he seen a genuine smile on her face.

She stared out the window rather than at him as she waited for his answer. In the daylight he could see the faint signs of freckles beneath a soft layer of makeup. He had never dated a woman with freckles, he mused, and he would probably never date this one, either.

That thought was disturbing... because he wanted to date Juliet Harper. It was why he had squeezed his way into the ID card office and why he had climbed aboard a bus going to a campus he had no reason to visit.

"Since you were nice enough to include me in your family Thanksgiving, I thought maybe I could ease the hassles of registration by taking you to lunch." He could see that his suggestion had caught her totally off guard.

"Lunch? It's very nice of you to offer, but I'm afraid I really don't have the time," she answered politely. "I have to finish registering, then get back to work." She glanced nervously at her watch.

Ross could see she had no interest in going anywhere with him. It shouldn't have been a surprise. After all, she wasn't exactly the kind of woman he usually asked out. She worried about schedules and etiquette. And she was fastidious. She was probably the kind of woman who had a fit if a guy dropped his clothes on the floor rather than folding them neatly before going to bed. He should be relieved she said no.

He wasn't.

"Look at it this way," he tried again. "If you get into a registration line now, you're probably going to have a long wait because half the clerks will be at lunch. But if you were to get a bite to eat, then hit the lines, say around one o'clock, the office will be at full staff and lines will be much shorter."

She glanced again at her watch. "Then I'd have to line up at the cafeteria as well."

"You won't have to wait in line for lunch."

She raised her eyebrows skeptically. "That's not what Brenda told me."

He reached for the signal cord, then grabbed her by the hand. "Come on. We're getting off."

"Getting off? But..." She didn't get to finish her protest, for the bus had stopped and Ross was pulling her down the aisle and out the door.

"There had better be a good explanation for this," she told him as a cold gust of wind made her turn up the edges of her collar. They stood on the sidewalk in front of a warehouse, watching the bus whoosh away.

"It's cold, isn't it?" He, too, turned up the collar of his leather jacket. "Don't worry. We don't have far to go." He started walking down an adjoining street, and Juliet hurried after him. They had only gone about half a block when he stopped in front of a metal sign swinging back and forth in the wind.

"The Bar?" Juliet read the name aloud.

"Not a very original name, is it?" Ross said with a grin as he held the door open for her. "This place has been here for ages. Apparently years ago when the original owners first opened the place, they couldn't agree on a name, so they simply called it the Bar. It's been called that ever since."

He could see by the look on her face that the Bar's atmosphere didn't exactly impress her, and with good reason, he thought. It looked like no one had done a thing to the place since it had first opened. It was old and run-down, and suddenly Ross realized that a congressman's daughter might not appreciate its comfortable, worn atmosphere.

"The food's good," he told her, feeling the need to defend his choice of eating spot. "And there's never a crowd."

As he led her over to a booth in the back corner, the bartender called out to him, "It's about time you showed up."

Ross waved at the man, as well as a couple of other older gentlemen sitting on bar stools. Before he sat down, he hung both of their coats on the hook protruding from their booth and asked, "Well, what do you think?"

"It's different," she told him, trying to smile but failing.

"At least there aren't any queues."

The bartender wandered over to them, a flour-sack apron wrapped around his bulging middle. "Know what you want?"

"Why don't you give us a couple of minutes, Ed?" Ross suggested, noticing that Juliet was unsuccessfully looking for a menu.

"You going to be having a beer?" Ed asked.

Ross looked at Juliet, who said, "Maybe a diet cola."

"One diet cola, one beer," Ross told the bartender, who nodded and left. "They don't have menus. You can get hamburgers or pork tenderloin sandwiches anytime, and then there's a daily special. That's written on the blackboard behind the bar. Today it's chili," he told her as she craned her neck to see.

"I'll try the chili," she told him after only a moment's hesitation.

"Good choice. Ernie makes the best chili in town. He's the cook—besides being Ed's brother."

"How did you find this place?" She glanced around the small tavern filled mostly with older men.

"My landlord told me about it. I live about a block from here."

"Do you come here often?"

He shrugged. "It's a nice break from being around students. Besides, Ernie's a better cook than I am." A wry smile lifted one corner of his mouth. "Although I'm not sure he can match your culinary skills."

She blushed at the compliment, especially as she recalled her treatment of him that day at the house. She needed to apologize, to explain that she had misjudged him. The problem was, how did she tell him she had thought he was simply one of the boys in the band who didn't have any direction in his life?

"Ross, there's something I wanted to tell you." She fidgeted with the silverware as she spoke. "When you came to dinner on Thanksgiving, I didn't behave very well. You see, I didn't know that you were a teaching associate at the university."

"And now that you do know?" He looked at her curiously.

"I feel rather foolish." She kept her eyes downcast. "I'm afraid I wasn't very cordial, and I'm sorry."

"Apology accepted," he said easily, although it made him wonder if she was the kind of person who was overly concerned with social position. He didn't want to think that she was pretentious, yet from the minute she had glared at him in the White Wolf, he had had the feeling that she was looking down her nose at him.

There was an uneasy silence between them, and Ross was relieved when Ed arrived with two huge steaming bowls of chili and a loaf of French bread topped with melted cheese.

"Well?" He held his own spoon in midair as he waited for her to taste the chili.

She took several spoonfuls before saying, "It's wonderful, but then you knew it would be, didn't you?"

There was no smugness in his smile, just genuine satisfaction. "For a moment there you had me worried. The way you were looking around the place I thought maybe you were going to ask to inspect the kitchen."

For the first time her smile didn't look forced, and his heart skipped a beat.

"I'm studying to be a dietitian, not a health inspector," she told him.

"What made you decide on nutrition?"

"Motherhood." When he cast a puzzled look in her direction, she explained, "When Sara was about three she went through a stage where she wouldn't eat anything but French toast and applesauce—for breakfast, lunch and dinner."

She paused to take a sip of her cola, then went on, "I was so worried she was going to end up with some serious vitamin deficiency, I read everything I could get my hands on regarding nutrition. Unfortunately, that only confused me. The magazines contradicted the newspapers, the newspapers contradicted the books, and the books contradicted the magazines."

"So you decided to find out the truth for yourself, eh?"

"It's a fascinating subject," she said with a nod. "And my previous credits gave me a good start on the prerequisites for the program."

"You've had other college experience?"

"I went to a small private college after my graduation from high school, but I dropped out after my freshman year," she told him.

"That surprises me, considering your family background."

"Well, it didn't exactly win me any points with my father," she admitted, keeping her eyes on the food she was eating.

"So why did you quit?"

She stole a quick glance at him and saw that she had his complete attention. She supposed that to someone working on a Ph.D., there probably weren't many legitimate reasons for not completing an undergraduate degree.

"I got married," she said quietly.

"Ah," was all he said.

Juliet suspected he was wondering why marriage had prevented her from attending school. She didn't want to tell him that she had sacrificed her college education in order to put her husband through dental school. Instead of explaining that Tim had promised she could go back to college when he was finished, she simply shook her head in regret.

"It wasn't one of my better decisions," she admitted soberly.

"Marriage or dropping out of college?"

Juliet met his questioning gaze. She was spared from having to answer when an elderly gentleman wearing a rumpled fedora called over to Ross.

"Hey, sax man. You up for a game when you're finished?"

"Maybe another time, eh? The schedule's tight today," Ross called back to him.

Juliet was looking at him with a puzzled expression. "Darts," he said in answer to her unasked question. "Archie challenges me to a game every time I come in."

She glanced over at the man with the small hump on his back. He was looking longingly in their direction, his eyes mirroring his disappointment. "Go ahead and play if you like. I don't mind."

Ross shook his head. "It's all right. Archie's here every day."

The expression on the little old man's face made Juliet say, "It wouldn't take long just for one game, would it?"

Ross shrugged. "Are you sure you don't mind?"

"No, please. Go ahead."

When Ross hesitated, Ed called out, "Ernie says the winner gets the last piece of banana cream pie."

"You like banana cream pie?" Ross asked Juliet. When she nodded, he stood up and said, "Don't plan on getting any. Archie's unbeatable when pie's on the line."

As the bent-over man climbed down from his bar stool, Juliet felt a tug on her heartstrings as she noticed for the first time that his shoes had holes in them. He was tired-looking and a good foot shorter than Ross, but he managed to win not one, but three games.

Every time Ross threw what Juliet thought was a perfect dart, Archie would outdo him.

When the contest was over, Ross gave Archie a pat on the back, then returned to the booth where Juliet sat. As he slid in across from her, she thought she detected a gleam of satisfaction in his eyes.

"Did you let him win?" she asked.

"Not at all. I told you—Archie's good."

Juliet didn't know whether to believe him or not. The longer she sat talking to him, the more she wanted to believe everything he said. Looking into his eyes she realized why. She was attracted to him—plain and simple. A wave of guilt washed over her. How could she be attracted to her sister's boyfriend?

Feeling extremely uncomfortable, she excused herself and took refuge in the washroom. If she had had her coat, she would have sneaked out the door and run all the way to the bus stop. Unfortunately, she had no choice but to return to the booth. As she sat down, Ed set a piece of banana cream pie down in front of her. "Archie wants your girl to have this," he announced.

"Oh, I couldn't . . ." Juliet started to refuse the offer, but one look at Archie's face gazing at her in anticipation had her saying instead, "I couldn't think of a better way to top off that wonderful chili." She smiled at Archie and mouthed a thank-you.

When she glanced at Ross, he was looking at her with an emotion she didn't want to see on his face. He was her sister's boyfriend. She had no business sitting across from him and feeling the way she did. She quickly averted her gaze.

"Do you want coffee to go with that?" Ed asked as he cleared away the dirty dishes.

Juliet shook her head. "Oh, no. I'm fine."

"You don't look fine," Ross said a few seconds later when Ed had gone. "You're looking at that pie as though it were a class-registration card."

She smiled weakly. "It looks delicious, but I don't know how I'm going to be able to eat it. I'm afraid I ate too much cheese bread."

"Ernie makes great pie," he said, trying to tempt her.

Juliet was silent for several moments, then asked, "Do you think you could get Ed to bring me another plate?"

Ross signaled for the bartender. As soon as he had brought her the additional plate, Juliet sliced the pie into two wedges and gave one back to Ed, telling him to give it to Archie.

She watched the old man's face brighten as Ed set the pie down in front of him. He tipped his hat and smiled his toothless grin.

This time there was no mistaking the admiration in Ross's eyes, and she quickly turned her attention to the pie. While she ate, Ross left to make a phone call. On his way back, she noticed that he had stopped at the bar and several of the old men were clapping him on the back affectionately. When he went to sit down across from her, she noticed several of them gave a thumbs-up gesture.

Puzzled, she asked, "What was that all about?"

"Just guy talk," he said evasively.

"Guy talk?" Juliet repeated. She knew she should let the subject drop, but some perverse curiosity made her ask, "Were they talking about me?"

"Not in the way you're thinking."

Her fork dropped to the plate. "And how would you know what I'm thinking?"

"Because those blue eyes of yours tell me more than your lips ever do."

Juliet turned away. "I think I'd like to go, if you don't mind." She gathered up her purse and gloves from the booth.

Before she could reach her coat, he had it in his hands and was holding it open for her so she could slip her arms into the sleeves. "I'm sorry, Juliet. I shouldn't have brought you here."

"Why did you? So some dirty old men could snicker about me behind my back?"

"They're not dirty old men and they weren't snickering," he told her coldly. "If you must know, they were telling me how lucky I was to have found such a good woman. They think you're my girl."

"Why? Because I had lunch with you?"

"I've never brought a woman here before."

"Not even Brenda?"

"No, not Brenda. Just for the record, I don't make a practice of taking my students to lunch, and I know better than to bring any minor into a bar."

They had reached the entrance and were face-to-face in a closet-size space glowering at each other. "Is that why you arranged for a nineteen-year-old to return your van to you at a place like the White Wolf?" she demanded in a self-righteous tone.

"I didn't want her coming down to the White Wolf, but she insisted. I told her I'd pick it up on Thanksgiving Day, but she said she'd get one of her older sisters to come down with her." He thrust his fists on his hips. "Look, why don't you just tell me what's really eating you? Ever since the first time we met you've been looking at me as though I'm something the cat dragged in."

Juliet couldn't prevent the blush that washed across her cheeks. "I think you know."

"The only thing I know is that every time I look at you my hormones take off like cruise missiles."

She looked into his eyes and saw no flirtatious sparkle. She had wanted to think she had misread his interest in her, that she had imagined the physical attraction that had flared between them. Now she knew it wasn't true. Ross wanted her. It was there in his eyes and it excited her.

"This isn't right. I have to go." She quickly reached for the door.

He followed her outside, calling to her to wait, but Juliet refused to slow down.

As she hurried to the bus stop, she expected him to come after her, but he didn't. As luck would have it, there was a bus arriving just as she reached the door. Breathless, she climbed aboard and took the first available seat, never once glancing back over her shoulder.

CHAPTER FOUR

ALL AFTERNOON JULIET was plagued with regret over having run into Ross on campus. By the time she had picked up the girls from the baby-sitter's, her emotions were in a tangle. She felt guilty over being attracted to her sister's boyfriend and angry that Ross Stafford was putting her in a position to feel guilty. Why couldn't he just leave her alone?

"Mommy, I'm hungry," Sara whined as Juliet parked the car outside the two-story house.

"Sara, please don't whine. We're all hungry," she answered, suddenly weary from the long day.

"But my tummy hurts," Sara insisted.

"We're going to eat as soon as we get inside." Juliet climbed out of the car and went around to the passenger side, where she unstrapped Annie from her car seat. "Don't forget to bring in the tote bag," she reminded Sara, who was climbing out the back door.

They were halfway up the walk when Sara screeched in delight. "Oooh, look, Mommy! Christmas lights!"

Juliet glanced across the street at the house decorated with strings of colored lights. "I see them. Aren't they pretty?"

"Are we going to decorate Grandma's house?" Sara asked eagerly, skipping up the walk.

"Oh, I don't know. We'll see," she said absently.

"You always say we'll see when you really mean no," Sara said a bit petulantly as she followed her mother inside. Juliet chose to ignore the remark, but Sara continued to press the issue. "Melissa Owens said her dad already put up their lights. I wish we could have lights on our house."

"Sara, I don't know how to hook up electrical lights," Juliet explained as she helped Annie out of her snowsuit.

"Maybe Auntie Brenda knows how."

"I doubt it." She tucked mittens into coat sleeves, then hung the outerwear in the closet. "Why don't you take Annie into the bathroom and wash up for dinner while I set the table?"

Juliet headed for the kitchen, her senses attuned to the aroma that should have welcomed her entrance. As she pushed through the swinging door and flipped on the light, her eyes focused on the stove. She quickly crossed the parquet wood floor and pulled open the oven door. A warm blast of air greeted her, but there was no baking dish on the shelf. She let the door slam shut, then rushed out into the foyer and hollered up the staircase.

"Brenda, are you up there?"

A few seconds later a stocking-footed Brenda came padding to the top of the stairs, a cordless phone tucked close to her chest. "What is it, Juliet? I'm on the phone."

"What happened to the meat loaf?"

A hand flew to her mouth. "Oh, shoot! I forgot all about it."

"You forgot? How could you forget? I left a note for you on the table. I even set the oven on time bake. All you had to do was take the meat loaf out of the refrigerator and slide it into the oven," Juliet sputtered angrily.

"I'm sorry, but I forgot!"

Juliet threw her hands in the air. "Well, this is just terrific. Now what are we supposed to do for dinner? Sara and Annie are starving."

"Can't you put it in the microwave?"

"No, I can't put it in the microwave," she retorted obstinately. "It was made for the oven."

"Why don't I run and pick up some hamburgers for the girls?" Brenda suggested. "Just let me get off the phone." Without waiting for an answer, she disappeared.

Juliet could only shake her head in disappointment. By the time Brenda came downstairs, she had opened a can of soup and was grilling sandwiches.

Brenda looked baffled. "What are you doing? I said I'd go get hamburgers for everyone."

"If you want to get yourself a burger and fries, be my guest. I'm making the girls soup and sandwiches." Juliet couldn't keep the irritation out of her voice. "They don't need all that fat in their diet."

Brenda dropped her purse onto the table. "Well, *excuse me* for wanting to help out," she drawled sarcastically.

Just then Sara and Annie came running into the kitchen, preempting their argument.

"How come you have your coat on?" Sara asked when she saw Brenda.

Juliet shot Brenda a warning glance, which she wisely heeded.

"I just had to run out to my car for a minute," Brenda answered, shrugging out of her hot-pink ski jacket.

"Oh, good," Sara said, sitting down at the table. "'Cuz I wanted to ask you something."

"Oh? What's that?" Brenda took the chair opposite Sara.

"Do you know how to hang Christmas lights?"

"You mean the ones on the tree?"

"Uh-uh. The ones you put outside on the house. You know, like sometimes you wrap them around the trees and stuff." She spoke with her hands, her fingers bending and twisting like the claws of crabs on the move.

"I've never done it before, but I suppose I could if I had some help." She looked over at Juliet expectantly.

"I hate ladders, and I'm not exactly crazy about doing anything outdoors at this time of year," Juliet said before her sister could even ask the question.

"I bet Mom's Christmas decorations are still in the attic," Brenda said, rising to get the milk from the refrigerator.

"Those decorations haven't been up since Dad died," Juliet reminded her.

"That's because Dad was the one who always put them up. Maybe Donovan could help us," Brenda said, filling Annie's and Sara's glasses with milk.

"Maybe," Juliet replied dubiously.

"Do you think Grandpa Donovan knows how to make them blink on and off?" Sara wanted to know.

"I'm sure he does. We'll ask him just as soon as he and Grandma get back from their honeymoon, okay?" Brenda said with a grin.

"How many more days is that?" Sara asked.

"Six," Brenda answered.

"Six!" Sara groaned. "But everyone else already has their lights on."

"Well, we're not everyone else," Juliet said as she set a grilled cheese sandwich down in front of her daughter. "And if you want lights, you'll just have to wait until we can get some help."

Sara heaved a long sigh. "We wouldn't need any help if I had a dad."

"You have a father, Sara. He lives in California, that's all." Juliet tried to keep her voice even, but every time Sara mentioned her father, she felt the same rush of angry feelings.

"I wish you wouldn't have got a divorce," Sara said glumly, her cheek resting on her palm.

Juliet took a deep breath and said calmly, "Even if we hadn't gotten a divorce, your father would have still moved to California, Sara. That's where he wants to live."

Sara took a bite of her sandwich, her eyes downcast. Lately, the same look shadowed her face whenever the subject of her father arose, and it worried Juliet. To a six-year-old, divorce was a difficult concept to understand. During the two years Tim had been gone, Juliet had sought counseling for her on several different occasions, hoping to ease the pain the separation had caused her daughter. She knew, however, that the subject of her father still troubled Sara.

"Maybe we should go up to the attic and scrounge around just to see what's up there," Brenda interjected on a brighter note. "We could bring the Christmas things downstairs and see what works and what doesn't."

Sara's face brightened. "Could we plug in the lights?"

"Sure. Maybe we can even find that big old plastic snowman Grandma used to stick out on the porch. But first you have to finish your dinner," Brenda said, snatching a grape from Sara's plate.

"Aren't you going to eat?" Sara asked, noticing Brenda didn't have a sandwich.

"Not right now. I might be meeting a friend later, so I thought I'd wait in case we want to get something to eat then."

Juliet glanced suspiciously at her sister. "Who are you going out with?"

"I'm not exactly going out." Brenda's voice was defensive, as it usually was whenever Juliet asked about her personal life. "Wendy and I thought we might do something after she gets off work."

Juliet's immediate sense of relief that she wasn't meeting Ross disappeared when she realized the two girls might be planning on visiting the White Wolf. Suspicious, she asked, "What are you going to do?"

Brenda shrugged. "Find some action at one of the sororities, I suppose."

"Where's Ross this evening?"

"Probably at the White Wolf. Why?"

This time Juliet shrugged. "No particular reason. I just thought you might be seeing him tonight."

"What you really want to know is whether I took your advice, right?"

Juliet could hear the edge in her sister's voice, but decided to take the risk and asked, "What I want to know is how important he is to you."

"Too important for me to consider forgetting him simply because my sister doesn't approve," she stated defiantly.

Guilt reared its ugly head as memories of her lunch with Ross taunted Juliet. "It's not that I disapprove of him," she said evenly.

"Then what is it?"

What could she say? That she didn't want Brenda to be attracted to him because she was? She could see that Sara was following their conversation, and she chose her next words carefully. "I guess I'm uncomfortable with the age difference between the two of you. I think you should be dating boys your own age."

Brenda slumped back in her chair and sighed. "Well, you'll be happy to know that Ross and I aren't exactly dating."

Juliet felt as though a weight had been lifted off her chest. "What do you mean?"

"He likes me . . . I know he does," Brenda insisted. "But I can't seem to get him to quit treating me like a little sister. You saw the way he behaved on Thanksgiving."

As Juliet thought back to the holiday, she realized that Ross's attitude toward Brenda had been rather indulgent, only she had been too caught up in her own reaction to him to notice it at the time. "It's probably better he does treat you like a sister."

Brenda sighed impatiently. "Just because you don't like him doesn't mean you have to wish me bad luck with him."

"Why don't you like Ross, Mommy?" Sara asked, listening to the conversation with interest.

Juliet shot Brenda a look of reproach before saying, "I never said I didn't like him."

"I like him," Sara said innocently. "Especially when he plays the piano. Mommy, am I going to start my piano lessons pretty soon? You said I could when we had a piano, and now we have Grandma's."

"I know, Sara, and I'm going to find a teacher for you, but it takes time," Juliet explained.

"Ross gives music lessons," Brenda stated with a sly smile.

"He probably only teaches college students," Juliet said, giving her sister another hostile look. She attempted to change the subject. "Sara, finish eating so you can go up into the attic with Brenda."

"Do you want me to find out?" Brenda persisted.

Juliet was about to give a firm no when Sara cried out, "Annie spilled her milk!"

With lightning quickness, Juliet was on her feet and retrieving a sponge for the floor while Brenda soaked up the milk on the tray as best as she could with a napkin.

"I think she's going to need another sandwich. This one's all soggy," Brenda stated as she lifted Annie's plate from her high-chair tray. Annie immediately began to cry out in protest at the loss of her dinner.

"Give her mine," Juliet said from her crouched position on the floor.

Brenda gave Annie a piece of Juliet's sandwich, but it failed to calm the wailing child. As Juliet's hand swept across the pool of milk, a big chunk of grilled cheese sandwich landed with a splatter.

"I think she wants her soggy one back," Brenda said, trying to stifle her giggle.

"Then give her the soggy one," Juliet snapped irritably. Before she had finished mopping up the milk, the soggy sandwich was on the floor as well. "Oh, good grief," she said wearily, getting to her feet. "Are you hungry, Annie, or aren't you?"

"Teez," Annie cried out, pointing to Sara's plate.

"That's Sara's sandwich," Juliet told her, moving Sara's plate out of Annie's reach. "I'll make you another one."

"She can have the rest of mine," Sara insisted, shoving the plate back in Annie's direction. "I want to go to the attic."

"But you haven't eaten your soup," Juliet protested.

"I'm not hungry," Sara declared, climbing down from the chair.

Juliet wanted to remind her that only a short time ago she was complaining of a stomachache because she *was* hungry, but she was too tired to argue with a six-year-old. "Oh, all right. Go ahead. I guess you can always have a snack before you go to bed."

Sara took one last sip of milk, then went dancing out of the room with her hand tucked in Brenda's. Juliet looked over at Annie, who was contentedly chewing on Sara's half-eaten sandwich. As she reached for Sara's bowl of soup, Brenda poked her head back into the kitchen.

"By the way, I forgot to tell you. Some guy called for you when you were gone."

"Who was it?"

"I don't know. He didn't want to leave a message."

For a moment Juliet thought that it might have been Ross, but then she realized that Brenda would have recognized his voice.

"I figured if it was important, he'd call back."

"I guess he will," Juliet agreed absently, wondering why her first thought was that it had been Ross who had phoned. After everything that had happened, did she really expect him to be calling her? Did she want him to? She didn't think she wanted to know the answer to either question.

IF IT HADN'T BEEN for a tie clip, Juliet would never have made any attempt to see Ross again. While digging between the sofa cushions in search of Annie's barrette, she found the small gold object with the initials RAS engraved across the front. There was only one man it could belong to—Ross.

Having already arranged to have Brenda sit with the girls while she did some of her Christmas shopping that evening, she decided to return the tie clip to Ross. She would be driving right past the White Wolf on her way downtown, and all it would take was a quick stop—in and out.

This time Juliet used the front entrance to the White Wolf. Although it wasn't as crowded as it had been on her previous visit, the club was far from empty. Because it was still early in the evening, the stage was bare except for the instruments and speakers. She glanced about apprehensively, wondering where Ross might be. She was about to ask one of the waitresses when she felt a hand on her shoulder.

Startled, she turned around just as Ross said, "This is a surprise."

The look of pleasure on his face made Juliet's heart thump in her chest. Now that she was face-to-face with him, she forgot everything she had planned to say. He looked so damned attractive. Once again he was wearing black, but this time it wasn't leather.

"Are you alone?" he asked.

She nodded. "I'm going shopping."

"Then you're not staying?"

He looked disappointed, and Juliet felt her stomach lurch. "I wasn't planning on it." She reached into her purse for the tie clip and handed it to him. "I came because I found this in between the cushions on my sofa. I thought it might be yours."

Ross scrutinized the tiny gold object. "It's mine, all right. I didn't even realize I had lost it. I guess that tells you how often I wear a tie." He shoved the clip into his pocket.

Juliet stood staring at him, thinking that he didn't need a suit and tie to improve his appearance. He looked great just as he was. She searched her mind for something clever to say, but found nothing.

Ross was the one who spoke. "Do you have time for a drink?"

She checked her watch. "I really shouldn't," she began, but he cut her off.

"Why shouldn't you?" he asked point-blank.

"I'm supposed to be Christmas shopping. The stores will only be open for a couple more hours this evening."

"And one drink will put you off schedule?"

He made it sound as if being on any kind of schedule was something too ridiculous to worry about.

"It's the least I can do to repay you for returning my tie clip," he cajoled softly.

She shrugged. "I guess one drink would be all right."

The look of satisfaction in his eyes made her heart race as she followed him to a small table not far from the stage. Ross's eyes skimmed her figure appreciatively as she removed her coat, and she was glad she was still wearing the long jacket and short skirt she had worn to work that day. It was one of the few additions to her wardrobe this fall, and it did wonders for her self-confidence. As she looked around her, she knew that this time she didn't look out of place.

"What would you like?" Ross asked as a waitress approached them.

"Maybe just a glass of white wine," she told the young woman.

Ross ordered a beer for himself, then said, "You know, you're really not very much like Brenda at all."

"No, I have red hair, freckles and I'm bigger," she quipped.

His dazzling smile made her breath catch in her throat. "That's not what I meant and you know it." He leaned closer to her when he spoke, making her feel as though they were sharing something more intimate than drinks in a jazz club.

"Brenda wears spandex tube dresses and I prefer skirts and sweaters?" Again she tried to sound flip, but failed.

"Brenda's a child and you're a woman," he said softly.

She shifted uneasily beneath his intense gaze. "She *is* only nineteen." Her mouth felt dry, and she was relieved to see the waitress coming with their drinks.

"I know. Brenda told me you're twenty-seven," Ross said as the waitress set two glasses on the table. "I guess that means you and I have done a lot more living than Brenda has."

While Ross exchanged a few words with the waitress, Juliet took a sip of her wine, then said, "What time do you have to play?" She glanced up at the stage.

"Not for a while."

"Have you been doing this type of work very long?" she asked politely, trying to keep the conversation on an impersonal level.

"This isn't work, Juliet. I like playing the sax, especially in a club like this one."

"It's very trendy, isn't it?" Her gaze swept across the room.

"The people here appreciate good jazz." He leaned forward, his expression changing from good-natured to speculative. "Juliet, why did you really come here?"

"To return your tie clip."

"I see Brenda every day in class. You could have given it to her."

She blushed. "That's true, but I thought it might be a good idea for me to return it." She took another sip of wine. "There's something I think we should talk about."

Ross looked at her steadily. "And what might that be?"

She took a deep breath and said, "Brenda's feelings."

He leaned back, his expression guarded. "What are you trying to say?"

"That Brenda has a crush on you."

"I realize that. She hasn't exactly tried to keep it a secret." He rubbed a hand across his jaw. "Look, if you're worried that I'm going to do something to encourage her, you're worrying over nothing. I'm not interested in Brenda in that way."

"Then why did you come to Thanksgiving dinner?"

A look of annoyance crossed his face. "You think that because I accept a dinner invitation from one of my students it means I'm hoping to start something up with her?''

"Are you?''

"No!'' It came out fast and sharp. "Is that why you've been so hostile toward me? Because you thought I was sleeping with your sister?''

"Every time she talked about you she made it sound as if the two of you were going out.''

"Well, we're not,'' he said firmly. "Brenda's my student, not my girlfriend. The only reason I came to dinner on Thanksgiving was because I thought she had invited several members of the theater department, not just me.''

"She told you that?''

"That's what she implied. Is that why you didn't want me coming on to you?''

A sparkle of understanding shone in his eyes, but Juliet didn't see it, for her eyes were on her fingers as they pleated her paper napkin. His hand reached over and stilled hers.

"Juliet, is that the reason you didn't want me coming on to you? Because of Brenda?''

She met his gaze. "Partly.''

"What's the other part?''

"Ross, I'm a divorced mother with two small children.''

"Is that supposed to make you unattractive or something?'' When she didn't say anything, he said, "Or is it that you think I'm not suitable for a divorced mother with two children?''

"I hardly know anything about you.''

"That's because you were in the kitchen while I was giving my life history to your grandmother on Thanksgiving.''

"I'm sorry about Thanksgiving. I told you, I had no idea you were Brenda's teacher...." She shrugged, embarrassed.

Several of the musicians had climbed onto the stage to warm up. Seeing Juliet watching them, he asked, "Do you like jazz?"

"Sometimes."

"Spoken like a politician's daughter," he said with a wry grin. "You're usually not so polite when it comes to me. Why don't you just say what you really think?"

"All right. I'm not particularly fond of jazz. I prefer classical music."

"That figures."

She bristled at his tone of voice. "What's wrong with classical music?"

"I didn't say anything was wrong with it."

"Then why did you say 'that figures'?"

"Because it does. You seem like the type who would prefer structured music. Lots of people do. Jazz can be a little too improvisational for some people's tastes."

"But that's what you like about it, isn't it? You like to do things on the spur of the moment . . . like getting on a bus for no apparent reason." The memory caused an inward smile.

"Oh, I had a reason, Juliet," he said seductively. He held her gaze for several seconds, then added, "I like jazz for several reasons, but I have to confess that being able to take a melody and improvise is what I like best."

"You play the saxophone beautifully." Her compliment was warm and sincere.

"I'm glad you like it. If you stick around, I'll play something special for you."

Again she stole a glance at her watch, and Ross said, "I think you look at your watch more than anyone I know."

"With two small children, I have to." She slipped her arms into her coat sleeves. "I wish I could stay to hear the music, but I really can't."

"Not even for one song? You wouldn't have to sit here by yourself. You could come backstage."

"If I go home without any packages, Brenda's going to be suspicious." As she rose to her feet, he came around to hold her chair.

"Aren't you going to tell her you stopped by?"

She shook her head. "I don't think it's a good idea."

"Juliet, I'm not dating your sister."

"I know." She buttoned her coat, keeping her eyes on her fingers.

"I'd like to be dating you."

He was only putting into words what they both already knew. "I know that, too."

"But you don't think it's a good idea."

Her teeth tugged on her lower lip. "I...I..." she stammered, wanting to say yes. "No."

He stared at her for several seconds, then said, "I bet when you were a little kid you never wanted to color outside the lines, did you?"

She just looked at him, then primly recited, "Thank you for the glass of wine." She reached for her gloves and purse.

"I'm glad you stopped in, Juliet." He walked with her to the exit, where he held the door for her. "You'll have to come back some night when you have more time.''

''I will,'' she answered, knowing perfectly well that she probably wouldn't. ''Good night,'' she said as she slipped through the door.

But he followed her outside saying, ''Where are you parked?''

''In the lot across the street.''

''I'll walk you to your car.''

''You'll freeze,'' she said, looking at the thin shirt covering his torso.

''Not if we hurry.'' He grabbed her by the arm and started for the parking lot. By the time they reached her station wagon, he was shivering.

''Thanks. I'm fine now.'' She flashed him a grateful smile as she unlocked the door. Expecting him to run back inside, she was surprised when he stood watching until she had started the engine and was ready to drive away. Just as she was about to put the car in reverse, he tapped on her window.

When she opened it, he said, ''By the way, I happen to like classical music, too.''

THE NEXT EVENING, Juliet was sitting at the kitchen table with her textbooks and notes spread out in front of her when Brenda waltzed in. Not having mentioned seeing Ross at the White Wolf, Juliet hoped her sister wouldn't bring up his name. Ross Stafford was one subject she wanted to avoid at all costs. Unfortunately Brenda didn't share her feelings.

''Did Ross call you?'' she asked, pulling a soda from the refrigerator.

''No,'' Juliet quickly denied. ''Why would he?''

Brenda popped the top on the can and took a sip. "I told him you were looking for a piano teacher for Sara."

Juliet groaned. "I wish you hadn't."

"Why not? You've heard him play. He's a fabulous musician and a good teacher."

Juliet searched her mind for a quick answer. "That's exactly my point. He's a wonderful musician. He doesn't need to be giving lessons to a six-year-old."

"He gives private lessons, Juliet. He told me he worked his way through college teaching piano."

"How nice," she muttered, not intending for the words to come out quite so sarcastically.

Brenda boosted herself up onto the counter, leaving her legs dangling as she eyed Juliet curiously. "I still don't understand why you don't like him."

"Can we just change the subject here? I've got twenty pages to read before my exam on Saturday."

"Excuse *me,*" Brenda said in an exaggerated drawl. "I thought I was doing you a favor, and I know Sara wants to play the piano."

Juliet pushed her bangs off her forehead and sighed in resignation. "Look, I'll talk to Ross about it if he calls, all right?"

For the next few days, every time the phone rang Juliet's heart skipped a beat. But Ross didn't call, and she felt a strange mixture of relief and disappointment.

She chastised herself for feeling anything at all. There was no room in her life for a Ross Stafford—in any capacity.

Ross, however, didn't share her sentiments. Just when Juliet thought she wasn't going to hear from him again, the postman arrived with her mail. Among the Christmas cards and bills was an envelope with no return address, her name written in a bold, unfamiliar handwriting.

She ripped open the flap and extracted a glossy rectangle with the words Admit One stamped across one end. She quickly scanned the fine print indicating it was a ticket for the St. Paul Chamber Orchestra's classical music concert the following Sunday afternoon at the Ordway Theater. It was a concert she had been wanting to attend, but she hadn't been able to justify the price of a ticket on her budget.

Juliet looked once more inside the envelope for a note or a card, but found nothing. There was only one person who could have sent it. The question was, did she dare use the ticket? She hesitated only a moment before picking up the phone to arrange for a babysitter.

To Juliet's relief, Brenda left early Sunday morning to go skiing with friends, eliminating the need to tell her how she was going to spend her afternoon. The only explaining she had to do concerned Sara, who didn't understand why her mother couldn't take her to see Santa at the mall rather than go to some dumb old concert.

But it wasn't just any old concert, Juliet thought to herself as she hurried into the lobby of the elegant Ordway Theater. Glittering lights and garlands of greenery set the tone for the music she was about to hear. She gave her ticket stub to an usher, who led her down the center aisle to the correct row. As she expected, Ross was sitting in the seat next to hers. When he saw her, he rose to his feet and stepped into the aisle so that she could take her seat.

"You look surprised to see me," she told him when they were both seated.

"I didn't think you'd show up," he admitted.

"I didn't think I would, either," she retorted, shrugging out of her coat. He reached behind her to help her, his arm gently grazing her shoulder in the process.

"I'm glad you did." His gaze held hers, and the message she saw there made her glad they were in an auditorium filled with people.

Juliet was relieved when the lights were dimmed, for she didn't know what else to say. Had she made a mistake in coming? Her worries faded, though, as the music worked its magic, and soon she was captivated by the orchestra's performance of some of her favorite works. During intermission, Ross took her to the lobby, where they had a glass of wine and discussed the selection of music on the program.

She wasn't sure whether it was the wine or their conversation that had her mellowing by the second half of the program. When Ross reached for her hand and held it in his, she didn't offer any resistance.

At the end of the concert, she turned to him and said, "You really do like classical music, don't you?"

"That surprises you?" he asked as he helped her on with her coat.

"What surprises me is your interest in theater arts. Music seems to be a big part of your life."

"That's a long story...one that would be better told over dinner. I know a great place not far from here that serves the most wonderful pasta." He looked at her expectantly.

Juliet wanted to say yes, but she knew it wasn't going to work. "I'm sorry, but I can't."

"What about a cocktail at the lounge across the street?"

She shook her head. "I told the baby-sitter I'd be home by six," she said apologetically. "Sara and Annie need dinner."

She expected him to make some wisecrack about being on schedule, but he didn't. He simply said, "Then I guess we'll have to save the story for another time."

As he escorted her to her car, he made no mention of when that other time would be, and Juliet began to suspect that his statement was his way of saying, "I'll call you sometime." But just as she was about to say goodbye, he pulled her into his arms and kissed her.

At first she thought it was because he had caught her off guard that the kiss left her breathless. But as his mouth intimately teased hers, she realized that she was reacting to Ross, not surprise. By the time his lips left hers, she was clinging to him, her insides quivering with delight.

"Drive carefully." His voice sounded as weak as she was feeling, and she knew that he had been as affected by the kiss as she had.

She nodded and mumbled, "Thanks for the concert," then got in her car and started up the engine. As she drove away, she could see him in her rearview mirror, and she was filled with regret that she couldn't invite him to come home with her.

CHAPTER FIVE

EACH TIME THE PHONE RANG the following week, Juliet expected it to be Ross. What she didn't expect, however, was that he'd show up on her doorstep.

It was Wednesday evening, the night she set aside for laundry. She had changed out of her working clothes into an old faded pair of sweats and was folding underwear and socks at the kitchen table when Brenda came bouncing through the swinging door.

"Ross is here," she declared with a gleam in her eyes.

"Ross Stafford?" Juliet repeated inanely.

"Yes. Come on. He's in the living room and he wants to talk to you."

Juliet felt her heart start to pump vigorously. Why had he come to the house? What could he possibly want to say to her in front of Brenda? Reluctantly she followed her sister through the swinging door.

He was seated on the sofa, sandwiched between Sara and Annie. Sara was showing him a drawing she had done in school that day and Annie was trying to get his attention by waving a rag doll in his face. He smiled at Juliet as she walked in.

"Brenda said you wanted to talk to me." She glanced warily from Ross to her sister.

"Maybe we should talk privately," he suggested, which only increased her apprehension.

"Brenda, why don't you take the girls into the kitchen for some cookies and milk?" Juliet nervously glanced from her sister to her daughters. Brenda cheerfully consented and reached for Annie's and Sara's hands.

Both girls scrambled off the couch and followed their aunt out of the room, waving at Ross as they left. Brenda flashed Ross a beguiling smile and said, "Be back in a bit."

As soon as Juliet was alone with Ross, she asked, "Does she know why you're here?" She deliberately kept her voice low.

"She's the one who asked me to come. She said you were looking for someone to give Sara piano lessons," he explained.

Juliet felt an odd mixture of relief and disappointment. He hadn't simply come to see her. "And you're interested?"

"I'm interested," he repeated, although the look in his eyes hinted that he was interested in more than Sara's piano lessons.

Juliet felt the now-familiar rush of pleasure as his eyes swept over her. "I'm not sure it's such a good idea," she said.

Impatiently, he heaved a sigh and said, "I've had plenty of experience. Would you like to check my references?"

"Of course not," she replied quickly. "It's just that you're used to teaching college students."

He shrugged. "I've taught children as well."

"I was thinking more along the lines of a college student who would be willing to come to the house." Her voice was tentative.

"I'll come here if you like," he offered.

She shook her head emphatically. "I couldn't impose on you that way."

"It's no imposition. I enjoy giving lessons. All you have to do is tell me what time is convenient for Sara and I'll work my schedule around yours." When she hesitated, he added, "I'll have her playing Beethoven before you know it." He went over to the piano and played the first four notes of Beethoven's Fifth Symphony.

"Ross, I know you play the piano beautifully, and it's kind of you to offer to teach Sara, but the truth is I'm not in a financial position to pay for professional lessons. That's why I was hoping to find a student who was interested in making some extra money."

"If you're worried about paying me, I could always take it out in trade," he offered. Seeing the look of alarm on her face, he added quickly, "I meant a home-cooked meal in exchange for a lesson."

She chuckled. "I couldn't let you do that."

"Why not?"

"Because it wouldn't be fair to you."

"Why wouldn't it? I have a late class at the university, and I usually skip dinner on the nights I play at the White Wolf. If I stopped in on my way, I could give Sara her lesson and you could give me dinner."

"You're serious, aren't you?"

"We could start tonight, if you like."

"We've already had dinner," Juliet said apologetically.

"I could give her the lesson tonight and come back for payment later," he suggested with a challenging gleam in his eye.

"It's really kind of you to offer, but . . ."

"You're going to say no, aren't you?"

Just then Sara came skipping into the living room. "Ross, will you play 'Jingle Bells' for me?" she asked, seeing him standing next to the piano.

"I will if you'll sing while I play. Is it a deal?" he asked, pulling out the piano bench and sitting down.

Sara climbed up beside him and said, "Deal."

They were halfway through the song when Brenda came in with Annie. She joined in the singing, bouncing a giggling Annie in her arms. When the song came to an end, they all looked at Juliet.

"Does this mean he's hired?" Brenda asked pertly.

Before Juliet could answer, Sara said, "Can Ross be my piano teacher, Mommy? Please?"

Juliet knew she was outnumbered. "All right," she conceded, annoyed not so much with the fact that Brenda and her daughters had forced the issue, but because the thought of Ross coming to dinner generated more excitement than she wanted to admit.

So Ross gave an attentive Sara her very first piano lesson and agreed to return the following night for payment. The next day, Juliet told herself she shouldn't do anything different for dinner just because Ross would be there. Nevertheless, instead of one of the quick meals she usually prepared on weekdays, she put a beef roast in her slow cooker and baked a chocolate cake for dessert. But if she expected Ross to treat her as anything other than the mother of one of his pupils, she was in for a disappointment. When he arrived at the house, Sara immediately latched onto him, wanting to show him what she had done with only a couple of hours of practice.

Throughout dinner, Ross's attention seemed to be divided between Brenda and Sara. Brenda kept the conversation centered around theater-arts topics that Juliet knew little about, and Sara talked of nothing but the titles of songs she wanted to learn how to play. Except for complimenting her on her dinner, Ross didn't say much to Juliet, and it wasn't long after the dessert was served that he left for the White Wolf.

Juliet was beginning to think she had only imagined he was interested in her as a woman, but a short while later the phone rang. It was Ross.

"I just wanted to let you know that Sara and I got off to a good start," he told her. "I'm looking forward to working with her."

"That's nice to hear, although I'm wondering if she isn't overdoing it a bit. She seems to be a little obsessed with practicing."

"That's not unusual for beginners. It's the excitement of being able to make music." His voice sounded unusually husky, and it sent a tiny shiver down her spine.

"I only hope the enthusiasm lasts."

"We'll work on it." There was a commotion in the background and then he said, "Juliet, I had two reasons for calling tonight. Tomorrow's my night off and I was wondering if you'd like to go with me to the Chanhassen Dinner Theater?"

A date. He had come right out and asked her for a date! It had been months since she had gone out with a man. Pleasure was followed by the sobering realization that she couldn't accept. Memories of how Brenda's face had lit up every time Ross spoke to her at dinner reminded her that her sister had a very real crush on him.

"I'm sorry, Ross, but I've already made plans for tomorrow night," she lied.

"I understand," he answered, although Juliet didn't think he could possibly understand how difficult it was for her to say no.

She tried to explain. "Brenda would be..."

Before she could finish he cut her off. "I said I understand, Juliet, and I do." There was more noise in the background, and he said, "Look, I have to go. We're about ready to go on. I'll see you next week."

With a click he was gone, and Juliet swore softly beneath her breath. How could he possibly understand? She certainly didn't.

ON FRIDAYS, THE OFFICES where Juliet was employed closed at one-thirty. She and Annie often spent the afternoon at the parent-child center not far from the university where special classes were offered in swimming and exercise for mothers and toddlers.

On this particular Friday, however, Juliet decided to skip the sessions. Annie appeared to be coming down with a cold, and with Christmas only a few weeks away, Juliet needed the time at home to work on the matching dresses she was sewing for her daughters.

When she arrived at the house, she was surprised to find Brenda curled up on the couch reading a magazine.

"How come you're not in class?" Juliet asked as she unwrapped Annie's scarf from around her neck.

"I cut it," Brenda answered a bit sullenly.

"Brenda! Finals are just around the corner," Juliet chided.

"Get off my case, Jules. I don't need your permission to cut a class," her sister retorted defiantly.

"You're right. You don't." Juliet quietly finished unbundling Annie, then started up the stairs toward her room. She had only gone halfway up the staircase when Brenda called out to her.

"By the way, that guy called again—the one I told you called last week."

"Did he leave his name?"

"Uh-uh. As soon as I said you weren't here, he hung up. You know, it almost sounded like it could have been Tim."

Juliet's heart skipped a beat at the mention of her ex-husband's name. "I haven't heard from him in almost two years. Why would he call me now?"

Brenda shrugged. "I don't know, but something about this guy's voice reminded me of Tim."

The rest of the afternoon Juliet was distracted by the possibility that her ex-husband might be trying to reach her. After their bitter parting two years ago, she hadn't expected to hear from him again. Although the judge had granted him visitation privileges at the time of their divorce, not once had he made an effort to see his daughters. The only contact she had had with him was through his sporadic child-support payments and the birthday and Christmas presents he had sent by mail. Not that Juliet believed Tim had anything to do with the gifts. She guessed that it was his parents who were responsible for remembering their grandchildren.

Just the thought of him made her angry, and every time the phone rang that afternoon, she jumped. Fortunately all the calls were for Brenda, except the one that came right after Sara had arrived home from school. Juliet was pinning the partially constructed velveteen dress on her daughter's small shoulders when Brenda announced that this call was for her. Out of Sara's range of vision, she mouthed, "It's him."

Juliet carefully removed the straight pins holding the dress in place, then went to take the phone in her bedroom. Before saying hello, she took a deep breath.

"Juliet, it's Tim."

His face came to mind with startling clarity. She flattened her hand against her chest, as if she could slow her racing heart. "What do you want?" she asked, her voice barely above a whisper.

"I called to see how Sara and Annie are doing."

"They're doing just fine," she said curtly.

"I bet they're getting big."

Juliet didn't comment. She waited, wondering what he was going to say next.

After a brief pause, he said, "It's been awhile since I've seen them."

"That's not my fault."

"I didn't say it was." He exhaled a long sigh. "I think we should at least be civil here, Juliet."

"Civil about what?" she asked suspiciously.

"About my visitation rights."

Juliet's heart rose into her throat. Panic bubbled up inside her. "What are you saying?"

"I want to see my daughters."

Her grasp tightened on the receiver. "You're coming to Minnesota?"

"No, I was hoping the girls could come out here."

She took another deep breath, trying to calm nerves that were threatening to pop like firecrackers. "You expect me to bring them to California?"

"You wouldn't have to come. They could fly out, and I'd be there at the airport to meet them."

"No!" Her objection was immediate. "You don't send a six-year-old and a two-year-old on a plane trip two thousand miles by themselves!"

"Calm down," he said in a patronizing tone that Juliet had always found annoying. "If you don't want them traveling alone, I could come to Minnesota and get them."

"No!" she repeated even more firmly. "They're not leaving this state, Tim."

"Juliet, I have visiting privileges," he reminded her.

"For every other weekend, here in Minnesota," she said angrily. "And you haven't wanted to see them in two years!"

"That's not true. I've been busy getting my practice established out here. I couldn't leave. I don't see why they couldn't come out here during Christmas vacation for a few days."

"The answer is no."

"Juliet, be reasonable. They're my children, too."

"How convenient for you to remember," she mocked in a sugary-sweet voice. "It's only taken you two years."

"There's no point in getting hostile," he said in a deceptively calm voice.

Juliet could imagine his eyes narrowing and his chin jutting forward as they had so often in the past whenever they argued. She was sorely tempted to hang up on him, but exercised every bit of self-restraint she possessed. "The terms of our agreement say you can see them every other weekend, here in Minnesota," she repeated evenly.

"I realize that, but will you at least think about letting them come out here? They'd love it. It's sunny and warm, and Gloria has a daughter the same age as Sara."

At the mention of his new wife, Juliet felt as though a fist had been thrust into her stomach. She had heard that he had remarried, but she hadn't known that he'd gotten a new daughter into the bargain.

"There's nothing to consider. You know the terms of the divorce agreement. We go by the rules or not at all," she said, hating the fact that after two years he still had the power to upset her.

He made a sound of exasperation that crackled over the line. "I want to talk to Sara," he demanded.

Juliet contemplated saying she wasn't home from school, but knowing how Sara still felt about her father, she couldn't deny her the chance to speak to him. She didn't realize she hadn't answered him until he said again, "Juliet, I want to talk to Sara."

"All right. I'll get her, but only if you promise not to mention anything about flying out to California." Reluctantly he agreed and she called her daughter to the phone.

When Juliet saw the way Sara's face lit up when she discovered it was her father calling, she wanted to grab the receiver from her hand and slam it down in the cradle. For months after the divorce she had prayed for Tim to call and talk to Sara, to ease the emotional stress she was suffering because of their separation. Now that he finally had, she was frightened of the consequences. Sara needed a father in her life, but one who was dependable and caring. Not a part-time parent who'd put in an appearance whenever it was convenient. Not a father who would only bring her heartache—which is exactly what she thought Tim Harper would do.

Tim was a user. As long as people filled a need in his life, he kept them around. The minute he didn't need them, he tossed them aside. It had happened to all three of them once before. She didn't want it to happen to her daughters a second time. The sad part was, there really wasn't anything she could do to prevent it.

SHORTLY AFTER TIM'S phone call, Kate and Donovan, newly returned from their honeymoon, arrived to hook up the outdoor Christmas lights. As excited as Sara was about the event, she was more interested in telling her grandmother about her phone conversation with her father. When she was finally bundled into her snowsuit, Brenda took her outside to watch Donovan string the lights up and down the columns on the porch. Juliet made her mother a cup of tea and told her about Tim's request.

"You aren't going to let him take the girls out there, are you?" Concern lined her mother's face as she sat across from Juliet at the kitchen table.

"No, of course not. I don't even want him coming here to Minnesota, but I'm afraid he's going to show up if I say the girls can't visit him."

"Maybe you should call Harvey for advice," Kate suggested.

Harvey Wilkens had been her father's law partner, and at Kate's request had handled the divorce for her. At the time, he had refused to accept payment for representing her in court, and Juliet was reluctant to call him without having money to pay for his services now.

"Harvey is a corporate attorney, Mom. He only handled my case because of Dad."

"It's because he did handle your case that you should call him and ask him what rights Tim has. He's familiar with the details."

Juliet ran a hand through her tousled curls. "I suppose you're right, but I don't want to be anyone's charity case."

Kate reached across the table and covered Juliet's hand with hers. "Harvey would be offended if he heard you talking that way. He's very fond of you."

"I know. That's why it's so difficult to talk to him about all of this."

"Juliet, you misjudged a man's character. That doesn't require a lifetime of penance." Kate's green eyes were brimming with compassion. "The point is, you need legal advice, whether it be from Harvey or a total stranger. Does Sara know that Tim wants her to visit him in California?"

Juliet took a sip of tea and shook her head. "Not yet." She rubbed her forearms as though warding off a chill. "I've got this horrible fear that when she does hear, she's going to want to go, and then I won't know what to do. I'm afraid I might not even see them again if Tim gets them out there."

"That does it." Kate abruptly rose from the table. "I'm calling Harvey myself. You can't be worrying about Annie and Sara's safety."

Juliet watched her mother as she talked on the phone, her auburn head nodding and shaking several times during the conversation. When she was finished, Kate said, "He wasn't in, but I talked with his partner and he's going to have Harvey call you first thing in the morning."

Juliet shook her head disconsolately. "I can't figure out why Tim's so interested in Sara and Annie all of a sudden. He didn't want anything to do with them before, but now he's putting on his great paternal act."

She bit down on her lower lip. "If only I didn't have this awful feeling that he was up to something."

"Why don't I take the girls overnight and you can go out with a friend this evening," Kate suggested. "It'll help you take your mind off all of this."

Juliet gazed affectionately at her mother. "I can't let you do that, Mom. You and Donovan just got back. You don't need two kids underfoot."

"They are never underfoot when they're with Grandma. Besides, I've missed them. It's been a long time since I've had them overnight."

"What about Donovan?"

"Oh, I'm sure he won't mind. Besides, he told me he might have to go down to the station after dinner." When Juliet hesitated, she said, "Let me take the girls. You can use the time for yourself—take a bubble bath, indulge in a good book. You'll be able to get to your class tomorrow without the hassle of fixing breakfast and bundling them off to the baby-sitter," she added temptingly.

Juliet reached over and squeezed her mother's arm. "All right, but I don't think I'm going to be very good company—not even for myself."

"Maybe you and Brenda could go to a movie," Kate suggested. "Go see something funny."

"If I know Brenda, she's already made plans to go to some party on campus, but I'll ask."

Juliet's suspicions were confirmed when a short time later Brenda came in from the cold and announced she had to get ready to go out with friends. When Kate asked if Juliet might like to go along, the two sisters exchanged leery looks.

"No, thank you," Juliet spoke up. "I don't need to be a baby-sitter to any teenagers."

Brenda pretended mock indignation, but Juliet knew she was relieved her big sister wouldn't be tagging along.

"Maybe Meridee's at loose ends this evening?" Brenda suggested.

"Uh-uh. I talked to her earlier this week and she said Richard was taking her to see the *Nutcracker* at Northrop Auditorium," Kate answered.

"Juliet, why don't you go for 'mom's night out'? That's tonight, isn't it?"

Kate looked perplexed by Brenda's question. "What's 'mom's night out'?"

"The mothers in the baby-sitting co-op get together once a month for a night out," Juliet explained.

"You never mentioned that to me before," Kate commented.

Juliet shrugged. "Their idea of a good time doesn't exactly jive with mine."

"Why is that?"

"Because Juliet thinks they only want to go bar-hopping to all the singles places," Brenda answered for her.

"I thought some of them were married," Kate remarked.

"Only one of them is married, Mom. The others are all divorced or separated," Juliet told her. "Basically, they're a lot of fun, but I'm a little tired of the singles scene. I haven't exactly had terrific luck with the men I've met in the bars."

"Then why don't you suggest they try something different—like a dinner theater or a comedy club?" Kate asked.

"Because these women don't want to go to the theater. They want to go where there are men." Juliet tried to keep the censorious note from her voice but failed.

"Sounds like they have their priorities straight if you ask me," Brenda said lightly. "I only wish I were old enough to get into some of those places they visit. Being a minor is so boring."

Kate frowned at her youngest daughter, then turned to Juliet. "Well, whether you go out or not, I'm still going to take the girls overnight."

The plan met everyone's approval, but later, when Juliet found herself alone in a too-silent house, she wished that she had kept the girls with her. The phone call from Tim had been too unsettling for her to relax and enjoy her unexpected privacy. She needed to be around people, and after a couple of unsuccessful attempts to reach friends, she decided to call Lyn Tyler, one of the mothers from the baby-sitting co-op.

As it turned out, the group was meeting at a place called Dino's, a newly opened nightspot that had a limited dinner menu but a big dance floor. A local rock band was appearing, and Lyn told Juliet they were "fabulous."

So Juliet dressed in a black-and-white jumpsuit and let her red curls frame her face instead of pulling them back in a clip. While she waited for Lyn to pick her up, she tried not to think of all the bad times she had had at singles bars.

There were five women in the baby-sitting co-op, but only three went to Dino's that night. To Juliet's surprise, the atmosphere at the club was nonthreatening, and with the place only half-filled, she was beginning to think her friends were wrong when they told her it was *the* place to be.

With an air of studied nonchalance, Juliet made a survey of the crowd, which was steadily increasing as it got closer to the time for the music to begin. Most of the patrons were in their twenties and thirties, and although there were some couples, most of them were singles—or pretending to be singles.

"Didn't I tell you there'd be lots of guys here?" Lyn said enthusiastically when a couple of good-looking men passed their table.

"That won't do us much good if they don't like to dance," Gwen Nilson, the third member of their group, commented. The band was getting ready to play, and Gwen was wiggling and bouncing as though they couldn't start soon enough. "Hey... check out that guy in the yellow shirt."

Heads turned, but not Juliet's. She was only half-tuned in to their conversation, wishing that she hadn't given in to the loneliness that had prompted her to call Lyn. Suddenly she wished she was at home putting the finishing touches to Sara's and Annie's holiday dresses instead of listening to women dissect men as though they were choosing meat at the market.

As she made a mental list of everything she wanted to accomplish during the weekend, Lyn grabbed her by the shoulder.

"Are you having another one?" Lyn asked, and Juliet looked up to see the waitress waiting for her answer.

"No, I'm fine," Juliet answered, placing her palm over her glass of white wine.

Apparently Lyn hadn't noticed her distraction. She was looking around like a child in a candy shop. "What do you think of this place? Isn't it great?"

"The food was good," Juliet answered, trying to sound as upbeat as she could.

Her answer seemed to satisfy Lyn, whose attention span seemed to be about as long as Annie's when single men were in the same room.

"Oh, my gawd!" Lyn drawled. "Would you look at the gorgeous creature talking to the singer. Do you suppose he's in the band?"

"I've heard this group before and I don't recognize him," Gwen remarked.

"He's got a great body—not too big and not too muscular. Just right," Lyn pronounced with a coy giggle.

"Something about him seems familiar to me," Gwen said contemplatively. "I wonder if he's somebody famous."

Lyn tried to guess his identity, then finally asked Juliet. "What do you think? Is he a local celebrity?"

Juliet was sitting with her back to the band and didn't feel much like turning around to gawk at some Adonis. But Lyn wasn't going to let up until she took a look. Reluctantly she twisted around in her chair.

The man was none other than Ross Stafford. Juliet couldn't prevent her eyes from widening when she saw him. She would have liked to pretend she didn't know him, but she knew Lyn had seen the recognition on her face.

"Do you know who he is?" she asked excitedly.

Juliet quickly turned her back to the band and said, "That's Ross Stafford. He teaches at the university."

"He's a teacher? Maybe we ought to go back to college, eh, Gwen," Lyn suggested, nudging the blonde with her elbow. "How well do you know him?" she asked Juliet.

"I don't really *know* him," Juliet hedged. "My sister's in one of his classes."

"Is he single?" Gwen demanded.

Juliet had never been much good at lying, but right now she would have liked to have told them Ross had a wife and three kids. She did the next best thing. She shrugged and said, "It's hard to believe a man who looks the way he does is available."

"Well, he's definitely not unattached. There's some blonde with him," Gwen observed unhappily.

Again, Juliet turned around, this time to get a glimpse of the woman hanging onto Ross Stafford's arm. It was the same blonde she had seen cuddling up to him backstage at the White Wolf the night she had returned his van. Juliet felt a strong twinge of envy.

"Wouldn't you know? The good-looking ones are always taken, aren't they?" Lyn said, pouting, then quickly turned her attention to another man on the opposite side of the room.

Not wanting Ross to notice her sitting at the table with the others, Juliet excused herself to go to the ladies' room, taking a rather long way around to avoid running into him. After powdering her nose and debating whether or not she should use her emergency twenty-dollar bill to take a cab home, she decided to return to the table and hope that she would be lost in the crowd.

The band had already started playing by the time she sat down. Juliet's eyes scanned the dance floor, but there was no trace of Ross or his date. Lyn and Gwen, on the other hand, had both been asked to dance, leaving Juliet sitting alone at the table.

She did her best not to feel conspicuous, but she felt as if she had a red bull's-eye painted on her forehead. Feeling totally out of her element, Juliet decided it was definitely time to use her twenty.

As soon as she was able to get Lyn's attention, she told the other girl she wasn't feeling well and was leaving. Lyn didn't try to talk her into staying. If anything, she looked relieved, and Juliet guessed her friend was anticipating spending the rest of the night with the man clinging to her side.

Feigning a cheerfulness she wasn't feeling, Juliet said good-night and headed toward the coat check. By now there was standing room only in the nightclub, and everywhere she looked there were people. With a series of "excuse me's" she began elbowing her way through closely packed bodies, trying not to make eye contact with anyone.

She was almost to the coat check when she spotted Ross. He was directly in her path, but his back was to her. She looked around, hoping to find a way to avoid walking past him, but it was inevitable. When he turned and saw her, she knew it was useless to pretend she didn't see him.

He smiled with obvious pleasure, then shoved his way around the people separating them, a glass of beer clenched in his left hand.

"I didn't expect to see you here," he said, his eyes raking over her in a manner that told her he was glad he had.

"I could say the same for you," she responded. "I thought you had theater tickets."

"I did, but the woman I wanted to be with turned me down." His gaze penetrated to her very soul, and Juliet couldn't resist the urge to like him. She wished she had accepted his invitation and that they were seated in the Chanhassen Dinner Theater rather than in the midst of a crowded dance hall.

He gave a cursory look around her. "Where are you going?"

"To the coat check. I'm leaving."

"You can't go home yet," he said in a seductive tone. "We haven't had a chance to dance."

This time it was Juliet who looked around, wondering what had happened to the blonde.

The band was about to begin a new song. Ross reached for her hand and said, "Dance with me, Juliet."

His eyes beckoned, his smile persuaded. Fleetingly she wondered what Brenda would say if she knew her sister was at Dino's dancing with the man she idolized? Maybe it was wrong, but what harm could there be in one dance? she asked herself.

"Just one," she said.

CHAPTER SIX

As ROSS LED HER out onto the dance floor, Juliet felt the rush of pleasure she experienced whenever she was with him. Her hand was warm in his as he took her to a small area in front of the stage. When the singer bent down to talk to him, Juliet looked on curiously, unable to hear the words.

"A friend of yours?" she asked when the singer had rejoined the other members of the band.

Ross smiled again. "We've played together a couple of times at the White Wolf."

She soon learned the reason for their brief conversation. When the music began, Ross cast a satisfied grin in the singer's direction as the harmonious chords of a love song filled the air.

Juliet immediately stiffened. It was one thing to dance to a fast rock song in which partners didn't need to touch; quite another to be held in Ross's arms, especially when the lyrics being sung by the sultry-voiced singer had a seductive power of their own.

Reluctantly Juliet went into his open arms, allowing him to pull her close, yet determined to maintain an emotional distance. She didn't succeed, for as soon as she felt his arms around her, her body betrayed her, melting against his as if it were the most natural thing in the world.

A musky aroma teased her nostrils, and for a moment she closed her eyes, fighting the warm sensations his scent stirred in her. With her breasts flattened against his chest, her knees shaking as her feet followed his, she tried to think of something mundane to say, but failed miserably.

All her thoughts were concentrated on how her body was pressed close to his. His flesh was enticingly firm underneath the silky-smooth shirt. A thrill shot through her as feelings she hadn't experienced in a long, long time warmed her insides. Being close to Ross was a heady sensation.

Gradually she relaxed, resting her head against his shoulder. He tightened his hold and sighed. "I knew you'd fit," he murmured.

The words were spoken so softly, Juliet wasn't sure if he was speaking to her or to himself. All she knew was that she agreed with him. She did fit, and it felt good to be in his arms—too good. They were two bodies in sync, two hearts beating to the same rhythm, two minds sharing the same thoughts as they danced in silence.

For a few minutes she closed her eyes and pretended there was no reason in the world why she shouldn't be enjoying the gentle touch of his fingers as they stroked her hair. Swaying to the sultry rhythm of the love song, she blocked out everything except the delicious warmth seeping through her.

Pressed close to Ross's lean frame, she realized that she wasn't the only one aroused by their proximity. He caught the tip of her chin with his finger, lifting her face to his, forcing her to look at him. Dark brown eyes conveyed his desire better than words.

Juliet thought that if she stayed in his arms one more minute, she'd find herself agreeing to just about anything. Fortunately the music ended and a round of applause brought her back to reality. "I really have to go," she said, pushing out of his arms.

He tried to stop her, but she eluded his grasp. "I'll walk you to your car," he stated, his arm snaking out possessively to steer her away from the other couples as they started dancing to a fast song.

"No," she said quickly. "That's not necessary."

"I know it's not necessary, but I want to do it," he told her in a husky voice.

"But I didn't drive my car here. I came with a friend."

"Are you meeting your friend out front? Is that why you're in such a hurry?"

There was a slight edge to his voice now, and Juliet knew he was assuming her friend was male. The thought that he might be disturbed by the idea of her being with another man set off a tiny shock wave of delight.

"I'm not in a hurry."

"Then why don't you stay? I can give you a ride home," he offered.

His hair had fallen rakishly across his forehead, and Juliet could feel her resolve weakening, wanting only to run her hands through its thickness. She resisted the urge. "I can't stay. Please don't ask me to." She took a step and so did Ross, blocking her path to the coat check.

"Are you involved with someone?"

"You mean a male someone?"

He nodded.

"Heavens, no," she said with a shaky little laugh. "The last thing I want in my life is an emotional entanglement."

"I feel the same way, but that doesn't mean we can't have fun together." He grinned wickedly as he caught her by the wrist and started to pull her back toward the dance floor.

"I don't want to stay, Ross," she told him, trying to ignore the sensations his touch was arousing.

He dropped her wrist, the teasing light in his eye disappearing. "You don't like it here, do you?"

She shrugged and was about to say something polite when he added, "Go ahead. Be honest. You're not going to hurt my feelings if you say you hate it."

"I don't hate it. It's just not my idea of a good time."

"I didn't think it would be. That's why I suggested we go to the theater." He followed her to the coat check. "Obviously your friend doesn't know you very well if he brought you here."

"My friend is a she. Her name is Lyn," she told him, then handed her token to the girl at the coat check.

His dark brown eyes gleamed with satisfaction. "Then *she* won't mind if I give you a ride home."

Privately Juliet thought Lyn would be green with envy if she knew Ross was even offering her a ride home. Aloud she said, "Lyn isn't leaving. I'm taking a taxi home."

"A taxi? Why? I can take you home."

When the coat-check girl returned, Ross was the one who reached for the wool parka, holding it open for Juliet so she could slide her arms into the sleeves.

"I *want* to take you home," he said close to her ear, his hands resting on her shoulders while she buttoned her coat, her back to him.

She slowly turned around to face him. "It's not a good idea."

She could see her answer didn't please him. "There you go again with that 'good idea' stuff." He shoved both of his hands into his pockets. "You can go ahead and take the cab, but I warn you, I'm going to be following it all the way to your place to make sure you get home safely." He pulled one hand from a pocket and flipped his coat-check token to the girl behind the counter.

He stood staring at her in silence until the girl returned with his jacket. "Well, what do you say?" he asked, pulling on the soft brown leather jacket. "You want to spend your hard-earned money in a cold cab with some stranger or go with me?" He added in a lower voice, "I'm neither strange nor cold."

Besides the fact that there were dozens of better ways to spend the twenty dollars, Juliet knew that the real reason she was going to accept his offer was because she wanted to spend more time with him. Her insides were still tingling from their close contact during the dance, and she was about to tell him she'd accept a ride when she remembered the blonde he had been with earlier in the evening.

"What about your friends? Are you sure they won't mind if you leave?"

"I came alone," he said with a face as honest as daylight. With a hand at her back, he started toward the door.

"You came alone?" she repeated skeptically.

"Yes. I'm not emotionally entangled with anyone, either."

"I thought I saw you with someone earlier," she said quietly.

They had stepped outside into the cold wintry air and were moving at a brisk pace, as most Minnesotans did in December. "You mean a female someone, right?" His words came out on a stream of white mist.

"A blonde. She was at the White Wolf the night I returned your van." Her breath, too, was making tiny white clouds in the frigid air.

"Oh, you must mean Shawna. She's just a friend of mine."

Juliet wondered if Shawna knew that that was how Ross thought of her. "I see," she mumbled through the collar of her coat as she fought to stave off the cold stinging her cheeks. She really didn't think it was quite as simple as that.

"Besides," Ross continued, "Shawna's more like a groupie. She fancies she's in love with practically every musician she meets. She's really just a sweet kid."

Juliet didn't think she'd describe someone who looked like a blond version of Cher as a "sweet kid," but she didn't argue the point. After all, what Shawna was or wasn't to Ross was really none of her business.

She tried to keep that in mind as Ross drove her home. Despite her efforts to steer their conversation away from the personal, however, Ross managed to get her to talk about herself. By the end of the ride, she realized they were more than casual acquaintances, and it came as no surprise when he asked her for another date.

"It's not going to work," she told him, wishing she didn't have to say no.

"I think it would," he said, leaning across the console separating the two front seats.

"It wouldn't."

"Why not?"

"Because my sister walks around the house talking about you as though you're her goal in life. Do you know what would happen to our relationship if she found out I had gone out on a date with you?"

He laid his arm across the back of her seat, his fingers dipping down to caress her shoulder. "I don't want to hurt Brenda, but what am I supposed to do? Pretend I don't have any feelings for you?"

"Feelings for me," she repeated weakly, her heart racing. "Ross, we hardly know each other." She looked away from his probing gaze, staring out at the blinking snowman on the front porch.

He gently pulled her face back toward his. "I want to know you, Juliet," he said in a husky voice. "I want to know everything there is to know about you...what makes you laugh, what makes you cry...what you do to stay warm on cold winter nights." He caressed her with his eyes, with his words and with the warm breath that fanned her cheeks.

Juliet knew he was going to kiss her. A thrill shot through her, and she began to tremble as she realized it was exactly what she wanted him to do. Instinctively her moist lips parted and she kissed his mouth. Slowly. Softly. Sliding her lips over his. Taking him by surprise.

Then suddenly his arms were pulling her hard against his chest, bending her body to his. His hands cradled her head while he kissed her deeply, his mouth moving in tantalizing ways, teasing, caressing and creating a longing in a private part of her only one other man had ever known.

It was that longing that made her pull away just moments before her hands could reach inside his jacket to touch him possessively. She had no right to feel possessive about this man, no right to be intimate with him. Yet that was how she felt, what she yearned for.

The realization was sobering. "I have to go," she whispered, trying not to see the passion clouding his eyes, eyes that begged her to stay.

"Wait." He held her arm as she reached for the door handle, his breath hot on her face as he leaned across her. "Will you come to the White Wolf tomorrow night?"

"I can't."

He groaned. "I only have to play for about an hour, then I'll be free."

Free? You'll never be free the way I want you to be, Juliet wanted to say. Instead, she was about to tell him it wouldn't be a good idea for her to be anywhere near him when he raised a finger to her lips.

"Don't say no," he pleaded, then took her mouth with a sweet gentleness before slowly releasing her. "If you come before nine, I can introduce you to the rest of the women."

"Women?" She gave him a puzzled look.

"Most of the guys in the band have wives or girlfriends who come to listen on Saturday nights. They all sit together at one table, and after the club closes everyone goes over to Bubba's place to eat. He's the big guy with the trumpet."

"You know I'm not exactly crazy about jazz," she teased.

"What if I could talk the guys into playing Beethoven? Then would you come?"

She sighed and rolled her eyes. "I can imagine how well that would go over with the audience," she said dryly. "You'd probably get stuff thrown at you."

"I'd risk it if it meant having you there."

She felt her resolve weakening and quickly said, "I really have to go in." She dug in her purse for her house key. When Ross reached for his door handle, she added, "You don't have to get out."

"No, and I don't have to eat bran flakes for breakfast, either, but I happen to like bran flakes," he told her, slamming the door behind him.

She slammed her door as well and met him at the front of the van, shrugging off his hand as he tried to rest it ever so lightly on her shoulder. Ignoring the pleasure she was feeling because of his gentlemanly behavior, she hurried up the porch steps.

When he held the storm door open for her, she was forced to acknowledge his presence. "Thank you," she said in a not-so-gracious tone.

"You're welcome," he said in kind.

She shoved her key into the lock until it clicked, then gave the big oak door a push. A rush of warm air greeted her, and as she turned she saw him silhouetted in the colored Christmas lights. Never had he looked more attractive. She was tempted to invite him in, but the possibility of Brenda arriving home early changed her mind.

"Well, good night," she said uneasily.

"Good night, Juliet." He waited, as if he expected her to ask him inside.

"I can't ask you in."

"Did I say I wanted you to?"

She blushed, then her lips tightened. "Thank you for the ride home," she said brusquely.

"The pleasure was all mine," he replied. Then he blew her a kiss and walked away.

ROSS'S INVITATION was on Juliet's mind on Saturday afternoon as she drove over to the Cade house to pick up Sara and Annie. It caused her to fantasize what it would be like to walk into the White Wolf and sit at a table reserved for the women of the guys in the band. It also tempted her to ask her mother to keep the girls another night.

For a fleeting moment she allowed herself to consider what it might be like to be Ross Stafford's woman...to be the one he wanted in his bed at the end of the day. The thought was enough to bring a warm flush to her cheeks and make her tingle all over.

As she parked her car in front of the Cade home, she was grateful for the blast of cold air that greeted her when she pushed the door open. Through the sheer drapes in the living room, she could see her mother and Donovan sitting together on the leather sofa while Sara and Annie sat on the floor watching a cartoon video.

Marriage to the commissioner had put a sparkle back in her mother's eyes. Smiles came more easily to her lips and contentedness was etched in her gentle features. Juliet felt a twinge of envy.

It wasn't that she begrudged her mother happiness. On the contrary. She had been in favor of the marriage. The trouble was, she was having a little difficulty adjusting to the fact that ever since Donovan had come into their lives, things had changed. The mother-daughter bond, although still strong, had undergone subtle changes that left Juliet with an undefined sense of loss.

Neither Brenda nor Meridee seemed to be affected in the way she had been. They didn't feel as though any distance had crept into their relationship with Kate. Maybe Juliet felt differently because she had always been able to relate to her mother in a way Brenda and Meridee hadn't understood. Juliet wasn't sure if it was something in her emotional makeup or simply the fact that she was the only daughter who had been married and had children. And when her father had died at the same time Juliet was about to lose a spouse, mother and daughter had shared more than grief. They had learned to cope without the men they had thought would be their lifelong partners. Loneliness had actually strengthened their relationship.

Only now her mother wasn't lonely anymore. Unlike Juliet, she had found someone to fill the emptiness, and Juliet, too, wanted someone to belong to, someone strong and dependable who would love her children as his own, someone who could put the sparkle back in her life.

Immediately she thought of Ross. He definitely could put sparkle in her life, and she had no doubt that he could be strong and dependable if he chose to be. The problem was he wanted no obligations, no duties, no promises. He moved from city to city, doing what he wanted, when he wanted. He was not the kind of man for a mother of two. Yet Juliet wanted the other things he had to offer, especially when she saw the chemistry between her mother and Donovan.

When Juliet stepped inside the Cades' warm, comfortable home, Kate insisted she stay long enough to have a cup of cappuccino. While the girls finished watching their video, she took Juliet into the kitchen and asked her about her night out with the mothers from the baby-sitting co-op.

"So, did you meet anyone nice?"

Juliet hoped her mother bought her feigned look of boredom. "Mom, there are no nice men left. I tell you that every time you ask that question."

"I guess that means you didn't meet your Prince Charming, huh?" she asked as she uncovered the cappuccino maker.

Again, Juliet thought of Ross, and fleetingly debated whether she should tell her mother about him. Knowing that men were a subject they seldom agreed on, she decided she couldn't take the risk. She did her best not to make it sound as though the evening was a total disaster, giving Kate enough details to satisfy her curiosity but omitting any mention of Ross.

"Are you all right, dear? You're looking a little peaked," Kate observed during a lull in their conversation.

Juliet shook her head. "I'm fine, Mom. I'm probably just a little run-down."

Kate reached over to cover her hand with hers. "You're trying to do too much. What you need is rest. Maybe I should keep the girls another night? Would that help?"

Juliet was tempted to say yes. She wanted to say yes. And memories of Ross's kisses nearly made her agree until she happened to glance up and notice her mother's calendar. From where she was sitting, she could see the notation, "Jacobsons'—8:00" written on today's date.

A wonderful feeling of tenderness rose in Juliet's throat at the thought that her mother would sacrifice her night out for her. But Juliet couldn't let Kate cancel her plans to baby-sit her children just so she could have some sparkle in her life.

"After last night, I think what I really need is to be with my daughters. I'm going to take them home and do what we used to do when we were kids," Juliet told her.

"What's that?"

"Remember how whenever one of us had a problem or was upset about something you'd let us crawl into bed with you and we'd have hot chocolate with miniature marshmallows while you read us stories?"

"And one of you would always end up spilling," Kate reminisced fondly.

"But you always let us do it anyway."

Kate smiled. "Sheets and pillowcases are easily laundered."

"I'll keep that in mind for later this evening." She stood up and carried her empty cup to the sink. "Thanks for taking the girls overnight, Mom," she said gratefully. "I know how much they like being with you."

"They're great kids, Juliet." She came to stand beside her daughter. "Before you go, though, I wanted to talk to you about Sara."

"What about Sara?"

"She's been asking questions about Tim."

Juliet's muscles tensed. "Such as?"

"Like whether mommies and daddies who get divorced ever get married again."

Juliet groaned. "What did you tell her?"

"I said I didn't know any that had, but apparently she had seen some television program where the little girl wished for her mommy and daddy to stop being divorced and it happened.''

"Just terrific." Juliet dropped her head into her hands.

"She doesn't know Tim has remarried, does she?"

Juliet shook her head. "I didn't see any point in bringing up the subject, since he hasn't wanted to have anything to do with us anyway."

"She's going to have to be told she has a stepmother," Kate said gently.

The thought sent a chill up and down Juliet's spine. "And a stepsister."

"Tim's new wife has children?"

"Just one. A six-year-old girl."

"Is he going to bring them when he comes here?"

"How should I know? I don't even know if he *is* coming," Juliet snapped irritably, then immediately felt contrite. "I'm sorry, Mom. I shouldn't be taking it out on you. I guess the subject of my ex-husband is better left alone."

Kate pulled her close and gave her a reassuring, gentle squeeze. "Try not to worry so much. Everything's going to be just fine."

Juliet forced a weak smile to her face. "You always say that."

"Because it's true."

Juliet's face revealed her skepticism. "I wish I had inherited your optimistic streak."

"You have, you just like to fight it." Kate gave her arm an affectionate pat. "Oh, by the way, Sara told me she's taking piano lessons."

Again, Ross's face popped into Juliet's mind, and she couldn't prevent the rush of guilt that accompanied it. "Didn't I mention it to you?"

Kate shook her head. "No, but I think it's a wonderful idea. She loves music."

"Yes, well, let's hope she has more talent than her mother ever did," Juliet said dryly, lifting her coat from the back of the chair.

"You would have done just fine if I could have gotten you to stick with it. I always had to fight with you to get you to practice," Kate reminded her.

"I don't think that's going to be Sara's problem. I'm surprised she doesn't have swollen fingers."

"I promised her I'd stop over next week and hear her play. When does she have her next lesson?"

"Wednesday." Which meant that's when she would see Ross again. And cook dinner for him. And...

THE THOUGHT OF SARA'S lesson had Juliet trying to think up reasons why she could be absent from the house when Ross came over. Unfortunately there were none. In exchange for Sara's lesson she had promised him a meal, a bargain she needed to keep—for Sara's sake.

Since he had scheduled Sara's lesson for five-thirty, Juliet planned dinner for six-thirty, hoping that he would have to leave for the White Wolf as soon as they had finished eating. With Brenda present, she doubted there would be any occasion for him to speak to her privately, although judging by the last time he had dined with them, she didn't need to worry about him being overly attentive to her anyway.

Shortly after five, Brenda rushed in the back door with a "Hi, I won't be able to wait for dinner." She hurriedly shook out of her jacket and boots, dropping them in the middle of the floor. "A bunch of us are going to the hockey game, and I've got to be at Williams Arena by six.''

Before Juliet could respond, Sara popped through the swinging door, asking, ''How many more minutes is it now, Mommy?'' Ever since Juliet had picked the girls up from the baby-sitter, Sara had been asking how long it would be until Ross arrived for her piano lesson.

''Only fifteen more minutes,'' Juliet answered absently, still reeling from Brenda's announcement.

''Fifteen more minutes?'' Sara echoed the words with a groan, then marched out of the room.

''Oh! That reminds me,'' Brenda said, lowering her voice. ''Ross told me to tell you he's going to be running late tonight.''

''How late?''

Brenda shrugged and said, ''I don't know. He didn't say.'' She lifted the lid of one of the pans on the stove and said, ''Umm. This smells good. What is it?''

''It's a new tomato sauce one of the women at work gave me. I'm making lasagna.''

''Too bad I don't have time to eat, but if I don't change and leave right away, I'm going to be late,'' Brenda said before scurrying through the swinging door.

Juliet glanced at the clock and sighed. She had counted on Ross being there at five-thirty. She wished he had called and told her what time to expect him so she could have planned dinner accordingly.

The later it got, the more annoyed she became, especially as Sara repeatedly complained about his absence. When it was nearly six-thirty and there still was no word from him, she decided she would feed the girls. They were just about finished when the door-bell rang.

"I'm sorry I'm late." Ross stood on the doorstep, a full-length wool coat covering most of his lean frame. On his head was a felt derby that gave him the appearance of a mob man. It had started to snow, and fluffy white flakes drifted around him. "Is Sara ready for her lesson?" He flashed her a charming smile that was a combination of contrition and enthusiasm.

Juliet would have liked to have said no, but upon hearing the doorbell, Sara had raced into the living room and plopped her tiny body in the center of the piano bench. From where she stood, Juliet could see her waiting for Ross to come inside.

Without saying a word, Juliet stepped aside and indicated to Ross that he should come in. She took his hat and coat from him, trying not to notice how the knit shirt he was wearing hugged his chest.

"I really am sorry, Juliet," he said again, this time without a smile. He could see by the stiffness of her shoulders that she was angry.

"Why don't you two get started?" she said brusquely. "I have to see to Annie. She's in the kitchen finishing her dinner."

Ross watched her walk away, wondering if she realized how incredibly sexy she looked in her faded sweatshirt and jeans. He had a hunch that she had deliberately tried to make herself look unappealing, for all traces of makeup were gone and her hair was pulled back and tied with a scarf. Could it be that she was still trying to discourage him? Maybe that was the reason for her cool treatment tonight. Or maybe she was simply angry that he was late.

He learned the answer from Sara. As he sat down beside her, she looked at him with eyes that were the same brilliant blue as her mother's—and equally devastating in their effect on him—and said, "You're late."

"I'm sorry, Sara. I hope that doesn't mean you don't want to have your lesson?"

"Uh-uh." Her blond curls danced back and forth as she shook her head. "I want my lesson, but I'm not sure you're going to get anything to eat. My mom says lasagna isn't any good if it gets cold."

"She could be right," he said, his glance straying in the direction of the kitchen.

"Maybe you can have a peanut butter and jelly sandwich," she suggested.

Ross couldn't hide his grin. "Maybe I can." He was tempted to go in and smooth Juliet's ruffled feathers, but he could see the excitement on Sara's face at the thought of her lesson. When she asked him if he'd teach her a Christmas song she could play for her grandma, he knew Juliet would have to wait for explanations.

By the end of her lesson, Sara had captured Ross's heart, just as her mother had managed to do. Not once since he had sat down with her had Juliet come into the room, and he wondered if she was going to renege on dinner.

He wished now that he hadn't gone to the audition that had made him late. To a woman like Juliet, punctuality ranked right up there with honesty. He contemplated leaving quietly, without collecting for the lesson, but she had taken his coat and hat and tucked them out of sight. He had no choice but to send Sara to find her mother. While he waited, his fingers gently moved over the piano keys in one of his favorite Brahms lullabies. When he saw Juliet come into the room, he automatically lifted his hands from the keys.

"That was lovely," she told him. "Why did you stop?"

It made him feel good to know that she liked hearing him play. "Would you like me to finish?"

She nodded, then added, "I just put Annie to bed, and I think it'll help her fall asleep."

He didn't comment, but started the piece from the beginning, noticing out of the corner of his eye that she had seated herself in the wing chair. When he finished, he turned to see Sara curled up on her lap. There was something about the sight of mother and daughter sitting together so peacefully that made him wonder what it would be like to be a parent.

He quickly pushed the thought from his mind. There was no place in his life for a wife and kids—at least he had never expected there would be.

"Will I be able to play songs like that?" Sara interrupted his train of thought.

Ross got up and walked over to them. "I believe you will, Sara."

There was an odd look on Juliet's face, and Ross wondered if she had forgiven him for being late.

"Sara, say good-night to Ross. It's time you went upstairs and got ready for bed," Juliet said.

Sara thanked him for the lesson, flashing him a dimpled grin.

"She's a wonderful child," Ross said softly as he watched her giggle and dance her way out of the room. "And she's doing very well with her music."

"Good." Juliet had stood, too, and nervously ran her hands up and down her arms. "Do you have time to stay for dinner or do you have to leave for the White Wolf?''

He had a pretty good idea that she was hoping for the latter. Normally he wasn't the kind of guy to stay where he wasn't wanted, but some stubborn streak in him refused to make it easy for her.

"I can stay," he said innocently, watching her mask her emotions with a polite smile.

"Very well," she said noncommittally and led him into the kitchen.

Few words were spoken between them as she moved around preparing his food. He asked her several questions, to which she responded with one-word answers, and finally he gave up trying to make small talk. When she set the plate down in front of him, he reached for her wrist.

She snatched it away as if his touch burned.

"Aren't you going to join me?" he asked.

"I already ate with the children."

He knew from Sara that she hadn't. "Why are you angry with me? Because I put you off your schedule?"

"I'm not angry," she denied. "And I wish you'd quit acting as though I have a major character defect because my life is organized."

"Organized?" He sighed. "I'm afraid that's one thing my life has never been . . . organized."

"Surprise, surprise," she muttered dryly, a ghost of a grin flickering across her face.

Ross ignored the sarcasm, giving her an engaging smile. "Please sit and talk to me. It's a little uncomfortable eating dinner alone in someone else's home."

Reluctantly she pulled out a chair and sat down across from him. He would have liked to talk about her, to find out more about her likes and dislikes, but instead he discussed Sara's music lessons. When he did finally manage to steer the conversation into a more personal vein, she excused herself, saying, "I'd better go check on the girls."

He nodded, then said on a note of resignation, "Bring my coat when you come back."

Ross finished his dinner, wondering why he was beating his head against the wall trying to get somewhere with a woman who obviously wanted nothing to do with him. But then he remembered how she had responded to his kisses and he knew exactly why he was still here.

When she returned, she was carrying his coat and hat. Seeing his empty plate, she asked, "Would you like anything else?"

Ross stared at her for several seconds, then got up from the table and walked toward her. He wanted to pull her close, to mold her curves against his own hard length, to kiss her until her eyes flashed with passion instead of apprehension.

Instead, he said, "I guess that'll be all for now." He took his coat and hat from her and put them on. "I missed you at the White Wolf Saturday night."

"I...I...couldn't get a baby-sitter for Sara and Annie," she stammered.

He didn't know if she was telling the truth or not. He hoped she was. "Maybe another time?"

She nodded tentatively. As he started for the door she asked, "What about next week? What time should we plan on seeing you?"

He thought he detected a trace of annoyance in her tone. "Same time all right with you?"

"Does that mean five-thirty or six-thirty?"

"You're still upset, aren't you?" He stared at her intently and she quickly averted her gaze.

"No, I'd just like to know so I can plan dinner," she answered, busying herself with clearing away dishes.

"I'm really sorry about being late tonight, Juliet. It wasn't something I could prevent. I had a last-minute audition."

She finally looked up at him. "For a theater part?"

He shook his head. "For a job in Chicago." He could have told her it was only a two-week engagement, but something inside him wanted her to think he had considered moving away. "Ever been to Chicago?"

"Yes. It's a great city," she answered.

"I like it, too." He watched for a hint of emotion in her face, but tonight she was guarding her feelings carefully. "Well, guess I'd better go. I'll see you next week."

"All right."

He was halfway out the back door when he turned and said, "By the way, you make great lasagna." He blew her a kiss and left.

CHAPTER SEVEN

THE FOLLOWING FRIDAY evening Juliet took Sara and Annie downtown to see the holiday decorations and to visit one of the local department stores whose auditorium had been transformed into a fairy-tale garden. After having their pictures taken with Santa, Juliet bought them each a gingerbread man and a cup of warm apple cider. By the time they had visited the toy department, the girls were ready for bed, and Juliet wisely headed for the parking ramp. They were asleep before the car even made it to the bottom of the circular exit.

To get out of the city, it was necessary to drive past the White Wolf. As usual, a crowd stood outside the door and traffic moved slowly in the streets. While she sat at an intersection waiting for the light to turn green, Juliet's thoughts drifted back to the last time she had been inside the jazz club, and as usual the memory made her pulse leap.

As the traffic slowly inched forward, she looked longingly at the flashing neon sign over the White Wolf and tried not to think about what was happening inside the club. She didn't want to know if Ross was playing his sax or if Shawna might be sitting at the table reserved for the musicians' "women." Although it was of little comfort, she reminded herself that she was the one who had passed up his invitation to be his guest last Saturday. And after the way she had treated him at Sara's piano lesson, she'd be lucky if there ever was another.

She glanced in the rearview mirror at Sara's sleeping face, then across to Annie's, and thought about how different her weekends were from Ross's. While he played to the wee hours of the morning in a smoky jazz club, she was at home with two children.

Only on this particular weekend night, he wasn't at the White Wolf, but sitting in her driveway.

She saw his van the minute she turned onto her street, and as she pulled her battered old station wagon into the drive she could see the vague shape of his body in the dark. As soon as her car was alongside his, he climbed out of the van and came toward her, pulling her door open just as she turned off the engine.

"Ross, why are you here?" she asked quietly as she got out of the car. She gently closed the door so as not to wake Sara and Annie. "I thought you'd be at the White Wolf."

"Friday's my night off," he said, sounding a bit frustrated.

"How long have you been here?"

He shrugged. "Maybe an hour?"

"An hour?" Her eyes widened. "Why?"

"I needed to see you." He took a step closer to her. "Juliet, this is driving me crazy."

"What is?"

"What's going on between us. Or maybe I should say what isn't going on between us. I don't know where I stand with you."

She shifted uncomfortably. "Ross, you shouldn't have come here. What if Brenda came home?"

"We're not doing anything, Juliet, except standing in the middle of your driveway shivering. What could she possibly interpret from that?"

It was cold, and Juliet felt her teeth begin to chatter. "I'd better get the girls inside," she told him, then went around to the passenger side and opened the door to release Annie from her car seat.

Ross, noticing that Sara was sleeping in the back, reached inside and lifted her into his arms. Following Juliet's lead, he carried the sleeping child into the house. Sara stirred briefly, her eyelids fluttering open to see what was happening. As soon as she saw Ross, she smiled, then nuzzled her head comfortably against his shoulder. The sight of her tiny hands clinging to him so trustingly sent a warm shiver through Juliet's body.

"Which room?" he asked softly when they had reached the landing on the second floor.

"Last one on the right. Just lay her on the bed."

He nodded, then headed down the hallway while Juliet took Annie into the room that was once Meridee's but now was decorated with teddy bears and balloons. She quickly changed Annie into her pajamas and put her in the crib, then went to check on Sara.

The room was in darkness except for the pink glow from the night-light. As Juliet entered, her glance went to the canopy bed with its ruffled valance. At the same time that she noticed it was empty she heard the rhythmic creaking of wood on wood. She looked to the opposite corner, where Ross was sitting in the rocker with Sara on his lap, gently moving back and forth.

Juliet walked over and knelt down beside them. "Sara, come," she said softly. "It's time to get ready for bed."

With a whimper, Sara awoke and went into her mother's outstretched arms. Juliet carried her over to the bed, whispering words of comfort.

As Juliet began to undress her daughter, Ross got up to leave. "I'll wait downstairs," he said quietly.

Juliet nodded, then turned her attention to Sara. It only took a few minutes before she was tucked into bed, and Juliet left to search for Ross. She found him browsing through the books in the walnut-paneled library.

"I hope you don't mind that I came in here?"

She hesitated a moment before saying, "No."

"Are you sure?"

She nodded. "It's just . . ." She paused as she swallowed the emotion in her throat. "This was my father's room. Every time I come in here it's as though I can still smell the scent of his pipe tobacco."

"I'm sorry. I didn't realize. I was looking for a phone to use, and the collection of World War II books caught my eye."

"It's all right," she told him, liking the way he looked standing in the room that had always been a favorite of hers. "All of the books in here belonged to my father."

"He must have been a World War II buff," Ross observed as he looked around the room at the various memorabilia from that era.

She smiled in recollection. "There's also a video collection of movies and documentaries." She walked over to a cabinet and swung open the doors. "See."

Ross's eyes scanned the titles with an appreciative whistle. "I thought I had seen just about every World War II movie ever made, but there are some here I haven't even heard of."

"Somehow I wouldn't have thought you were the type to like war movies," she noted, a bit bemused by his interest.

"They're not just war movies, Juliet. World War II was a fascinating period in history."

Her eyes took on a slightly wistful expression. "You sound like my father."

"Is that good or bad?"

Her shrug was accompanied by a slightly crooked smile. "He was a good man. Of course, that's a rather biased opinion."

"From the way people talk about him, I'd say it's an accurate statement. I'm sorry I never had the chance to meet him."

"I think he would have liked you." The words came out without conscious thought, surprising Juliet.

"What makes you say that?"

Again she shrugged. "Just a feeling I have."

"A feeling, eh?" He moved closer to her. "Your feelings are why I came over here tonight."

As he moved closer, she inched backward until she was up against the desk. "You really shouldn't have come here, Ross. I'm not sure what time Brenda's going to be home."

"You can relax. I have an excuse ready if she should walk in. I brought over the sheet music Sara wanted for her Christmas carol." He leaned closer to her in a suggestive way.

"You did?"

"Yup. It's in the van. I'll get it for you in a minute, but first I need to ask you three questions, and I want honest answers." He had her pinned against the desk, his body just centimeters away. "First of all, do you like me?"

She only hesitated a moment, moistening her lips before saying, "Yes."

"Good, because I like you, too." Without otherwise touching her, he gave her a quick kiss on the lips, then said, "Next question. Do you like being with me?"

"Yes." This time there was no hesitation in her response.

"Good, because I like being with you." He kissed her again, but this time more intimately, forcing her lips to part beneath his, his hands gently cupping her face. "Now the last question. Do you want what's happening between us to continue?"

She hesitated before answering, and he quickly added, "If you get this answer right, you win a prize."

She was trembling slightly, but she managed to arch one eyebrow and ask, "Are you the prize?"

He ran a finger across the smooth skin on her chin. "No fair. Can't answer a question with a question. I need a simple yes or no."

Boldly, she wrapped her arms around him and whispered against his lips, "Yes, but..."

His lips silenced any protest she was about to make, his mouth taking hers with an urgency that surprised both of them. Juliet moaned as her body instinctively arched against his.

His hands were rough yet stimulating as they traveled the length of her back, coming to rest at the hem of her sweater where bare skin met bare skin. Juliet shuddered as his fingers sought the warm flesh beneath the angora. When she felt a hand cup her breast, she whimpered and sagged against him.

With a groan, Ross pressed his hips into hers, letting her feel what she was doing to him. Without saying a word, he told her in no uncertain terms what he wanted from their relationship.

Juliet gave in to the feelings she had been fighting, wanting to experience the comfort of being held, of being desired, of being intimate. However, it was the realization that intimacy was where they were heading that made her pull away from him a few minutes later.

Afraid of what he might see in her eyes, she focused on her fingers, which had found their way inside the brown leather jacket and were splayed across his chest. She could feel his heart beating unevenly beneath her fingertips.

"I'm glad you said yes, Juliet." His voice was ragged when he spoke. "I want to be with you."

She closed her eyes, wishing she could deny the feelings she had for him, but she couldn't. "I want to be with you, too," she confessed. "But..."

"But what?"

"I think I should make something clear." She kept her eyes level with his chin. "Just because I'm divorced and the mother of two children doesn't mean I'm looking to domesticate every man I date."

"Are you trying to tell me you want no strings in this relationship?"

She lifted her eyes to his. "I can't afford any at this time in my life."

A grin spread slowly across his face. "That's all right by me. Domesticity and I haven't exactly hit it off so far." He kissed her again. "Now, tell me when I get to see you again. What about tomorrow?"

"I have classes at the U."

"In the afternoon?" When she nodded miserably, he asked, "Can't you cut them?"

"They're review sessions for finals." She bit down on her lower lip, as conflicting emotions had her feeling confused.

"What if I told you I could get tickets for the matinee performance of *A Christmas Carol* at the Guthrie?" His eyes still devoured her hungrily.

She moaned as she deliberated her decision.

He lifted her chin with his finger. "If I know you, you haven't missed a single class this quarter and you have all your notes memorized." He had her hands in his and lifted them to his lips.

There was a long moment of silence as she debated what she should do. She looked up at him almost shyly, as if it were an effort to speak, then said, "I'll go."

His eyes glowed with delight. "Good. I'll pick you up around one."

"Why don't I just meet you at the university after I finish my morning class?"

His thumb gently massaged the back of her hands as he held them. "You're worried about Brenda, aren't you?"

"It'd be easier for me if I met you over there."

"I understand that," he insisted, but a line of disapproval etched itself between his eyebrows. "I have a better idea. Since you're going to be over at the U, why don't you come to my place and we'll go from there?"

Her muscles tensed slightly at the thought of going to his apartment. Here, in this house, she felt safe with him. With two kids upstairs and the possibility of her sister walking in on them, nothing much would happen. But in his apartment... The thought was both tempting and frightening. "All right," she finally agreed.

"Good. My apartment's on Fourth Street. Just go straight past the Bar and take the first left. You can't miss it. It's the only residential building on the block." He kissed her once more, a kiss that did little to alleviate her fears. Then, with a sigh, he released her. "I'll see you tomorrow."

Juliet nodded and watched him walk toward the door.

He stopped in the doorway and turned around. "I almost forgot. The prize." He raised and lowered his eyebrows as he reached into the side pocket on his jacket. He pulled out a cassette tape and said, "Here. Catch."

She caught the plastic box he tossed in her direction and looked at it curiously. It was an audio cassette tape. Across the top was a slim label indicating what was on side A. It read "For Juliet."

"You made me a tape?"

He leaned lazily against the doorjamb and said, "If Muhammad won't come to the mountain, the mountain must come to Muhammad."

A wry smile lifted one corner of her mouth. "Thank you. I'm sure I'll enjoy it."

"I think you'd enjoy the real thing more, but—" he gave her another of his sexy smiles "—that'll do...for now."

As soon as he was gone, Juliet hurried to the stereo system in the living room and dropped the cartridge into the cassette player. Because the girls were asleep, she plugged in the headphones and slipped them over her ears.

Sounds of Ross's saxophone surrounded her, and she smiled as she made herself comfortable on the sofa, imagining how he looked as he played the instrument. It was classical music, but after establishing the theme of the piece, he began to improvise, until the original melody was obscured.

The longer she listened, the more enchanted she became. In between pieces, Ross gave a brief explanation of his interpretation of the music. Every number on the tape had its own appeal, and her respect and admiration for Ross as a musician grew.

So engrossed was she with the tape that she didn't hear Brenda come in. It was only when she felt a hand on her shoulder that she realized she wasn't alone. She sat up with a tiny shriek, pulling the headphones from her ears.

"Brenda! You frightened me." Her hand flew to her rapidly beating heart.

"Sorry. I thought you were asleep. You had your eyes closed and this dreamy look on your face." Brenda flopped down onto the chair beside the sofa. "What are you listening to at this time of night?"

Juliet quickly got up and went over to remove the tape from the stereo system, guilt flooding through her. "Just some lecture notes I taped," she lied, slipping Ross's cassette into her pocket.

Brenda snorted. "I should have known you'd be studying on a Friday night."

Annoyance at her sister's flippant attitude toward studying took a bit of the edge off her guilt. "Yes, well, maybe if you'd spend a few weekends hitting the books rather than the parties, you'd be a few credits closer to your degree." She tucked the headphones back into the cabinet and switched off the stereo system.

"Degree, degree," Brenda said, looking bored. "That's all you and Mom ever talk about. I know lots of kids who have worked their butts off getting through college only to graduate and not be able to get a better job than the kids who never went to college."

Suspicious of the direction of the conversation, Juliet put her hands on her hips and asked, "And what's that supposed to mean?"

Brenda gave her a sullen look before saying, "It means I hate school and I really can't see the point in going." She gave Juliet a defiant look, then said, "I guess I might as well tell you. I'm dropping out after this quarter."

"You can't just quit!" Juliet exclaimed, her fingers digging into the back of the sofa.

"Why can't I?"

"Because you need an education, that's why!"

"Well, I happen to disagree with you."

"Well, you're wrong!" Juliet didn't mean to sound so high-handed, but the thought of her younger sister tossing aside a college education was almost more than she could bear.

Brenda stretched her arms over her head and grimaced. "It's too late to be discussing this. We're only going to end up fighting." She attempted to get up from the chair, but Juliet stopped her with a hand on her arm.

"Wait a minute!"

"Jules, I'm in no mood for any lectures."

Taking a deep breath, she composed herself. "I'm not going to lecture you, but I really think we need to talk."

Brenda exhaled an impatient sigh. "It won't do any good. My mind's already made up."

"I can see that," Juliet said pensively. "Have you told Mom?"

Brenda shook her head. "Not yet. I wanted to wait until after Christmas. No point in spoiling her holidays."

"Whether you tell her now or wait until after Christmas, she's not going to be happy. You must realize that."

"I know she's going to be upset," Brenda snapped irritably, "but I can't live my life according to what Mom wants."

"So how *are* you going to live your life? What are you going to do? Get a job?"

Brenda hesitated briefly. "I'm going to be a model."

"A model?" Juliet's jaw dropped open. "Brenda, you're barely five feet tall. Most models are almost a foot taller than that."

"It depends on what kind of modeling you want to do. I'm not trying to get on the cover of *Vogue* or anything."

"What *are* you trying to do?"

She shrugged. "Maybe TV or newspaper ads. Shelly Novak told me there's this agency here in town that's looking for local talent. They've hired her sister, and she's already done a bunch of the Christmas ads for the newspaper."

Juliet raised her eyebrows skeptically. "But you haven't had any experience."

"I took an acting class this quarter." She laughed uneasily. "It's one of the few classes where I'm getting a passing grade."

"Oh, Brenda, you're not failing any classes, are you?" Brenda didn't need to answer; her averted eyes said it all. Juliet stifled her groan. "Do you know what that's going to do to your grade-point average?"

"It can't be helped. It's too late to drop any classes for no credit." She rose to her feet. "Look, Jules, I'll never be the brain you are. Did you ever think that maybe I'm just not cut out for college?"

"That's not true and you know it. If you liked the acting class and you're doing well in theater arts, why not change your major?"

"Because I don't want to be a theater-arts major," she said impatiently. "I want to be a model. Can't you at least pretend you're a little bit happy for me? For the past year I've been trying to figure out what I wanted to do with my life, and now I know."

"Brenda, modeling isn't exactly a lifelong career. It's something women do when they're young. You can have five, maybe ten productive years and then you're considered old and get replaced by some teenybopper."

"Oh, don't be such a pessimist!" Brenda dismissed her sister's comments with a wave of her hand. "You always look at the negative side of everything."

"I'm being practical," Juliet stated soberly. "I hate to see you pass up an opportunity to finish your education just so you can pose in front of someone's camera."

"Well, I can't see staying in school and taking boring classes just so I can get a piece of paper that says I'm educated."

Juliet saw that nothing she could say was going to change her sister's mind . . . at least not tonight. "It is too late to be having this discussion," she said with a weary sigh, rubbing two fingers across her temple. "Why don't we go to bed and talk about this later?"

"There's no need. I'm not going to change my mind," Brenda said, lifting her chin.

Juliet fought to control her emotions. For too long now she had watched her younger sister take for granted opportunities she'd wanted for herself. Brenda didn't have to struggle to make her tuition payment. She hadn't had to work at a full-time job during the day and go to school at night. She didn't have to worry about whether or not her paycheck would stretch to cover groceries and baby-sitting expenses. Yet she was the one dropping out of college.

Juliet tried to understand her sister. After all, she herself had quit school when she was nineteen—the same age as Brenda. The only difference was she had left because of a marriage, not because of some starry-eyed dream to become a model. But hadn't she been as starry-eyed as Brenda? And as a result she had spent her college tuition trying to make a man happy. At least Brenda wasn't leaving school in order to put some guy through college. Still, Brenda's decision was a bitter pill for her to swallow.

"We'd better go to bed," she said in resignation, not wanting to say anything she might regret.

"You have to promise me you won't say anything to Mom before I've had a chance to talk to her," Brenda begged.

Juliet sighed. "I won't, but I really think this is a decision you ought to discuss with her before canceling your registration."

Brenda lowered her eyes. "It's too late. I've already done it."

Again Juliet groaned, but she bit back the angry lecture that leaped to mind.

"Are you going over to Mom's tomorrow?" Brenda asked.

Juliet nodded. "She's watching the girls while I'm in class."

"Whatever you do, don't say a word about this, all right?"

"I've already told you I wouldn't," Juliet snapped, annoyed with her sister for putting her in such a position.

However, Brenda wasn't the only one withholding information from her mother, as Juliet soon discovered when she dropped the girls off at the Cade home the next morning. When Kate saw that Juliet was wearing a woolen dress rather than her usual blue jeans and sweater, she inquired as to the reason.

Like Brenda, Juliet found herself reluctant to tell her mother the truth. How could she confess she was cutting her afternoon class to go to the theater? It would only raise questions, for her mother knew how conscientious she was in her schoolwork and would certainly suspect there was a man involved. The last thing Juliet needed was for her mother to be asking about her love life. It was the one topic on which she and her mother were invariably at odds.

Juliet didn't understand why. As far back as she could remember, she had always been able to talk to her mother about anything, including sex. Since her divorce, however, something had changed between them. Juliet suspected that it was because of Sara and Annie. Maybe Kate looked at every man she dated as a possible father to her granddaughters. Whatever the reason, Juliet knew that in order to preserve her relationship with her mother, there were certain things she needed to keep quiet. Such as the fact that she was on birth control pills. And that she was meeting Ross today.

So instead of telling her mother about her plans to go to the theater, she made some vague references to seeing people between classes regarding internship programs. Kate didn't question her explanation, although Juliet suspected she didn't quite believe it.

From that moment on, guilt became Juliet's constant companion. It followed her around the university campus, interfering with her concentration in the class she did attend and making her miserable as she thought about the one she was about to skip. It haunted and taunted her until she finally decided she couldn't go out with Ross. She found a pay phone and dialed his number to tell him she'd have to break their date.

There was no answer, and she slammed the receiver in place. She had three choices. She could meet him at one o'clock as planned and tell him face-to-face she wasn't going, she could do nothing and simply stand him up, or she could drive over to his place and leave him a note. She chose the third option.

Ross's apartment was in an old, run-down building that looked to be about the same vintage as the Bar. There was no security system in the fourplex, and Juliet was able to walk right in the front door. From the age of the building, she expected the halls to smell musty, but she detected a hint of pine, and the wood-work, although old, gleamed with polish.

She checked for Ross's apartment number and started up the stairs to the second floor. The wooden risers creaked, and her footsteps echoed despite the plastic runner on the steps. Since Ross's apartment was the only one on the upper level, the stairs led directly to his door.

She stared at it curiously for several seconds, wondering what it looked like on the other side of the heavy, wooden door. Then she pulled the note from her pocket and bent down to slip it through the crack separating wood and floor. She froze. The faint sound of music could be heard and her brain registered the fact that Ross was at home. She couldn't just slide a piece of paper under his door and leave . . . or could she?

Before she could make up her mind, the glossy wooden door opened and she glanced up to see Ross gazing down at her, looking just as disconcerted as she was feeling.

CHAPTER EIGHT

"YOU'RE EARLY," he said, and she blushed, for he was standing in front of her barefoot and bare chested, wearing only a pair of black slacks. A belt dangled unbuckled from the waistband.

"I tried calling, but there was no answer," she said shakily as she rose to her feet.

"I was probably in the shower." He took her hand and pulled her into his apartment, saying, "Come on in. It'll only take me a few minutes to slip on some clothes."

"That's not necessary," she told him, and he lifted an eyebrow in surprise.

"You don't want me to get dressed?" He gave her a devilish grin that invited her to grin back.

She did, but weakly. "That's not what I meant," she said almost shyly.

"What did you mean?" He pulled her closer, and Juliet caught the fresh scent of soap and noticed the dusting of hair across his chest. Surprisingly it was blond, a direct contrast to his dark head.

She searched for the right words to tell him she had changed her mind about the theater, but she couldn't seem to find any words at all. Something was happening to her. A strange, giddy pleasure was rushing through her, dissolving the tension that had weighed on her all day. When the gleam in his eyes softened to something warm and curious, she found herself reluctant to say anything that would make them cool and distant.

"I... I could wait downstairs," she offered hesitantly.

He shook his head and laughed wickedly, pulling her into his arms. He bent his head and brushed his lips across hers. "I think I'd rather you wait here where it's nice and warm. Why don't you take off your coat." He started to undo the buttons for her, and Juliet's heartbeat accelerated. "Sit down on the couch—" he slid his hands inside the open coat and wrapped them around her "—have a glass of wine—" his hands slid over her back in a caress "—and I'll put on my shoes and socks."

He kissed her once more, then led her over to the couch where a decanter of wine and two glasses sat on the coffee table. After helping her off with her coat, he poured her a glass of wine and handed it to her.

"Don't go away. I'll just be a minute," he told her, then disappeared into the bedroom.

Until Juliet entered Ross's apartment, she had always regarded him as a musician. Now she could see the influence of the theater in his life. It was there in the arrangement of the furniture—furniture that looked as though it could have come out of her grandmother's house. Funny, she would have thought his taste would have leaned more toward the modern—futons and sofa sectionals, not camelback sofas and upholstered armchairs. Privately she was glad he had slipcovers and throw pillows. She loved old furniture, and even though he might have rented his with the apartment, she preferred to think he had chosen it himself.

Track lighting created small spotlights at regular intervals around the room, and as Juliet drifted around she had the sensation of being on a stage. Instead of paintings on the wall, there were framed playbills, and a mobile of papier-mâché masks dangled from the high ceiling. At the far end of the room sat a high-tech sound system, the state-of-the-art speakers looking a bit out of place among the comfortable, old furniture.

A large archway opened onto the dining area, but the room was empty except for an antique chandelier that hung from the ceiling. There was a row of cardboard boxes stacked against the back wall, the kind of boxes movers used, and Juliet wondered if Ross had any intention of unpacking them. Built-in china hutches sat empty, and Juliet had the uneasy feeling that this room, too, said something about Ross. He was only here temporarily.

On the opposite side of the dining room was the kitchen, which was small but modern. After a quick perusal, during which she noticed there was a box of bran flakes sitting next to an empty beer bottle, she returned to the living room. She looked inquisitively down the hallway, wondering which of the three doors led to the bathroom.

She was about to open one of them when Ross reappeared. He wore a black turtleneck that on some men would have looked ordinary, but on him looked better than any shirt and tie. His dark hair was slicked back, and she could smell the scent of after-shave. When his eyes met hers, Juliet's pulse leaped.

"I...I was just looking around. I hope you don't mind?" Over his shoulder she caught a glimpse of an unmade bed in the room darkened by drawn shades.

"Not at all," he lied, pulling his bedroom door shut as he noticed the direction of her gaze. He wished he had taken the time to straighten the apartment before he had gone to bed last night, but he hadn't expected that she'd arrive an hour early.

"I was looking for the bathroom," she said softly, and he gestured toward the door across the hall. She smiled shyly, then slipped inside. As the door closed behind her, he prayed she wouldn't find a pair of dirty shorts at her feet.

While she was in the bathroom, he rushed back into his bedroom and quickly dragged the covers up over the mattress, raised the shades and kicked the pile of clothes that had been scattered across the floor under the bed. Then he went out to the living room to get himself a glass of wine.

"This is a nice place," she said when she joined him a few minutes later.

He shrugged and looked around, trying to see it through her eyes. "It's old, but it's roomy."

"I like these old places," she said, looking up at the high ceilings. "They're full of character." She was carrying her wineglass and nervously took a sip. "What's in there?" she asked, pointing to a door that had a railroad-crossing sign on the outside.

"Come on, I'll show you." He took her wineglass from her and set it down beside his on the coffee table. As he opened the door, he pointed to the sign and said, "My grandfather worked for the railroad."

He didn't mind taking her into the room he used for a workshop, for he knew that, unlike the rest of the apartment, it would be neat. When her eyes spotted the huge round table with several three-dimensional models scattered across the top, she exclaimed, "How interesting! Are these yours?'' She bent down to examine the designs more closely.

''They belong to my students. They're called renderings, and they are every student's nightmare. The assignment is to take a floor plan for a stage setting and turn it into a three-dimensional perspective of how it will look when it's constructed as a set.''

''It's sort of like having a dollhouse,'' she commented. ''Did Brenda do one of these?''

''She hasn't turned hers in yet.'' He didn't want the thought of Brenda to put a damper on their time together and quickly added, ''These are from *Hamlet*. The university's going to be doing it in the winter quarter.''

After studying the renderings, Juliet looked around the room at the various drawings lining the walls as well as the photographs scattered across the cork bulletin board over his desk. ''Have you always been interested in set construction?'' she asked.

He shook his head. ''I never went to any theater productions when I was a child. It wasn't until I was hired to play the saxophone at a college performance of *The King and I* that I realized how fascinating it could be behind the scenes. Putting a play together is one of the most exciting experiences I've ever had.''

''So you changed your major from music to theater arts?''

He shook his head. ''I never was a music major.''

''You weren't?'' She cocked her head in surprise.

''My undergraduate degree is in history.''

''History?'' she echoed.

''My graduate work is in theater arts, but what I'm doing now is sort of a combination of history and theater arts. Even though I'm teaching a class on scenery construction, my thesis involves reconstructing old pieces of scenery, not creating new ones. It's what brought me here to Minnesota."

"Old scenery?"

"Yes. Extensive research is being done here on scenery that's been recovered from some of the original theaters built in this part of the country. You'd be surprised at the big caches that have been found."

"And that's what interests you? The historical aspect?" She still looked a bit bewildered by the discovery.

He grinned. "Now you know why I was so fascinated with your father's collection of history books." There was an odd look on her face, and he asked, "What's wrong? Don't I fit the part?"

He thought he'd get some polite, suitable answer, but she surprised him by saying, "No, you don't." He chuckled at that. "History majors have crew cuts and thick-rimmed glasses and wear brown suits with narrow ties."

This time he laughed outright.

"And from the way Brenda talked about you, I thought you were more of a performer. I think she sees you as the next Mel Gibson."

"It just goes to show you how little she knows about me," he told her pointedly.

"I realize that now," she said, emphasizing the last word.

He shoved his hands into his pants pockets. "Are you disappointed I'm not aspiring to be an actor?"

"Not at all." She waved her arm in an encompassing gesture. "This is very impressive."

"And respectable?" His voice sounded far more skeptical than he intended.

"What's that supposed to mean?" she asked. "You think I'm pretentious and that anything academic impresses me?"

"I didn't say that."

"Well, then, what are you saying? Ever since we met you've been acting as though you think I'm more concerned with what people are rather than who they are. Well, I'm not." She turned away from him, but he reached for her stiff shoulders and forced her to look at him.

"I'm sorry. I didn't mean to upset you. It's just that I have this feeling that you think I'm not good enough for you." He looked at her directly, his dark eyes intent.

"Why would you think that?"

"Look at your family. Your mother works for Senator Billman and your stepfather's the commissioner of police. We don't exactly move in the same social circles."

"So we know different kinds of people."

He gave her a crooked smile. "You haven't exactly been overly friendly toward me at times," he reminded her. "You did look down your nose at me on Thanksgiving."

"That was because I thought you were my sister's boyfriend, and I was feeling all sorts of things I wasn't supposed to be feeling—especially for my sister's boyfriend," she said coyly.

His fingers traced her face. "I would imagine they were the same kinds of wonderful things I was feeling. A warm tingling deep inside that made me want to forget about everything except getting to know you better." He slowly lowered his head and brushed his lips across hers. "Juliet, I don't know why it happened like this. I wasn't expecting to walk into your life and not want to walk out of it again.''

"Me, neither," she admitted throatily.

He held her tightly to him, his eyes darkening as he gazed into hers.

"But I am in it, Juliet, and I like being in it."

She sighed as his lips moved across the line of her jaw and downward to the smooth column of her throat. "Mmmm, you smell good," he murmured close to her ear, then nibbled at the soft flesh of her lobe.

"It's a French perfume my sister had made especially for me when she visited France last summer," she whispered, remembering how Meridee had told her only to use it when she went out with men she wanted to lust after her body.

"Whatever it is, I like it." Again he nuzzled her neck, saying, "I especially like the fact that you don't notice it until you have your nose right here. That way I won't have to worry about other men coming on to you at the theater. Speaking of which—" he reluctantly lifted his head "—we probably should be leaving."

She nodded in agreement and asked, "This play we're seeing this afternoon ... is this part of your research?"

"Not the kind of research you mean."

Juliet thought about his words often as they watched the Guthrie's performance of *A Christmas Carol*. Ross seemed fascinated by the special stage effects, and when she looked at him his eyes were often gleaming.

The play was wonderfully staged, and being with Ross and seeing how much he enjoyed the production made the experience all the more pleasurable. She was sorry to see it come to an end. But most of all she hated to think about going home to spend Saturday night alone.

Ross seemed just as reluctant to see their date end. "Can you come in for a few minutes?" he asked when he parked his van outside the fourplex.

She shook her head. "I wish I could, but I have to pick up the girls. I'm already later than usual."

"I enjoyed today, Juliet," he said huskily, his hand reaching out to caress her cheek.

"I did, too," she told him, turning her blue eyes in his direction. When she saw the emotion in his, she added, "I wish it didn't have to end."

Then he pulled her into his arms and kissed her, a deep, passionate kiss that had both of them breathing heavily by the time it was over. He leaned his forehead against hers and whispered against her lips, "I have to play at the White Wolf tonight."

"I know," she whispered back.

"Will you come?" he asked.

She pulled back slightly. "I've been away from Sara and Annie all day. I don't think I can leave them again tonight."

He nodded as if he understood, but Juliet wasn't sure he really did.

"What about tomorrow?" he asked.

"It's Sunday...I usually spend the day with family..." she trailed off.

"And evening?"

There was a brief hesitation before she said, "Why don't you call me?"

"All right." There was disappointment in his voice, and then he kissed her once more before letting her go.

JULIET KEPT GLANCING at the clock all evening, unable to stop thinking about Ross. She wanted to be at the White Wolf, and no matter what she did to try to forget, she was taunted by the thought that she could be sitting in the jazz club listening to him play.

She found herself short of patience with Sara and Annie and feeling guilty that she didn't want her Saturday night entertainment to consist of playing two games of Snakes and Ladders and making Play-Doh cookies. As soon as they were asleep, she pulled out her textbooks and forced herself to study for her final exams. It only took her a short while to realize that it was useless. She simply couldn't concentrate.

Instead, she put Ross's tape into the stereo system. Rather than soothing her restlessness, however, it fueled the fire burning inside her, the longing that brought to mind the taste of his warm, sweet lips.

She debated whether she should call the neighbor girl and have her come sit for a few hours. The question wasn't really one of whether she should hire a baby-sitter, but whether she was ready to take such a big step in her relationship with Ross. For she knew that if she showed up at the White Wolf, she would eventually end up at his apartment, and this time she wouldn't leave after only a few kisses. She reached for the telephone.

"Mrs. Karlin? It's Juliet. I know it's late, but I was wondering if Tracy could come over and sit with the girls for a bit?"

ROSS LOOKED OUT at the packed house sitting in the blue haze of smoke and wished it was closing time. He didn't know how many times he had looked at a certain table in the corner, but each time he looked he had felt a stab of disappointment. Juliet wasn't there, and she wasn't going to be there, no matter how many times he stared in that direction.

Music had always come so naturally to him it felt strange that tonight he should have trouble getting into it. But right now playing his sax was not what he wanted to be doing. Maybe he had just had too many late nights, too many smoke-filled rooms and too many complimentary drinks.

He tried to remember the last time he had stayed home on a Saturday night...and he couldn't. In fact, there were few nights he sat at home. Between his theater work and his music, he had little choice but to be a night owl. Unfortunately Juliet was a day person. Again his thoughts were on her. Lord, what had been happening to him these past few weeks? She seemed to be in his thoughts to the detriment of everything else.

He couldn't let that happen. He closed his eyes and threw himself into the piece he was playing, taking his frustrations out on his saxophone. All his emotions came pouring out of his horn as the combo played a medley of blues numbers. When it was over, he realized he hadn't once looked at the table in the corner.

"You expecting someone?" Big Bubba had come across the stage and was murmuring close to his ear.

Ross looked over to the corner table but saw only the same four women who had been there all evening.

"She's over there," Bubba told him in his gravelly voice. He cocked his head toward the exit door near the back of the stage.

Ross looked at Juliet and felt his heart swell with emotion. She looked like a frightened doe, standing in the crowd of heavy-smoking, Scotch-drinking jazz lovers. She waved her fingers and he smiled.

"Are we ready to break?" Ross asked no one in particular.

"Didn't we just take one?" another member of the combo quipped, exchanging glances with Bubba.

"I guess this is my chance to ham it up on my horn," Bubba said with a knowing grin, then clapped Ross on the back and said, "You go see to your woman."

My woman. Ross repeated the words over and over in his head as he set down his sax and discreetly left the stage. When he reached Juliet's side, he had already decided that he was going to make those words come true. He was going to make her his woman.

If there hadn't been hundreds of people crowding around them, he would have pulled her into his arms and made love to her right then and there. But what he was feeling for her at this moment was too private to share with anyone, so he simply slipped his arm around her and whispered close to her ear, "I'm glad you came. You found a baby-sitter?"

"The teenager across the street. I'm sorry I'm late. I wanted to come earlier, but I had to wait for the girls to fall asleep."

He tightened his hold on her. "I'm just glad you're here. Do you want something to drink?"

"Maybe just a soft drink. Shouldn't you be up there?" She gestured to the stage, where the trumpet player was in the spotlight.

"Not for a few minutes. This is Bubba's solo. Come with me." He pulled her through the velvet curtain beneath the red exit sign into the area behind the stage. There he kissed her, a long, intimate kiss.

"I really am glad you came tonight." He gave her a devilish grin and added, "I need a ride home."

"You knew I'd come, didn't you?" she accused, unable to hide her own grin.

"I was hoping you would. Does this mean you're coming back to my place after I'm through here?"

Her eyes held his as she nodded her answer, and she could see the gleam of satisfaction there. "How late will you be playing?"

"We're on our last set. It'll only be about another half-hour. Why don't I take you out front and introduce you to a couple of the other guys' wives. You can sit with them."

The minute Juliet saw the women, she knew she wasn't going to have much in common with them. They were older, tougher, and judging by the way they chain-smoked and downed gin and tonic, at home in the jazz club's atmosphere. To her surprise, however, they were warm, funny individuals who made her feel welcome and didn't question her relationship with Ross.

As usual, whenever she listened to Ross playing, she felt as though she were taking a magical journey. Whether or not it was her imagination, she thought his music seemed more lyrical, and she secretly wondered if it was his way of playing for her.

As it turned out, the combo played for more than half an hour, as the audience refused to let them leave without several encores. When it was finally closing time, Bubba announced to the small group of musicians that everyone was invited back to his place. To Juliet's surprise, Ross declined for both of them without asking her if she wanted to go.

She asked him about it later when they were in her car and on the way to his apartment.

"If you want to join the others at Bubba's, it's all right with me," she told him.

"Are you kidding? I'm not sharing you with anyone."

His words made her cheeks flame, and her nerves began to riot. She knew what was going to happen once they arrived at his apartment, and suddenly she began to worry that she would be a disappointment to him. She wanted to tell him that it had been a mistake for her to come tonight. She wasn't ready for what he was expecting of her.

It was only a brief distance from the White Wolf to his apartment, and they spoke little. He made a couple of trivial comments to which she responded in monosyllables. The closer they got to his house, the more nervous she became. She couldn't go inside with him. She rehearsed in her mind various excuses as to why she couldn't, but when they pulled up in front of the fourplex, she found herself reluctant to use any of them.

Ross had sensed a change in Juliet the minute they left the club. At first he had thought maybe it was just the awkwardness of her having to drive him home. He was no chauvinist, but he would have preferred to be driving her in his van. Now, in the light of the street lamp outside his apartment, he could see the panic on her face. Was he rushing her? Gently, he asked, "Need to get home?"

She nodded anxiously. "I didn't tell the baby-sitter what time to expect me, and it is getting pretty late."

Ross's heart dropped down to his toes. She wasn't going to be his woman tonight. "Maybe you should come inside and phone her before you leave here?" he suggested, wanting to prolong every minute with her.

He thought she'd say no, but she surprised him by saying, "Maybe I should."

He quickly came around and helped her out of the car and up the stairs to his apartment. As he unlocked the door, he kept one hand firmly intertwined with hers, wishing she weren't wearing gloves so he could feel her smooth skin.

The place was in total darkness as he shoved the door open, and he pulled her carefully inside. "Wait here and I'll get the lights," he instructed, then groped for the small lamp on the end table. When a soft glow lit the room, he motioned for her to step farther into the apartment.

But she didn't. She stood near the entry, as if frozen in place.

"There's a phone in the kitchen," Ross announced, shrugging out of his jacket.

She took off her gloves and dropped them on the couch, along with her purse, yet she didn't move toward the kitchen. "Ross, I . . ." she began, but trailed off, staying rooted to her spot on the carpet.

"Need an escort to the phone?" He walked toward her, taking both of her hands in his. They were ice cold, and he held them up near his mouth and blew on them. "Brrr. How come they're so cold? You were the one who had gloves."

"Poor circulation, I guess," she said with a weak smile.

He rubbed them between his fingers, then lifted them to his lips, pressing a kiss on each knuckle. "Any other cold parts that need to be rubbed?" He was hoping his levity would chase away the somber lines on her face, but she looked as though she were in a dilemma of some sort. "What's wrong, Juliet?" He slowly inched his way backward, leading her in the direction of the phone.

She kept her eyes downcast as she spoke. "I keep thinking I shouldn't be here."

Ross hooked a finger beneath her chin and tilted her face up to his. "Well, there's your problem. You're thinking." His other hand managed to slide inside her coat and cup a breast, but his eyes never left hers. "You should be feeling." They were still moving slowly across the room.

At the touch of his fingers, her body quivered and her eyes darkened. Then he lowered his mouth to hers, and as she slid her arms around his neck, she met his kiss with an intensity that sent a shiver coursing through his own body. He wanted to touch her—all of her. Without breaking the kiss, Ross slowly led her across the room, his hand frantically working to undo her coat buttons. As they passed the sofa, he eased the coat from her shoulders and let it fall to the cushions.

Suddenly aware of their change in direction, she lifted her mouth from his to ask, "Where are you taking me?"

"To the phone," he answered, then reclaimed her mouth before she could protest.

Juliet's lips parted in an intimate invitation, and he nearly groaned when she slid her palms down the solid wall of his chest, across his flat, hard stomach to the waist of his jeans. She moved restlessly against him, and Ross had to pull away from her for a moment or risk losing control. Reaching for her hands, he led her down the darkened hallway, his desire mirrored in her eyes.

Instead of the kitchen, they ended up in his bedroom, where moonlight cut through the blinds like prison stripes. When she realized where they were, she said in a husky voice, "I thought you were taking me to the phone."

He bent down and turned on the bedside lamp. "I did." He gestured to the piano-shaped phone beside the clock radio.

"Oh!" was all she managed to say. Her lips were swollen from his kisses, her hair was mussed from his restless hands, and her eyes were darkened with passion.

With his gaze locked on hers, Ross took her hands and returned them to the place they had been only moments ago. "I don't want you to leave yet, Juliet," he told her.

She stared into the eyes that seemed to have a mystical power over her. She knew that if she were going to call a halt to things, she needed to do it now.

She could feel his desire as though it were a tangible thing, enveloping her with its magical glow. She wanted him, oh, how she wanted him. To fill the void loneliness had left in her. To ease the ache she felt for him every time she looked at him. To love and be loved.

"I don't want to go," she whispered, her fingers moving along the waistband of his jeans to pop the snap open.

It was all the invitation he needed. Slowly he lowered them both to the bed, his mouth hungrily exploring hers, telling her of his need. Words of passion were whispered between them as simultaneously they freed each other of their clothes. Hands trembled as buttons came open and cloth was dragged away from skin burning with anticipation.

When nothing remained between them except the delicate stretch lace of her lingerie and the smooth knit cotton of his briefs, Ross paused to feast his eyes on the beautiful picture she made. He had expected she'd wear modest white undergarments, not delicate wisps of purple lace that barely hid her womanly secrets. Large, swollen breasts strained to be free of the bra she wore, and ever so gently he rubbed his thumbs across their tips.

Juliet sighed and closed her eyes, and Ross knew he couldn't just look any longer. He needed to feel skin against skin, and he slipped his fingers inside the lace, cupping and caressing the warm flesh. With one deft movement he flung the garment across the bed. For a long moment he stared at her nakedness before bending his head to her breasts.

Her fingers moved across the well-defined muscles of his shoulders, his arms and down his back. When they reached the snug-fitting briefs, he shuddered. Once they found their way inside the smooth cotton, he groaned. She tugged on the elastic waist, dragging the cotton downward. In the process her fingers grazed his swollen flesh and desire doubled its hold on him.

His hands swept down her belly to catch at her panties. Juliet lifted her hips to help him remove the last of the barriers between them.

Ross kissed her then, a slow, hot kiss that was meant to tell her they were going to explore each other without any hurry. But the fires of desire were reaching a fever pitch. Despite his attempts to slow the pace, there would be no way he could stand it much longer if she continued to touch him the way she was.

"Easy," he murmured, as her hands created exquisite feelings of pleasure.

She whispered back, "I don't want easy," and wrapped her legs around him.

Ross knew he was lost. As she lifted her hips, he entered her, sinking as deep as he could go. She sighed as her body adjusted to the intrusion, and he felt his control slipping as she began to move beneath him.

Carefully, slowly, he tried to savor every move he made, but she was arching beneath him, luring him toward the edge of sexual bliss. He trembled as he fought the urgency threatening to drive him to the brink of rapture. There were too many things he wanted to tell her, too many pleasures to show her.

They were good together, and he wanted to make it the best it could possibly be, but Juliet refused to let him hold back.

"Don't stop," she cried, pulling him deeper when he would have retreated. "Oh, please, Ross."

At the sound of his name, he was lost. He gave up trying to control anything and took the pleasures as they came. Just when he thought it could get no better, she rewarded him with sensations unlike any he had ever known. He felt like a man possessed, and he loved the feeling. When release finally came, it took his breath away and caused his body to tremble.

Neither one spoke for several minutes, content to savor the moment while they waited for hearts to slow and breathing to return to normal.

"How do you feel?" he asked, lazily outlining her smiling lips with his fingertips.

"Like all of my bones have melted." She sighed contentedly.

"Me, too. Especially one big one," he said, reluctantly rolling to his side. He propped himself up on his elbow and looked down into her face. "You are one sexy woman, Juliet Harper."

But Juliet turned her head to glance at the clock, refusing to meet his gaze. "I'd better go."

"Wait." Ross threw his arm across her as she started to sit up. He couldn't let her leave, not after what to him had felt like a union of their very souls. "Can't you stay just a few minutes? I need to hold you for a while."

The invitation was too tempting to resist, especially when Juliet saw the sincerity in his dark eyes. She relaxed and fell back into his arms. Now that the heat of passion had passed, the air felt cool on her skin, and unconsciously she shivered.

Ross reached for the edge of the bedspread and wrapped it around them cocoon-style. "Better?" he asked.

"Umm-hmm," she managed, wondering why she felt so shy around him. They had just made wild passionate love, yet she didn't know what to say to him.

Ross, on the other hand, was not at a loss for words and told her exactly how he was feeling. "I've never met anyone who could make me feel the way you do." He had turned her so that her back was pressed to his front, and nestled his cheek in the hollow of her neck.

"Is that good?" she asked, glad he couldn't see her face.

"It is if you're feeling the same way I am." When she didn't answer right away, he rose up on his elbow to gaze into her face. "I guess what I'm trying to tell you is that tonight was very special for me, and I don't want to see it end."

She reached up to lightly stroke the firm jaw where a hint of a beard was breaking through the skin. "It was special for me, too."

"Then let's make it the first of many special nights," he suggested huskily, turning his cheek so that his lips pressed a kiss into the palm of her hand.

"That might be easier said than done," she said, trying not to sound as apprehensive about their future as she was feeling.

"Why do you say that?"

"Ross, I'm a single mother with two small children." She glanced again at the clock and grimaced. "I shouldn't have stayed out this late. I've got to go." She shoved aside the spread, slipped off the bed and began to put herself back together.

Ross watched for a moment, a frown marring his handsome features. This was not how he wanted the evening to end. He reached for his pants and began to dress.

"What are you doing?" she asked, seeing him putting on his shoes and socks.

"I'm getting dressed so I can take you home."

"I have my car."

"I know. I'll follow you in my van."

"You don't have to do that." She was standing in front of his dresser mirror, finger-combing her hair. He came up from behind her and wrapped his arms around her, meeting her eyes in the mirror.

"I know I don't have to, but I want to."

She looked around nervously. "Do you know where my purse is?"

"I'll get it for you," he told her, then disappeared briefly. When he returned, he held her purse, gloves and coat in his arms.

"Will I see you tomorrow?" he asked as she applied a layer of red to her lips.

"It's Sunday—family day." She shrugged apologetically.

"What about Monday?"

"I usually study on Monday evenings."

"You could bring your books over here, and we could study together," he said with a grin. "There wouldn't be any kids to interrupt you."

"I'll have to see if I can get a baby-sitter," she said, the thought of another night with him making her pulse race.

"I could always go to your house," he suggested.

"No, it's better if we meet here."

Juliet's words made him realize that she was uncomfortable with the thought of sharing her family with him. He felt as though she were shutting him out of an important part of her life, and he didn't like the feeling at all. As he walked her to her car, he realized that despite what had happened in his bed, she still wasn't his woman. Yet.

CHAPTER NINE

ON MONDAY EVENING Juliet wasn't at Ross's apartment, but home nursing a child with the stomach flu. Earlier that day, the school nurse had phoned with the news that Sara wasn't feeling well, and Juliet had no choice but to pass up her opportunity to be with Ross. Maybe that was for the best. She wasn't sure where their relationship was going or if she should even be thinking about it going anywhere.

By Wednesday evening, butterflies were dancing in her stomach as she stood at the kitchen stove stirring the white sauce for the potatoes au gratin. Minutes earlier, Brenda had strolled into the kitchen wearing a skirt Juliet thought was too short and too tight, and a top that left little of her cleavage to anyone's imagination. When Juliet had asked her if she was going out for dinner, she had chuckled and said, "Are you kidding? Not with Ross here."

Restless, Juliet prowled around the kitchen, wondering what Brenda was up to while Ross sat at the piano giving Sara her lesson. Juliet's mind conjured up all sorts of images, none of which made any sense, but all of which added up to the same thing: she didn't want her kittenish sister hanging all over Ross.

Judging by Ross's behavior at dinner, he was as uncomfortable as Juliet with Brenda's coy act. The result was a tense, awkward atmosphere at dinner, and as soon as everyone had finished eating, Ross left. For Juliet, the last straw came when Brenda insisted on walking him out to his van.

Juliet was in the kitchen slamming cupboard doors when Brenda returned. When she would have passed through without offering to help clean up, Juliet couldn't resist speaking her mind.

"You could at least help me with the dishes," she snapped irritably.

"I've got stuff to do," Brenda replied sullenly.

"Your *stuff* didn't keep you from monopolizing Ross this evening. What were you trying to prove?" Juliet demanded, confronting her sister with her hands on her hips.

"I wasn't trying to *prove* anything. Chill out, Jules. What are you on my case for, anyway?"

"Because you made it downright uncomfortable for all of us. I could have crawled under the table in embarrassment."

"What are you talking about? I didn't *do* anything."

"You were throwing yourself at Ross," Juliet accused, trying to keep her voice from sounding jealous.

"I was being friendly."

"Hah!" She laughed sardonically. "You're chasing the poor man and he doesn't like it."

"And how would you know what he—or any man, for that matter—likes?"

Juliet ignored the barb. "He was here for Sara's piano lesson—not so you could drool all over him."

Brenda shot her a curious look. "You know what your problem is? You're jealous."

"Jealous?" Juliet's heart started to beat irregularly.

"You don't have any men in your life, so you don't want me to have any, either."

"That's not true!" Juliet said hotly, catching herself before she said something she would regret. She took a calming breath and said, "All I'm trying to tell you is that you're wasting your time with a man as old as Ross Stafford."

"And I've already told you, if I wanted any advice concerning my love life, I'd ask for it. So butt out. You're not my mother." Brenda stomped out of the room, calling back over her shoulder, "I'm going out."

Juliet looked at the mess in the kitchen and threw up her hands in frustration. "Just terrific," she mumbled to herself, wondering what bothered her more—Brenda's flirting with Ross or her own guilt.

Juliet hated deceit. Several times in the past two days she had thought about sitting down with Brenda and telling her the truth about her relationship with Ross. But each time she had come to the same conclusion. There was no way she could reveal her relationship with Ross without hurting her sister and creating discord in the family. It was something she couldn't risk, especially so close to Christmas.

And there was always the possibility that her affair with Ross would end before anyone else needed to know about it. That thought was even more unsettling, and Juliet tucked it away, not wanting to admit to herself how deeply she was coming to care for him.

JULIET AWOKE to a depressing amount of falling snow the next morning. It came down in big, wet flakes,

making roads slick and decreasing visibility, which in
turn created traffic delays. By the time she reached
work, not only was she late, but she was irritable and
out of patience, having narrowly avoided several col-
lisions because of the slippery roads. As the day wore
on, conditions steadily deteriorated until finally the
schools announced early dismissals and businesses
began closing. Juliet didn't waste any time picking
Annie up from the baby-sitter and arrived home just
in time to meet Sara's school bus.

Both Sara and Annie were delighted to see the huge
flakes piling up on the front lawn. Juliet, however, was
less enthusiastic. She really couldn't afford to lose the
time from work, and the thought of having to go outside and crank up her father's old snowblower was
hardly appealing.

By Friday, the snow had ceased, but since the
snowplows still hadn't cleared the roads, schools were
forced to remain closed and Juliet couldn't get her car
out of the garage, thanks to a huge drift blocking the
door. When the sun finally peeked through around
midday, she bundled the girls into their snowsuits and
took them outside.

The sound of shovels scraping against sidewalks and
snowblowers spitting out showers of white greeted
them when they stepped outdoors. When Juliet had
lived in her apartment, snow removal had been taken
care of by the building superintendent. Now, as she
surveyed the task ahead of her, she sighed. Her sigh
became a groan when a few minutes later she discovered the snowblower wouldn't start.

She grabbed a shovel from the garage and started
pushing the snow away from the door. It wasn't long,
however, before she realized she wouldn't be able to

clear the entire driveway unless she had some help. Winded, she stuck her head inside the back door and called out to Brenda.

The teenager came bouncing into the kitchen dressed in bold-patterned stretch pants and a bright purple sweater.

"Oh, good. You're dressed. I need some help clearing the driveway," Juliet told her. "If you expect to get your car out, I suggest you help."

"Why don't you use Dad's snowblower?" Brenda asked.

"Because I can't get it started. If you put your jacket on and come out and give me a hand, it'll go a lot faster."

"I can't." She was blowing on freshly painted nails, her fingers spread apart. "I just did my nails and I'm waiting for Debbie to pick me up. We're going skiing."

It was then that Juliet noticed the overnight bag sitting near the door. "When did you decide this?"

She shrugged. "It was kind of a spur-of-the-moment thing. Her dad has that condo up at Spirit Mountain, and he said we could use it this weekend. With all the new snow, skiing should be fabulous."

Juliet was tempted to tell her driving conditions were poor and temperatures were expected to plummet well below freezing now that the storm had moved eastward, but she held her tongue. Lately their relationship had been tenuous at best, and Juliet didn't want to get into another verbal confrontation with her sister.

"Well, can't you wait for her outside and help me shovel until she gets here?" Juliet appealed to her.

"Oh, all right," Brenda agreed petulantly. "I'll be out in a minute."

A minute was more like ten, and when Brenda finally did show up outside, she wasn't much help. She spent more time throwing snowballs at Sara and Annie than she did helping Juliet shovel. By the time Debbie arrived, Juliet was almost relieved to see her sister leave.

After only a short time in the snow, Juliet could feel the cold seeping through her boots and her toes beginning to go numb. With more than half of the drive still needing to be shoveled, she contemplated calling her mother to ask for Donovan's help. She decided to try the snowblower once more, first.

That was where Ross found her, yanking on the starter cord with a look of determination on her face.

"Need some help?" he asked, and Juliet jumped, startled by his appearance.

"Ross! What are you doing here?"

"Do you know you ask me that question every time you see me?" A grin curved his mouth, his dark eyes twinkling like the snowflakes that had fallen yesterday. "As usual, I came to see you. I wanted to make sure you had survived the storm."

"Just barely," she told him, her cheeks even rosier than before. Now the tingling Juliet was experiencing had nothing to do with the cold. She glanced down at his feet and exclaimed, "You're wearing boots!"

"Isn't that what Minnesotans usually wear in the winter?" Amusement danced in his eyes.

"Well, yes, but usually those big rubber clunkers are on someone who's wearing a down-filled parka, not a leather jacket." With the exception of the boots, he looked like he was on his way to perform at the White Wolf.

"Am I breaking a dress code or something?"

She laughed. "Uh-uh. In Minnesota, anything goes." She looked at his bare head. "You really ought to have a proper hat, though. I could probably find one for you inside."

"I brought a hat along. It's in the van." He leaned closer to her and whispered conspiratorially, "It has ear flaps."

The thought of him in a cap with ear flaps brought a grin to her face. "As my father used to say, you can't worry about how you look if you're going to survive a Minnesota winter." She sighed and nudged the tire of the snowblower with her foot. "I think this machine is testing my winter survival skills."

"What seems to be the problem?" he asked.

"I don't know. It won't start," she said, glowering at the machine. "I know it works, because my mom used it last winter."

He glanced out at the partially cleared driveway and asked, "Did you do all of that with a shovel?"

She nodded, suddenly feeling weary.

"Why don't you let me take a look at this. I'm not very mechanical, but maybe I can get it to work."

Again she nodded, watching as he bent down to examine the machine. While his fingers fiddled with wires and knobs, she remembered how those fingers had played across her skin, and a sudden rush of warmth filled her.

"Did you put in fresh gas?"

"What?"

"Did you change the gas? If this is the first time you're using it this year, the old gas should be dumped and you should put in fresh stuff."

She shrugged rather helplessly. "I didn't know. It looked as though it had gas in it, so I didn't add any more."

He gave her a reassuring smile. "It's all right. It's a problem easily corrected." He glanced around. "Do you have a gasoline can? I'll run down to the station and get it filled for you."

Juliet was about to protest when she realized that there was no reason for him not to help her. Brenda was gone for the weekend, she needed assistance with the driveway, and with the exception of a warm house, what she wanted most right now was someone to help her with the drive.

"I'd like that," she said appreciatively, which evoked a look of surprise on Ross's face.

"You would?"

She nodded and smiled. "I would. My back aches, I'm cold and I'm tired."

He took the gasoline can from her hands. "And here I thought you were going to tell me you could do it yourself."

"I can't even get my car out of the garage."

He looked at the station wagon covered with salt and mud. "Just give me an hour and you'll be back in business." He winked, then trudged back to his van through the drifted snow.

True to his word, Ross did have the driveway cleared within an hour. Neither Sara nor Annie seemed bothered by the frigid temperatures, and both protested when Juliet suggested they go indoors. While the three of them built a snowman, Ross guided the big snowblower through the drifts until the driveway was lined with two walls of snow.

By the time he was finished, Sara and Annie were shivering and begged their mother to make hot chocolate for all of them. Juliet was hesitant about inviting Ross inside, but Sara had no such reservations, and Ross accepted with a grin, offering to start a fire in the fireplace while Juliet busied herself in the kitchen with marshmallows and cocoa.

When she walked into the living room to announce that their beverages were ready, her chest tightened at the picture that greeted her. Sara was sitting at the piano, her fingers plunking away at the keys, and Ross was in the wing chair with Annie on his lap, patiently listening to Sara's attempts at music. But it was the look on Ross's face that played havoc with her emotions. He looked content, as though being with her daughters was exactly what he wanted to be doing at that moment in time.

"Can't we drink it in here, Mommy? Please?" Sara begged when Juliet suggested they go into the kitchen. "I won't spill."

Juliet felt her resolve weakening. It was warm in front of the fire, and she was reluctant to disturb the picture of serenity they made.

"All right. I'll bring it in here, but you have to promise me you'll be extra careful," she warned. She cast a quick glance at Ross, who gave her a little grin of approval that sent her insides into turmoil.

When she returned with the serving tray, Ross said, "Sara tells me Brenda went away for the weekend."

"Yes, she did," Juliet confirmed as she passed out the mugs of chocolate.

"And she won't be back until Sunday?"

"That's right." She deliberately avoided his eyes.

"You forgot the marshmallows," Sara complained.

"Why don't you get them for us?" Juliet suggested, then turned her attention to Annie, who was still sitting contentedly on Ross's lap. "Annie, come sit with Mommy and I'll help you with your chocolate."

When Annie was reluctant to leave her comfortable spot, Ross said, "She's all right here."

"She usually spills," Juliet warned, setting two mugs on the small table beside the chair. He was wearing a pair of black slacks and a silky white shirt.

"Don't worry about it." He shot her an attractive grin.

Ross should have worried about it, Juliet thought a short while later when Annie managed to tip her mug and drench the white fabric with a stream of dark liquid. He did his best to wipe at it with a napkin, but Juliet knew the only way to prevent a stain would be to soak the shirt in cold water immediately.

So Ross removed his shirt and gave it to Juliet, who took it to the laundry room, sprayed it with stain remover and rinsed it out. While they waited for the shirt to dry, Annie and Sara both fell asleep on the rug in front of the fireplace. Ross offered to carry them up to their rooms, and it was while he was upstairs that the doorbell rang.

Not expecting anyone, Juliet gasped when she opened the door and saw her ex-husband standing on the porch. "Tim!" Her voice was barely a squeak. Air seemed in short supply.

"Hello, Juliet."

She couldn't believe how much he had changed in the two years since she had last seen him. His normally straight hair looked as though he had had it permed, and he now wore a mustache. As she stared at his angular face, she wondered what it was about him that had originally attracted her to him. Even having the benefit of California sunshine year round, he looked pale and insipid.

They stood looking at each other for several moments before she invited him in. "I wasn't expecting you," she told him as he stepped into the tiled foyer.

Unlike Ross, he hadn't worn boots, and he stomped the snow from his shoes on the small scatter rug near the door. "I wasn't sure I was going to be able to get here with the snowstorm and all. I'm sorry about coming unannounced, but I tried calling and there wasn't any answer."

"How did you get here? I thought the airport was closed."

He smiled, revealing perfectly straight white teeth. "It reopened early this morning. The landing was fine, but driving is treacherous. I had forgotten how awful winter can be in Minnesota."

He was looking at her as though he were happy to see her, which only caused her to eye him suspiciously. Had he changed? Was he suddenly a good-natured human being?

All signs of pleasantness disappeared, however, when Ross came down the stairs, bare chested and in his stocking feet. Juliet could see by the way Tim was looking at him that he was imagining the worst. The tone of his next words confirmed her suspicions.

"Who is this guy?" he demanded, his eyes narrowing, and Juliet wondered how she could have ever found him attractive. He had such beady little eyes; funny she hadn't noticed until now. Any civility she had been feeling toward him disappeared, for once again he was the pompous, demanding man who had made her life miserable.

Juliet waited until Ross was standing beside her before she made the introductions. "Ross Stafford, Tim Harper."

Tim seemed reluctant to shake the hand that Ross extended, and Juliet felt like giving him a swift kick in the pants. It was only after Ross identified himself as Sara's piano teacher that Tim reluctantly acknowledged the handshake.

"Juliet, do you think my shirt's dry?" Ross asked, then turned to Tim. "I was having hot chocolate with Annie and she tipped hers down the front of me."

Juliet thought Tim looked as though he didn't believe a word he was saying. With his eyes on Ross, he said, "Juliet, I need to talk to you."

"Why don't I leave?" Ross suggested, and she felt a slight sensation of panic. She didn't want to be left alone with Tim, yet she couldn't expect Ross to stay and do battle with her ex-husband for her.

She was reluctant to leave the room for even a couple of minutes, but she needed to get Ross's shirt from the dryer. When she returned they were still staring at each other like a couple of boxers ready to square off. As she handed the slightly damp shirt to Ross, he didn't bother to leave the room but slipped it on in front of Tim, leaving the long tails hanging outside his waistband.

As he slid his arms into his leather jacket, Juliet said, "Thanks for helping me with the driveway."

"You're welcome. I'm going to have to go out through the kitchen. I left my boots near the back door."

She nodded and instructed Tim to wait in the living room while she saw Ross to the door.

As soon as they were out of Tim Harper's sight, Ross grabbed her and kissed her hard on the mouth.

"I don't like that man," he growled when his lips finally left hers.

"That makes two of us," Juliet said, trembling slightly.

"Do you want me to stay?" he asked, tracing her jaw with his fingers.

She shook her head. "It's probably better if you don't."

"I'll leave as long as you tell me he's never laid a hand on you." His expression was carefully controlled, but a small muscle twitched in his jaw.

"He's not abusive, Ross," she said softly. "He's just a jerk."

He kissed her again. "I don't like leaving you with him."

"It's all right. Really."

She tried to convince herself of those words a few moments later when she rejoined Tim in the living room. But the look on his face made her feel anything but safe. "Why don't you tell me why you're here," she said to him, trying to sound more confident than she was feeling.

"Isn't it obvious?" he said peevishly. "I want to see Sara and Annie."

She bristled at his high-handed tone. "I'm not going to allow you to take them to California."

"I didn't come to take them from you. I just want to see them."

Juliet swallowed with great difficulty. "They're napping right now, but if you want to come back later, you can see them then."

"I want to take them for the weekend," he told her, and the lump in Juliet's throat felt as though it had swollen to the size of a grapefruit.

"What do you mean?" she asked weakly.

"I'm at a hotel not far from here, and I want them to spend the weekend with me. That was part of our custody agreement. I'm supposed to get them two weekends out of the month," he reminded her.

"I realize that, but we've already made plans for the weekend. We're getting the Christmas tree and decorating it. They've been looking forward to it all week."

"Juliet, I've come halfway across the country to see my daughters. I think you can wait to trim your Christmas tree until after I've gone."

There it was again. That same sarcastic, intimidating tone he had used on her all those years she had been married to him. Only this time it didn't have its usual effect. She didn't back down. She wouldn't cower.

"If the girls want to go with you, they can go. Otherwise they stay with me," she said firmly.

"Fair enough." He glanced at his watch. "I'll come back this evening and they can tell me themselves. And don't try to talk them out of coming with me."

"I'd never do such a thing!" she shot back indignantly.

His look said he didn't believe her. "If you need to reach me, I'll be at the Marriott."

Juliet agonized over the situation for the three hours he was gone, but it was all for nothing. Not only did Annie cry when her father tried to give her a hug, Sara, too, was reluctant to get too close to him. Although Juliet could see that Sara wanted to warm up toward her father, after their two-year separation she needed time to get used to the man she had once called daddy.

Juliet was relieved when Tim agreed to her suggestion that he pick the girls up in the morning and spend the day with them instead of having them overnight. When Sara expressed her concern over not being able to see her grandmother, Tim offered to take her to the closest toy store. To Juliet's dismay, his ploy worked effectively, making Sara forget about spending the day at the Cades'.

Juliet felt a bit saddened to think that her daughters might be too easily influenced by their father. He was in a much better financial position than she, and she wouldn't put it past him to try to make up for his absence by plying them with material things. And there was still the matter of his wanting them to travel to California. Was this visit solely to see the girls or was he seeing the attorney who had handled his divorce for advice on custodial rights?

Long after the girls were in bed that evening, she thought about Tim and what effect his presence would have on them. For two years she had pretty much been able to forget that he had any role whatsoever in their lives. She had finally managed to put together the broken pieces he had left behind when he deserted the three of them. Now she was faced with the prospect that he might be trying to create cracks in that hard-won emotional stability.

When Ross called, wanting to see her, Juliet discouraged him from coming over. With two finals the following day, she told him she needed an early night. But long past midnight as she lay in bed watching the illuminated digits on the clock slowly flip, she wished that he was there with her, holding her in his arms, reassuring her with his lips.

It was with considerable misgivings that Juliet allowed Tim to take the girls Saturday morning. As they climbed into the rental car and drove off, she had the horrible feeling she'd never see them again.

All day long, she worried and fretted over their safety. In between her finals at the university, she tried calling Tim's hotel, but there was no answer. She even went so far as to check with the desk clerk to make sure he hadn't checked out of his room. He hadn't.

Not wanting to return to an empty house, she drove over to her mother's as soon as she was finished with her exams. Kate was decorating Christmas cookies when she arrived and looked surprised to see her daughter.

"Where are the girls?" she asked, a tube of frosting in her hands.

"They're with Tim," she said quietly, slumping into a chair at the kitchen table.

"What?" A look of alarm crossed Kate's face.

"He arrived yesterday. That's why you didn't have to watch the girls today. He took them." She sighed and brushed her hair back from her forehead.

"Why didn't you tell me?"

"Because I didn't want you to worry. I've done enough of that for both of us."

Kate wiped her hands on her apron and sat down across from her daughter. "Where was he taking them?"

"To the zoo, I guess, and he promised Sara she could pick out anything she wanted at the toy store." She made a sound of disgust. "He's probably plying them with junk food. He never did have much food sense."

"Did you call Harvey?"

Juliet groaned. "Aw, Mom. What can Harvey do?"

"I don't know, but you need legal advice. You can't possibly feel comfortable while he has Sara and Annie."

"Of course I don't!" she burst out emotionally. "For goodness' sake, Mom, how do you think I feel? I've been so worried I could hardly concentrate on my finals."

Kate reached for her hands and squeezed them reassuringly. "I'm sorry. The last thing I want to do is cause you any more anxiety than you're already feeling."

"I don't want him anywhere near my daughters, but he *is* their father." She was so tense her skin was clammy.

"Yes, and we have to keep in mind that although Tim Harper was a lousy husband, he was never really a bad father," Kate rationalized. "You know how close he was to Sara."

"That's right, which is why I'm trying not to let my fear become paranoia. Besides, if I know Tim, he won't even *want* the girls for more than eight hours at a time. Can you imagine what he'll do if Annie throws one of her terrible-twos tantrums?" She forced a weak smile to her lips.

"Everything's going to be fine," her mother said soothingly, patting her hands. "Why don't I make us some coffee?"

"That would be nice," Juliet said gratefully.

"Is he going to get them again tomorrow?" Kate asked as she filled the coffeemaker.

Juliet shrugged out of her coat. "I suppose that depends on how today goes. I had promised the girls we'd go get our tree, but maybe they'd rather be with him." Worry lines creased her forehead.

"I'm sure Sara's going to want to put up the tree. She's talked of nothing else all week. Donovan and I should come along. We could go out to one of the tree farms and chop one down."

"The girls would love that. Are you sure Donovan won't mind?"

"Of course not. It'll be fun for us. I love the thought of going out into the woods and cutting down a real pine tree."

"Aren't you going to get one?"

She shook her head. "We're putting up Donovan's artificial Scotch pine. It's lovely, but..." Kate sighed softly. "This will be the first time we've ever had an artificial tree at Christmas."

"About Christmas, Mom..." Juliet began.

"What about it, dear?"

"Meridee was talking as though you're planning on having our family celebration here." She couldn't hide her disappointment at the thought.

"This is my home now," Kate said gently.

"It may be *your* home, Mom, but it's not our family home. Do you realize that none of us has spent a Christmas anywhere other than the house?"

"Then this year will be the start of a new tradition."

Juliet looked down at her coffee cup, not wanting her mother to see how distasteful the idea was to her.

Sensing her unhappiness, Kate added, "This is my first Christmas with Donovan. I want it to be celebrated here in our home. You can understand that, can't you?"

On any other day Juliet might have been able to empathize, but not today. With her whole life being turned upside down because of Tim, she didn't want to think about changes. She wanted things to be the way they used to be. She wanted Christmas in the home where she had had all of her Christmases.

Looking at her troubled face, Kate said, "It really means a lot to you to be at the house, doesn't it?"

Juliet nodded solemnly.

"I have an idea. Why don't we have Christmas Eve at the house and I'll cook dinner on Christmas Day over here? That way we can blend the old with the new."

Juliet got up to give her mother a hug. "Thanks, Mom. I think that sounds like a wonderful idea."

"It'll be a wonderful Christmas. You'll see."

Juliet returned her mother's smile, but somehow she couldn't ignore the sense of foreboding that this was going to be one holiday she would never forget.

CHAPTER TEN

JUDGING BY SARA'S comments, the reunion between father and daughters went better than Juliet had anticipated. However, one look at Annie revealed that things hadn't been exactly perfect. There were grape-jelly stains on her shirt, and having gone without a nap, the two-year-old was cranky to the point of being unmanageable. Juliet could see by the tight lines on Tim's face that the day must have had its trying moments. There were jelly stains on his shirt, as well.

Leaving Sara to entertain her father, Juliet took Annie upstairs to get her ready for bed. All the while, she thought about father and daughter together downstairs. She hoped Tim would show a bit more enthusiasm than he had when Sara had announced she'd play the piano for him.

However, when Juliet entered the family room, she could see that he hadn't. Sara was no longer sitting at the piano but holding up a portfolio of artwork she had been accumulating since the first day of school. Tim sat nodding. The closeness he'd once shared with his daughter was gone, and there was a look of boredom on his pinched features. As Juliet saw the two of them together, she remembered how indulgent Ross had been with children who weren't even his own, yet here sat Tim looking annoyed with his own daughter.

Anger rose inside her. She didn't want him in her house, and she especially didn't want him with her children. Why had he come back into their lives now, of all times. All she could think about was getting rid of him.

"Sara, you'd better get ready for bed," Juliet said quietly, not caring whether she was being fair to Tim or not.

"But I haven't shown Daddy all my papers," she protested.

"It'll have to wait until tomorrow," Juliet told her, scooping up the scattered crayon drawings from the coffee table.

"Are you coming back tomorrow?" She looked at her father with such an eager expression, it made Juliet's heart ache.

"I think that's up to your mother. She says you have plans to get your Christmas tree tomorrow," he answered smoothly, but Juliet could see the challenge in his beady little eyes.

Sara looked pleadingly in her mother's direction. "Couldn't Daddy come, too?"

Juliet and Tim exchanged wary glances. "Sweetheart, we're going way out in the country to a tree farm with Grandma and Grandpa. I'm not sure we'd be back in time for your father to catch his plane back to California."

"I'm not leaving until Monday," he took great pleasure in announcing.

"You're not?" Juliet swallowed her disappointment with difficulty.

"Then you can come with us to get our Christmas tree?" Sara asked excitedly.

"Since you've already made plans with your grandmother, why don't you call me when you get back and I'll come visit you tomorrow night?" he suggested. "If that's all right with your mother," he tacked on as an afterthought.

Seeing the look on Sara's face, Juliet could hardly say she didn't want him anywhere near their house tomorrow. "That'll be fine," she murmured, shooting a suspicious look in Tim's direction. "Sara, you go on upstairs and I'll be up in a few minutes."

Sara said good-night to her father, an expectant look on her face as she stood before him. Juliet knew she was waiting for him to give her a hug. He didn't, and Sara left the room with her shoulders bent.

"I want to talk to you about my plans," he said to Juliet as soon as Sara was gone.

Juliet felt her stomach roll over. The sense of foreboding that had been teasing her all day leaped out like a lion snarling at a lion tamer. "What are your plans?" she asked bravely.

"I want to take the girls—or at least Sara—back to California with me on Monday."

"No!" She repeated the word several times, shaking her head vigorously.

"Will you at least listen to what I have to say before you reject the possibility?"

"What's there to explain? You want to take her, I'm saying no."

"Did you ever think it might be good for her to visit her other set of grandparents? She does have other grandparents," he reminded her.

"I've never denied your parents any opportunity to see or speak to the girls."

"My mother would like Sara to spend Christmas with us."

"And what about what Sara wants? You think she'll want to miss Christmas with her family?" She raked a hand restlessly through her curls. "You haven't been in her life for two years, she knows nothing of your new wife and she's virtually a stranger to everyone out there. Don't you think it would be traumatic for her to be away from her home on a holiday like Christmas?"

With his thumbs beneath his chin and his fingers pressed to his lips, he stared at her, contemplating what she had said. "What about letting her come after Christmas? She has two weeks off from school, doesn't she?"

"I don't care if she has a month off from school. The answer's still no. I want her here with me, and she's staying here with me," she answered, her cheeks flushed with emotion.

"Isn't that a little selfish?" he said, his eyes narrowing.

Juliet stared at him dumbfounded. "I'll tell you what selfish is. Selfish is dumping your wife and two kids so you can fly out to California with no responsibilities, no worries. Selfish is a man who doesn't once in two years try to see his children." She had a full head of steam now. "Selfish is a father who ignores child-support payments and has no idea whether his children even have enough to eat."

Tim abruptly rose to his feet. "I can't talk to you when you're like this. You're out of control."

That had always been his response whenever she had shown any emotion. "Out of control? I'll show you out of control." She picked up a sofa pillow and heaved it at his retreating body. It missed its target.

"I'll let my lawyers handle the details from now on," he said, glowering at her.

There was a definite threat in his parting statement, and Juliet found herself trembling long after he was gone. As she went to tuck Sara in for the night, she pulled her daughter into her arms and hugged her extra close. She couldn't let her go to California. She wouldn't let her go.

Shortly after Tim left, the doorbell rang and Juliet's stomach tightened at the thought that he might have returned. However, it wasn't Tim standing on her front porch when she peeked through the pane of glass beside the door. It was Ross. Juliet nearly flew into his arms.

"Boy, am I glad to see you," she told him, hugging him close.

"What's this? No 'What are you doing here, Ross?'" He held her tightly within the circle of his arms.

She tipped her head back and asked, "What *are* you doing here?"

He chuckled, pushing her inside so he could close the door behind them. "I came to see you." He kissed her then, slowly and thoroughly.

"But what about the White Wolf?"

"I found someone to fill in for me."

"Then you don't have to go back?"

"Uh-uh." He nibbled on her ear, his breath warm against her neck. "Got any plans for this evening?"

"I was just going to plop down with the books and a can of soda."

"How about plopping down in front of a nice warm fire with this?" From his coat pocket he produced a bottle of sparkling white wine. "I thought maybe we could sip it slowly and talk about all the things we have in common."

"Such as?" she prompted.

"Such as how we both like this," he said, nuzzling her neck with his lips.

"I think that sounds like a wonderful idea," she said, closing her eyes as his mouth burned a trail of kisses down the smooth column of her throat. "Why don't you get the fire going and I'll get us a couple of glasses."

"You've got yourself a deal," he said, sealing the bargain with a kiss.

By the time Juliet had fixed a small plate of cheese and crackers and pulled two long-stemmed glasses from the cupboard, Ross had a fire crackling in the family-room fireplace. The only light came from the flames glowing in the darkness, and Juliet was caught up in the intimacy of the room the minute she stepped through the archway. Ross had taken off his shoes and sat cross-legged on the furry rug in front of the hearth. When she sank down beside him, he reached for the silver serving tray, setting it to one side.

In the firelight he looked a bit like a pirate with his loosely fitting shirt open at the throat. Juliet watched him fill the wineglasses, noticing how long and slender his fingers were. They were the fingers of an artist, and once again she was reminded of what those fingers could do to her skin.

"I'd like to propose a toast," he told her as he held the two glasses in his hand. Juliet waited for him to say something terribly romantic as he offered her one of the glasses. He lifted his glass in salute and said, "To the end of fall quarter."

She grinned. "Here, here." She took a sip of the wine, then sighed. "I only hope I didn't blow the quarter with my finals."

"They were that tough?"

"My problem was one of distraction."

"Distraction meaning your ex-husband?" he asked solemnly.

She took another sip of wine and gazed pensively into the fire. "I guess it was rather obvious we don't exactly have a friendly divorce agreement."

"He doesn't look like an easy man," he commented shrewdly. "Has he done anything to upset you?"

"The fact that he's breathing upsets me," she said bitterly, then quickly amended her statement. "To be honest, I don't care what the man does as long as it doesn't include Sara and Annie." Uncomfortable with what she had revealed, Juliet said, "Look, it's probably better if we don't discuss Tim Harper."

He reached for her hand. "Maybe it would help if you did talk about him."

She shook her head vigorously. "He's not worth any time we might waste. Besides, there aren't many Saturday nights when I have a sexy saxophonist all to myself." She reached over and teased his thigh with her fingers. "I don't want to spend it talking about my ex-husband."

"That's fine with me as long as his ghost isn't going to be in this room with us." He raised his hand to touch her cheek.

Juliet wanted to feel the strength of his arms around her, the taste of his lips on hers. She leaned closer to him and whispered, "It won't. I promise."

Ross held her to her word, refusing to let her think about anything but him. They made love and they talked, they made love again and talked some more until hunger struck somewhere around midnight. They raided the refrigerator—Juliet clad only in Ross's shirt, Ross wearing a pair of dark briefs.

As they sat at the kitchen table with a single candle glowing between them, Juliet listened to him talk about his music, his work in the theater and the various places he had lived in over the past ten years. He was the most interesting man she had ever met, and something in his stories of life on the road appealed to the wanderlust in her, a wanderlust that was buried deep beneath layers of obligations and duties.

It also made her realize how different their lives were. She was a homemaker, a mother, a woman who wanted roots and traditions. He moved from city to city without any attachments, without any responsibilities. It was a sobering thought, one that brought a slight frown to her face.

Seeing the apprehension replace the joy, Ross asked, "What's wrong? Are you thinking about your ex-husband again?"

She gave him a weak smile and shook her head.

He pushed himself back from the table and patted his knee. "Come here."

Juliet didn't hesitate; she went straight to his arms.

"What's bothering you?"

She leaned her head against his shoulder. "I was just thinking."

"About us?"

She nodded.

"I had hoped that after everything that's happened between us tonight, you'd have a smile on your face."

She couldn't resist lifting her head to grin at him.

He brushed a kiss across her cheek and said, "That's better."

Juliet sighed and leaned her head back against his shoulder. "This feels so right," she murmured, her fingers tracing the well-defined muscles of his chest.

"That's because it is right. Are you still worried about Brenda? Is that what's bothering you?"

"I've never liked keeping secrets from my family."

"Then maybe it's time we share the secret?" He touched her mouth with his fingertips, sending a tiny tremor through her.

"I'd like to, but I don't think we should do it before Christmas. I'd hate to cause turmoil in the family over the holidays."

"Does that mean I should accept Bubba's invitation to his Christmas feast?"

Again, she raised her head and looked into his face. "You're not going home to be with your family?"

"I'm not sure I know where home is anymore. As for family, there's not much of that left, either." Although he said it matter-of-factly, Juliet detected a somber note in his voice.

"Would you like to be a part of our Christmas celebration?"

Surprised, he asked, "Is that an invitation?"

"Everyone's coming over here on Christmas Eve."

"And you want to tell your family about us then?"

She quickly refuted that idea. "No, but I was thinking that since you're Sara's piano teacher, I could probably invite you to share in our family celebration. No one would think anything of it."

"This holiday stuff is important to you, isn't it?"

She bristled for a moment as she remembered him telling her right from the start that he and domesticity didn't mix. Maybe inviting him to the family gathering was a mistake. "You don't *have* to come if you'd rather not," she told him, her shoulders stiffening as she tried to get off his lap.

"I want to come," he insisted, trying to prevent her from standing.

"Are you sure?" She eyed him warily.

"I'll be there," he told her, gently brushing his lips across her.

"Wait." She pushed lightly on his chest. "There's only one problem. If I invite you, Brenda might become suspicious."

"Then have Brenda ask me...like she did for Thanksgiving."

"But if you and I are together in the same room, I'm afraid someone's going to guess what's going on. And I'm not sure I could stand a repeat of the way Brenda practically tackled you Wednesday night."

He sighed impatiently. "So what are you saying? You're inviting me but I can't accept the invitation?"

"You can't come as you."

He gave her a quizzical look. "If I'm not me, who am I?"

"Santa Claus," she announced with a mischievous grin.

"You want me to come to your party dressed up as Santa Claus?" he said in disbelief.

"Just think how much fun it would be," she said enthusiastically. "We could rent the suit and stuff it with pillows. And you could wear a fake beard and a white wig.''

Astonished, Ross said, ''You're serious, aren't you?''

She nodded vigorously. ''With you as Santa, no one would ever suspect you're at the house because you want to be with me. They'll think you're there for Sara and Annie's benefit.''

''What if Sara recognizes my voice?''

''Aw, come on.'' She playfully punched him. ''With your theater background, I bet you won't have any trouble disguising it.''

He lowered his voice as he said, ''What do I have to do... besides ho, ho, ho?''

''See, that's perfect!'' Juliet exclaimed. ''Even if Sara sits on your lap, she won't guess who you are.'' She looked at him eagerly. ''Will you do it?''

''You really want me to, don't you?''

She smoothed her fingers across the curve of his shoulders. ''I want us to be together at Christmas. Please say you'll do it.''

''All right.'' He had barely given his consent when she started raining kisses all over him.

''So what are you going to tell everyone?'' he asked when she was finished.

''The truth. That your family's not here for the holidays and you offered to play Santa. It's not going to be a problem. Remember how well you got along with everyone on Thanksgiving? Gran, Meridee and Brenda all think you're dishy.''

''Dishy?'' He pulled a face.

''Yeah, and they haven't even seen you undressed,'' she teased.

"What about your parents? Will they like me with my clothes on?"

"Of course they will. They're just average every-day people."

"Juliet, your stepfather's the police commissioner and your mother's an aide to Senator Billman. Those aren't exactly average-everyday-people jobs."

"You're not nervous about meeting them, are you?"

"I do have a couple of unpaid parking tickets," he joked.

"There are still five days before Christmas. Plenty of time to get them paid," she replied lightly.

"Tell me one thing. What kind of music do they listen to?"

She shrugged. "Donovan's always had big-band music playing whenever I've been over there. He and Mom go ballroom dancing quite a bit."

"If they like big-band music, they can't be all bad," he said with a wink.

She laced her fingers behind his neck. "Do you always evaluate people by the kind of music they like?"

"You don't think it's an accurate people barome-ter?"

"I guess I've never really thought about it. But it doesn't matter. My mother won't be able to resist your charm, and all you have to do is ask Donovan if you can see his orchid collection and you'll be in his good graces."

"Can I stay late after the guests have gone home?" he asked, his fingers reaching inside the shirt she was wearing.

"Brenda doesn't go home. She lives here," she said with a sigh of delight as his fingers made contact with her flesh.

"Then maybe we'd better make the most of tonight—or what's left of it."

"Our fire's probably just about out."

"Do you want me to revive it?"

"I've got a better idea," she said, then slid off his lap and led him upstairs to her bedroom.

THE FAINT BEEPING that woke Ross made him wonder if his alarm clock was on its last leg. Normally his digital clock sent such a shocking blast of noise into the air it could arouse a dead person. As he opened his eyes he realized it wasn't his alarm, but Juliet's. Immediately he was aware of a warm body pressed up close to his, and memories of the night before sent a delightful rush of pleasure through him.

Juliet stirred slightly, and he quickly reached over to shut off the alarm. When he saw the clock read four-thirty, he grimaced. He wanted nothing better than to go back to sleep in her arms, but he knew she was the one who had set the alarm. She wanted him up and gone before Sara woke up and found him in her bed.

He looked at the sleeping woman beside him and sighed. The last thing he wanted to do was leave her, especially the way he was feeling about her at this moment. This was a new experience for him—waking up next to a woman who was more eager for him to leave than he was.

The scent of wildflowers teased his nostrils as he buried his face in the luxurious red curls. He glanced again at the clock and ignored the little warning in his head that said it might not be a good idea to stay in such idyllic surroundings.

He needed more time with her. Maybe he could stay in bed just a little longer. Sara and Annie certainly wouldn't wake before six-thirty or seven. He wouldn't sleep, he'd just hold her and savor all that had happened between them in this wonderful, warm bed. He snuggled closer to her and listened to the rhythmic sound of her breathing, amused by the tiny little whistle that accompanied every third breath she took.

One moment he was listening to her breathing, the next he was hearing the sound of tiny fists pounding on wood.

"Mommy, how come you locked the door?" Sara's voice rose above the noise of the doorknob being jiggled.

At the same time Ross saw seven o'clock illuminated on the clock radio, he felt Juliet scrambling beside him.

"Good grief. It's morning," she murmured, jumping out of bed as if a fire alarm had just been sounded. She frantically raced around the room looking for articles of clothing, but only came up with a pair of dark briefs and a silky white shirt.

"Quick, into the bathroom!" she ordered Ross in a whisper, shoving the shirt and briefs into his hands as he rolled out of bed. "You'll have to use the fire escape," she told him, hurrying over to the closet for her pink chenille robe.

"The fire escape?" he whispered, still groggy with sleep.

"It's right outside the window." She motioned in the direction of the bedroom window. "I'll take the girls downstairs for breakfast and you can leave."

'Aren't you forgetting something? Like the rest of my clothes."

She squeezed her eyes shut. "Oh, no! They're down in the family room." She looked to the door, where Sara was still pounding, and called out, "I'll be right there. I'm in the bathroom."

"Maybe you should take Sara into Annie's room and have her help you with something, then I'll sneak downstairs, get my clothes and leave," he suggested in a calm whisper.

"You're right. That'll work." She practically pushed him into the bathroom, saying, "Give me a couple of minutes to get them safely out of sight."

He grabbed her chin and planted a quick kiss on her lips. "I'll call you later, okay?"

She nodded, then pulled the door shut and went to unlock her bedroom door. Ross could hear the conversation between mother and daughter as he pulled on his briefs.

"Mommy, why did you lock the door?" Sara repeated impatiently.

"I was wrapping Christmas presents before I went to bed," Juliet answered. "Come on. Let's get Annie from her crib. I have something special to tell the two of you."

Their voices faded and Ross waited until he heard the sound of a door closing before cautiously making his way downstairs. Quickly and quietly he finished dressing, pausing only to gather Juliet's clothes together and shove them under the sofa. With one last look at the now-cold fireplace, he sighed and left.

JULIET WAS IN THE MIDDLE of making oatmeal when the phone rang. Before she could reach it, Sara had already answered.

"Mommy, it's Ross," she announced. "He says he needs to talk to you about my lesson."

She shook her head, trying to look nonchalant. "Tell him I'll be right there," she said, putting the lid on the saucepan and then spilling a pile of Cheerios on Annie's high chair tray to keep her quiet until she served breakfast.

Juliet's eyes were on Sara as she picked up the receiver. "Hello, Ross."

"Hello, you sexy creature."

Juliet felt the warmth spread across her face. "Sara says you want to talk to me about her lesson?" She deliberately kept her tone businesslike.

"There are two reasons for this phone call. First, I wanted to tell you that last night was the best night of my life and if I should get hit by a bus today, I will die a happy man."

"That's nice to hear," she answered, aware of Sara's interest in the conversation. "I agree with you."

"I also wanted to tell you that I stuffed all of your clothes under your sofa. I thought it might raise a few questions if Sara were to find your bra and panties on the living-room floor."

"You're right. It would." She glanced again at Sara. "Thank you."

"You're welcome. Now, about Sara's lesson—I'll be there a half-hour later than usual, all right?"

"That's fine."

"You aren't going to make me wait three whole days before I see you again, are you?"

"I'll leave it up to you."

"Great. That's exactly what I hoped you'd say. How about lunch tomorrow? I can meet you at Tejas at noon."

"Fine. I'll see you then." She said goodbye, then turned her attention to dishing up oatmeal and answering Sara's questions regarding the phone conversation. She was in the middle of buttering toast when the phone rang a second time. Again, Sara answered it.

"It's my daddy," she said excitedly, and Juliet's stomach plummeted.

"I've changed my plans," Tim announced when she picked up the phone. "I decided that since the girls were busy today, I'd catch a flight back to L.A."

Juliet felt both relief and concern. She knew that Sara was expecting to see him again. "When are you leaving?"

"I'm going to catch the airport shuttle about an hour from now."

"Then you're not planning on coming over before you leave."

"There's not enough time for that."

Juliet looked at her daughter, who had brought crayons and paper to the breakfast table in order to make a picture for her daddy, and felt her stomach tense. "Sara's expecting to see you today."

"If you're so concerned about whether she gets to see me, you could always let her come with me to California," he said unpleasantly.

"You know that's not possible."

He made a disgruntled sound, then said, "I'm not going to fight you on the Christmas issue."

Relief washed over her, but it was short-lived.

"But sometime in the future both of the girls will come to California, I promise you that." His words sounded more like a threat than a promise, and Juliet shuddered.

Mindful of Sara taking in every word, she said, "Look, I know your time is limited, so why don't I put Sara on and you can talk to her?" She didn't give him the opportunity to object, but handed the phone to her daughter.

From her spot at the kitchen table, she watched the expression on her daughter's face change from one of delight to one of disappointment, her voice becoming less animated the longer she talked. By the time she had hung up the receiver, there were tears in her eyes.

"He's not coming over today," she said in a broken voice.

Juliet opened her arms and pulled her daughter onto her lap. "He has a plane to catch." She couldn't believe she was defending the rat.

"He says... *hiccup*... he's going to come back soon."

The news only made Juliet more uncomfortable, but she tried not to let her anxiety show. "Why don't you finish your breakfast and we'll get ready for Sunday school? It's the Christmas program today."

Talk of the Christmas program effectively distracted Sara, and soon she was eagerly looking forward to the day ahead of them. Except for a brief mention of her father's visit to her grandmother, Sara didn't talk of him again until Sunday evening when Juliet was tucking her into bed.

"Do you think my dad will really come back?" she asked, her blue eyes solemn.

Juliet felt a hand reach out and squeeze her heart. "He said he would, didn't he?"

"He's got another little girl," she said, her lip rolling over into a pout. "And a new mommy."

Juliet reached out to pull her into her arms. "I know, sweetheart." She gently stroked the blond curls.

"He told me I could come to California if I wanted to." She lifted her head and asked, "Is that true?"

Juliet swallowed with difficulty. "Do you want to visit him in California?"

"Not without you and Annie." She yawned and Juliet gently guided her back against the pillows.

"Well, why don't we wait and see what his plans are before we make any decisions, okay?"

"Okay." She reached for her favorite baby doll and tucked it in beside her. "You know yesterday when I told you I had a lot of fun with my dad?" Juliet nodded and waited for her to continue. "Well, it was kind of fun, but some of the time it was kind of boring."

"Boring?" Juliet frowned. "Why do you say that?"

"He kept asking me so many questions."

"Like what?"

She lifted her tiny shoulders. "You know, about school and stuff. And if I liked the baby-sitters and if I liked my piano teacher."

"He asked about Ross?"

"Umm-hmm," she said sleepily. "Are we going to be able to put presents under the tree pretty soon?"

"Maybe tomorrow." Although Sara had switched subjects, Juliet's thoughts were still focused on why Tim would be questioning her daughter about Ross. It annoyed her to think that he was pumping a six-year-old for information regarding her personal life, but then, considering his past behavior, she should have expected it. She was tempted to question Sara herself, but one look at the tired, angelic face changed her mind.

She would deal with Tim Harper in whatever way was necessary, but not at the expense of her children. At least for now he was gone, and both of her daughters were safe with her. She felt as though she had survived round one of a boxing match. Tomorrow she'd call Harvey and find out what tactics it would take to score a knockout punch.

For that's what she wanted for Christmas—to have Tim Harper out of her life. If only Santa could make that happen.

WHEN JULIET SET HER MIND to something, she never did it halfheartedly, which meant that the week before Christmas was filled with preparations for their holiday celebration. Besides making sure all the wooden floors were polished to a glossy shine and the glass chandelier sparkled like brilliant gems, she decorated the house with garlands of evergreen and strung dozens of tiny blinking lights throughout the spacious rooms. Giving in to her mother's request that she leave the cookie-baking to her, she put all her culinary skills into preparations for their gala Christmas Eve dinner.

As she stood in the kitchen stuffing phyllo pastry with avocado and crabmeat, she reflected on past holidays, remembering what it had been like when she had been a little girl and Christmas seemed to be one big, joyful noise. While her mother put the finishing touches on elegant cocktail hors d'oeuvres, her father would lead everyone in singing carols. She and Meridee would count the packages under the Christmas tree and try to keep their fingers away from the frosting on the Yule-log cake.

Twenty years ago, everything had seemed so simple. She had been secure in the knowledge that she had a mommy and a daddy who loved her more than anything else in the world.

Juliet sighed as she realized that as hard as she tried to make this Christmas special for Sara and Annie, she would never be able to re-create the sense of tranquillity she had felt when she was Sara's age. Her daughters didn't have a mommy and daddy who loved them more than anything else in the world—at least not a daddy. And despite Sara's outward appearance of being happy, Juliet couldn't help but worry about how she was really feeling now that her father had reappeared.

On the morning of Christmas Eve the postman brought several packages. Juliet knew immediately that they were from California. She debated whether she should let the girls open them right away or put them under the tree with the mound of brightly wrapped presents. Not wanting Tim's presence to intrude upon their holiday celebration, she opted for the first choice.

Inside one of the prettily wrapped packages was an expensive electronic keyboard that Sara had often begged Juliet to buy but budget limitations had always prohibited. Although she wanted to feel annoyed with Tim for sending the instrument, the joy on her daughter's face took the sting out of her emotion. She looked at the gift-giving in a practical way: at least it kept Sara and Annie from constantly asking her, "How much longer till we get to open our presents?"

By late afternoon the hors d'oeuvres were ready, the standing rib roast was in the oven and holiday music filled the rooms of the grand old Victorian home. All that remained to be accomplished was to get everyone into their party clothes. Singing "Santa Claus Is Coming to Town," Juliet hustled her daughters up the winding staircase and into her bedroom, where three velvet dresses were draped across her bed.

As she tied sashes into bows and wove ribbons through blond curls, she pushed all thoughts of Tim Harper from her mind and let the holiday spirit capture her. However, when Annie and Sara stood side by side, one in red velvet, the other in green, she felt a surge of pride. They were such beautiful children, she couldn't understand how any father could not love them more than anything else in the world.

Juliet's dress was also velvet, but black with a long full skirt that fell to midcalf on her slender legs and a sweetheart neckline that left her shoulders bare. Like her daughters, she wore her hair up so that the curls spilled over the top of her head and allowed her long, dangling earrings to dust her shoulders. As she stood in front of the mirror, she couldn't help but think of Ross and wonder how he was going to react when he saw her.

It wasn't the kind of dress he would expect to see her wear. She wanted him to be unable to keep his eyes off her, yet she knew it would be better if he did.

The last thing she wanted to happen this Christmas was for anyone to suspect that Ross was anything other than Sara's piano teacher. And not just because of what Brenda would say. She wanted her mother to get to know him before she discovered that he was more than a friend. Too often in the past she and her mother had disagreed on her choice of men. But Ross was different from the men her mother had disapproved of, and in time she knew her mother would accept her feelings for him. Tonight, however, was not the right time to reveal their relationship, and as much as she wanted to spend the holiday with him, she hoped she wasn't making a mistake by inviting him.

Her apprehension was quickly dispelled when Ross made his appearance. He played his role with a flourish that made Juliet wonder why he wasn't still acting in the theater. Whereas Sara was mesmerized by him, Annie cried and wanted nothing to do with him. But even dressed as Santa, he managed to win the approval of the rest of the members of her family, and Juliet discovered her worries were unfounded. Although he spoke to her often, there was no hint of sentiment in his voice or eyes.

About halfway through the evening, Juliet began to feel lonesome for him. He was in the same room with her but he wasn't really with her. As Donovan took photos of the group gathered around the Christmas tree, Juliet realized that she wanted Ross in the family pictures—and not as Santa. A slight frown creased her brow as she wondered if he would be one of the faces in this room next year.

Her confusion must have shown on her face, for Ross cornered her a few minutes later and asked, "Is anything wrong?"

"No, why?"

"Santa senses a little unhappiness."

Juliet glanced around nervously. "You're doing a wonderful job."

He acknowledged her compliment by bending at the waist. "Did you know your mother's going to mid-

night mass and taking Brenda and Meridee as well?''
His eyes twinkled mischievously beneath the thick
white eyebrows.

''Umm-hmm. It's a family tradition. Gran offered
to stay with Sara and Annie so that I could go, but I'd
rather take the girls to church in the morning.''

''I guess that means you'll be home alone around
midnight, eh?'' he asked in a suggestive tone.

''I guess it does...unless the real Santa decides to
pay me a visit,'' she teased.

''Don't be surprised if he shows up at your front
door. Your chimney's too hot.'' He winked and
walked away.

Juliet wore a smile the rest of the evening. As soon
as everyone left for church, she put the girls to bed,
then rushed back downstairs to put another log on the
fire. With the stereo softly playing Christmas music,
she was ready and waiting for the doorbell when it
rang.

''Ho, ho, ho. Merry Christmas,'' Ross drawled
when she opened the door to him. He was still in his
Santa suit and carried a small gold package as he
stepped into the foyer. ''Is the coast clear for Santa?''

''Why, yes, it is, Mr. Claus. Can I take your coat?''
she asked pertly, playing with the big black buttons on
the fur-trimmed red jacket.

''That and a few other things. But first...'' He
pulled her into his arms and kissed her.

Juliet giggled. ''That tickles.'' She tweaked his
mustache.

Neither saw nor heard a little girl who had crept out
of her bed at the sound of the doorbell. She was
kneeling on the landing at the top of the stairs, her

face pressed close to the railing as she took in the scene below.

Juliet led Ross into the family room, where the only light came from the miniature bulbs on the tree and the blinking strands draped around the room. When she closed the doors, Sara quietly crept back to bed.

CHAPTER ELEVEN

BEHIND THE CLOSED DOORS of the family room, Ross and Juliet celebrated their own private Christmas. With only an hour to spend together, they made the most of their time, laughing and sharing stories of Christmases past as they cuddled together on the sofa. Juliet told him that this was probably one of the best holidays she had ever had, and when it came time for him to leave, she wished she didn't have to send him away.

She wanted to spend all night with him, and all of tomorrow, too. Although spending the night with him was out of the question, she was delighted to learn that her mother, upon hearing that Ross had no plans for dinner on Christmas Day, had invited him to the Cade home.

"And you accepted?" Juliet looked surprised.

"Would you rather I hadn't?" he asked, his brows drawing together.

"Of course not! I want you there, Ross," she declared emotionally, hugging him tightly.

"That's what I wanted to hear," he said, his fingers stroking the softness of her skin.

"I'm not sure I'm going to be able to keep my hands to myself, though." There was a hunger in her gaze as she spoke. "Do you think anyone will be able to tell from the way we act around each other that we're..."

"Lovers?" He brought her fingertips to his lips. "Look, if you'd rather I didn't show up, just say the word."

"But you'd be all alone on Christmas Day."

"It wouldn't be the first time."

She clicked her tongue. "Ross, that's awful. No one should be alone at Christmas."

Again he kissed her fingertips and smiled indulgently. "You're awfully sentimental."

"Yes, I am, which is why I want you with me tomorrow." She hugged him even closer. "We won't mess up. That's all there is to it."

"I'll pretend I'm acting out a role." In a dramatic voice, he said, "To save zee life of zee woman I adore, I must pretend she eez simply zee mother of my pupil." He wriggled his eyebrows.

"Oh, how gallant!" Juliet crooned, batting her eyelashes. "Do you adore me?"

"You know I do. But you have my word that nothing we do or say will give anyone any reason to suspect it."

THERE WERE CONSIDERABLY more people at Kate and Donovan's for dinner the following day than there had been at Juliet's on Christmas Eve. Cousins, aunts and uncles all joined in their family gathering. With the additional guests, there was less opportunity for Ross and Juliet to be together, and by the time dinner was served, Juliet felt confident that no one would suspect a thing.

Sara had brought her electronic keyboard, which she insisted Ross play. Even without the automatic rhythms and preset sound effects, he would have made delightful music. Everyone was impressed with his talents, and Juliet felt a surge of pride as she watched him perform.

Because Sara wanted to sit near Ross, Meridee offered to trade places with her niece at dinner, and Juliet found herself next to Annie, at the opposite end of the table. All day Sara had looked as though she were keeping a great secret, and Juliet wondered if the six-year-old had figured out that it had been Ross in the Santa suit last night.

Other people, too, noticed Sara's playfulness, and it wasn't long after the soup was served that Kate said, "Sara, I think Santa must have left you silly pills. You've been doing an awful lot of giggling today."

Juliet shot her daughter a look of admonition, which she chose to ignore. Instead, she turned toward her grandmother and said, "I can't help it, Grandma. I know something real funny."

"And what's that?" Kate asked, much to Juliet's dismay.

"Santa came to our house last night. He came in right through the front door," Sara announced with a giggle.

Kate gave her an indulgent smile. "I know that, darling. Did you forget that I was there? And you know he came in the front door because there was a fire in the fireplace. Remember, he told us that when he came in."

By now, everyone's attention was on the conversation between Kate and her granddaughter, and Kate briefly explained how Santa had come to their Christmas Eve celebration.

"I'm not talking about when you were there, Grandma." Sara's expression had changed from coy to serious. "I mean after we went to bed. Santa came back. He rang the doorbell and walked right through the front door.''

The guests exchanged amused glances as Sara's expressive face revealed her exuberance. Juliet, however, was not amused. Her eyes widened in panic, and she quickly shot a glance in Ross's direction. There was no humor on his face, either.

"Did you talk to him?" Donovan asked. He, too, smiled indulgently at his granddaughter, unaware that Juliet and Ross were turning paler by the minute.

"Uh-uh, but Mommy did," Sara said with a shy giggle.

"Mommy did?" Kate repeated, looking in Juliet's direction.

Juliet felt her hands start to shake. She thrust them onto her lap, where they ferociously clutched her napkin. Forcing a brittle smile to her face, she said in an unsteady voice, "I can see why you've been so silly all day, Sara. That certainly is a funny story, but then dreams can be funny, can't they?"

"But Mommy, it wasn't a dream," Sara protested in earnest. "Don't you remember? You saw him, too. You opened the door for him." Her eyes were as wide as saucers.

"Are you sure you weren't dreaming?" Kate asked in a gentle voice.

"Uh-uh, Grandma. I was lying in my bed and I heard the doorbell. I thought maybe you and Grandpa forgot something and came back. So I got out of bed and went to the stairs, and that's when I saw Santa. He came right in the front door and did something really funny."

"Sara!" Juliet called out a warning, but her daughter paid no attention.

"Santa Claus kissed my mom!" she boasted in delight.

Before Juliet could utter a word of denial, Brenda jumped up from the table, tossing her napkin aside. "I don't believe this!"

"It's true! It really happened," Sara exclaimed, but no one heard her because Brenda was shouting at her sister.

"You and Ross? How could you do this to me? It's . . . it's disgusting!"

Kate stood immediately. "Brenda, stop right now," she said in a stern but compassionate voice. "This is Christmas Day and we have guests. This isn't the time for accusations or judgments or anger of any sort between family members."

"But, Mother, she knew how I felt about . . ." Brenda began.

Kate cut her off. "This is my dinner table and these are my guests," she said in a tone that brooked no argument.

"Excuse me," Brenda choked out before rushing out of the dining room.

There was total silence in the room.

"I think it would be better if we left," Juliet said, pushing her chair away from the table.

"Wait a minute." Ross, too, stood. "If anyone's going to leave, it should be me, since it's obvious I'm the problem here."

"No one has to leave," Kate insisted.

"Of course not," Gran seconded. "This is Christmas, a time for peace, not bickering between sisters. I agree with Kate. Let's be thankful for what we have and finish our dinner."

From opposite ends of the table, Ross and Juliet looked at each other. She could see the curiosity on her aunts' and uncles' faces, as well as Sara's total confusion.

"Would somebody tell me why everyone's so mad?" she finally asked.

Ross sat down beside her and said, "We're not mad, Sara. There's just been a misunderstanding, that's all."

Juliet, too, sat back down, but when she saw how stilted and uncomfortable the remainder of the dinner was, she wished she had taken Sara and Annie home. Despite her mother's pleasant demeanor, she could tell she was terribly upset. The rest of the guests did their best to act as though nothing had happened. Brenda returned to the table, but her puffy red eyes did little to ease anyone's concern.

When it came time for dishes to be cleared, Juliet headed for the kitchen, choosing to bury her hands in soapy dishwater rather than face the curious glances from the others. It didn't surprise her when her sisters followed her into the kitchen, for she knew it was only a matter of time before the inevitable confrontation.

"What is going on?" Meridee demanded as the three sisters converged in the kitchen.

"I'll tell you what's going on. She stole my boyfriend," Brenda declared angrily, dropping the plates she had been carrying onto the counter with a clatter.

"He wasn't yours to steal," Juliet retaliated.

"Then it's really true? You and Ross are seeing each other?" Meridee's face registered her disbelief.

"It's not what you think," Juliet answered, hating the look of condemnation on her older sister's face.

"No wonder you didn't want me to have anything to do with him," Brenda cried out. "You wanted him all to yourself!"

"I can't believe you'd do this to your own sister," Meridee admonished, sliding her arms around Brenda's shoulders as she again burst into tears.

Kate entered the kitchen, saying, "If you don't lower your voices, you're going to make this even more embarrassing than it already is." She set the meat platter on the counter, then said in a firm but quiet voice, "As I said before, this is not the time or place to be having this conversation."

Juliet turned her back on the others and started running water in the sink. "I came in here to do dishes."

"You came in here to hide," Meridee said curtly. "And with good reason."

Juliet spun around to face her sister. "What are you doing in here, anyway? This doesn't concern you."

"That's enough!" Kate raised her voice sternly. "Stop! Right now."

Just then Gran came waltzing into the kitchen saying, "We need more coffee."

"Brenda was just about to bring some out," Kate told her, shoving the silver coffee server into her youngest daughter's hands.

"I have to go to the bathroom first," Brenda said sullenly, and Gran offered to take the coffee in for her.

"Why doesn't Meridee do it?" Juliet spoke up. "I can clean up the kitchen by myself."

"Maybe you ought to ask Ross to help you," Brenda whined, which brought another reprimand from her mother.

"Brenda, that's enough." She turned to Meridee and said, "Why don't you help Grandma with the coffee? Juliet and I will clean up the kitchen."

As soon as the three of them were gone, Kate said, "All right. Why don't you tell me about this mess?"

"I never meant to hurt Brenda," Juliet said somberly.

"I guess I can safely assume, then, that you are involved with Ross Stafford?"

"Yes." The word had barely been uttered when Kate released a long sigh. Although Juliet wasn't looking at her mother, she knew she was shaking her head in disappointment.

"I didn't plan for it to happen," she said, a plea for understanding in her voice.

"Well, obviously you didn't do enough to prevent it from happening." Kate's voice was full of censure.

"I did everything I could to keep Brenda from getting hurt," Juliet said miserably.

"What you really mean is you did everything you could to keep Brenda from finding out about the two of you. If you had done everything you could to keep her from getting hurt, you wouldn't have become involved with the man."

Juliet couldn't believe her mother was taking Brenda's side without even giving her the opportunity to explain. "Why won't you listen to me?"

Instead, Kate launched another attack. "What is it with you and men? You always want the ones you shouldn't have."

"I do not," she denied. "You don't understand about me and Ross."

"No, I don't understand. There are some things a woman may borrow from her sister. Jewelry, clothing, makeup...men are not on that list."

"I didn't borrow him!" Juliet exclaimed indignantly. "Mother, Ross was never Brenda's to start with. He was her instructor at school, not her boyfriend. The only place he was her boyfriend was in Brenda's imagination."

"That's not what Meridee told me."

"And what would Meridee know about it?" she asked, annoyed that her older sister had spoken to her mother about Ross.

"She said Ross was Brenda's date for Thanksgiving."

"That's not true." It was Ross who answered, not Juliet. He had come into the kitchen with his jacket in his hands. "Mrs. Cade, I came to say goodbye. I'm sorry about what happened today, but you really shouldn't blame Juliet."

He came to stand beside Juliet, which only made her more nervous, for her mother was looking angrier than before.

"And whom should I blame, Ross? Santa Claus?" Kate asked with an arch of one delicate eyebrow.

Ross ran a hand around the back of his neck. "I wanted Juliet to tell you about us, but it was because she has such loving feelings and concern for her family that she didn't."

"Oh, please," Kate drawled, rolling her eyes toward the ceiling.

Juliet was shocked by the sarcasm in her mother's voice. It was so uncharacteristic of her.

"It's true, Mother. I knew that if the truth came out about me and Ross, Brenda would make such a big fuss none of us would have a very happy holiday. And I was right. Look what happened today.''

Kate shook her head as if to clear it of everything she was hearing. ''Maybe it would be better if I were to finish up out here by myself. Why don't you see your guest to the door?''

''Mother!'' Juliet said indignantly, but Ross led her away before she could say another word.

''It's all right,'' he told her as they stood on the back step saying their goodbyes.

''I can't believe she's acting like that!''

''She's upset. Look, what you don't need is me to be hanging around here. I'm going to take off.''

''Take me with you,'' she said, surprising herself as much as she did him.

''But what about Sara and Annie? Are they going to want to leave?''

''Ross, I can't stay...not now.'' She grabbed his arm. ''Will you take us home?''

''You didn't drive over?''

She shook her head. ''We came in Brenda's car.'' She was standing outside without a coat, and suddenly she started to shake.

''You're going to freeze if you stand out here much longer.''

''I don't want to go back inside.''

He took off his coat and draped it over her shoulders. ''Do you want me to get the girls for you?''

She contemplated the suggestion for several seconds, then said, ''I'd better do it myself.''

''I'll come with you,'' he said, reaching for the doorknob.

''No. Why don't you warm up the van? It'll only take us a couple of minutes.'' She gave him back his jacket, then kissed him lightly, wondering if her mother was watching through the kitchen window.

When she went back inside, she said as little as possible, announcing only that she was taking the girls home. Kate didn't try to stop her, which only added to Juliet's misery. The final straw came, however, when her mother said, "Are you sure you really care for this man or is he simply a way for you to get back at Brenda?"

Never had Juliet felt so alienated from her mother. As Ross drove the three of them home, she couldn't keep the tears from pooling in her eyes. She squeezed them shut, hoping to block out the faces she kept seeing over and over in her mind. Her mother's, etched with disappointment; Meridee's openly scornful; Brenda's, full of pain. Three of the people she loved most in this world were bitterly angry with her.

While Ross and Sara chatted, Juliet relived the horrible events of the day. How could such a joyous occasion end with such hostility? What she had hoped to avoid had become reality. But she hadn't upset only Brenda; she had never seen Meridee and her mother so openly derisive. Only Gran had given her a smile when she said goodbye.

When they arrived at the house, Ross saw that they were safely inside, then asked, "Would you like me to stay for a while?"

"It's probably better if you don't," Juliet answered. "Brenda will be coming home, and we're going to have to get this mess straightened out."

"That's why I want to stay." There was such a tender look on his face Juliet almost relented.

"It might be less embarrassing for Brenda if I talk to her alone."

He shrugged. "If you're sure that's the way you want it." She could tell by his voice that he didn't think it was the way it should be.

"It is," she insisted, although her inner strength was dwindling fast.

Ross debated about insisting he stay. He felt as though she was shutting him out again, refusing to let him be as close as he wanted to be. But she had already started to pull back from him emotionally, and there was little he could do about it. With a sigh of resignation, he said, "I'll call you tomorrow," and left.

AFTER ALL THE HOLIDAY excitement, both Annie and Sara went to bed early that evening, much to Juliet's relief. She thought it would be much better for them to be asleep when Brenda returned than to witness any ugly scenes.

While Juliet waited for her sister to come home, she sat on the sofa watching a videotape of *Miracle on 34th Street*. It was one of her favorite holiday movies, and she had shown it to Sara only two nights ago to make sure that Sara really believed there was a Santa Claus.

Well, Sara certainly did believe. Maybe if she had suspected that Ross was inside the Santa suit on Christmas Eve, she would have come to her mother with her suspicions instead of making her announcement at the dinner table.

As Juliet heard a car pull into the driveway, she stopped the VCR and turned off the television. To her surprise, it wasn't Brenda walking up the front walk, but Meridee. Juliet was at the door before she could ring the bell.

"I came to get Brenda's things," Meridee explained when Juliet greeted her.

"She's moving out?"

Meridee stepped around her and into the big house. "No, she just wants to spend the night at Mom's."

Juliet shrugged as if she didn't care, flicking on the light switch for the chandelier that lit the staircase. "You know where her room is." It came out sounding more hostile than she intended.

"Do you think maybe we could talk first?"

"I don't need any more lectures, Meridee," Juliet said with a weary sigh and started to walk away.

Meridee followed her into the family room. "Hey, I came to apologize."

Juliet spun around, surprised.

"Yes, I said apologize," Meridee repeated. "After everyone left, I had a talk with Brenda."

"And she admitted that she and Ross weren't seeing each other?"

"Not exactly, but after talking with her I realized that I hadn't given you a chance to tell your side of the story. So when Brenda told Mom she didn't want to sleep here tonight, I offered to come pick up her things." When Juliet didn't respond right away, Meridee added, "Come on, Jules. Talk to me. I'm not going to be able to sleep tonight if we don't get this resolved between us."

Juliet dropped down onto the sofa and leaned her head back against the cushion. She should have known Meridee would find an excuse to come over. Ever since they had been children and fought over dolls and buggies, she had been the one who insisted they settle their differences before they went to bed at night. It was probably the quality she admired most about her sister.

"Oh, Meridee, I can't believe this has happened. This is probably the worst Christmas we've ever had." Juliet's voice broke as the tears trickled down her cheeks.

Meridee reached over to place a comforting arm around her shoulder. "Oh, I don't know. There was the year Uncle Carl punched Uncle Leo in the nose. Don't you remember how Dad had to play peace-maker?"

Her reminder was of little comfort to Juliet. "Mom thinks I deliberately set out to hurt Brenda," she said, sniffling.

"Now *that* I don't believe."

"That mother said it or that I did it?" Juliet asked ruefully.

"Both."

"Well, the first is true, the latter isn't." She sighed. "I didn't want it to happen. The first time he asked me out I told him I couldn't go because of Brenda."

"And that's when he told you he wasn't dating her?"

She nodded. "The only reason he accepted the invitation on Thanksgiving was because he thought she had invited other members of the theater department as well. After he told me that, I confronted Brenda about her relationship with Ross and she admitted he treated her like a little sister, but she was confident romance could grow out of friendship."

"She's never suffered from a lack of self-confidence, has she?" Meridee observed dryly. "I guess I'm just a little surprised that you didn't discourage Ross's interest, especially when you knew that Brenda had such a big crush on him.''

''I did try to discourage him,'' she protested. ''Meridee, I didn't see Ross and think, Hey, he's really cute, I'd like to get to know him better.'' There was an edge to her voice. ''I didn't plan any of it. It was as if one morning I woke up and there he was smack dab in the middle of my life.''

''Do you want him to be in the center of your life?''

Juliet paused before finally admitting, ''I'm not sure. Logically, I know it's not a very smart idea to want that. Emotionally, it's another story.'' Again, she had to swallow back the tears.

''Oh, oh, Jules. It's been a long time since you've cried over a man.''

She blew her nose as if in defiance. ''Yeah, well, it's a little difficult to be happy when your sister's miserable.''

Meridee disagreed. ''Being happy with Ross shouldn't have anything to do with Brenda.''

''What?'' She shot Meridee a look of disbelief. ''How can you say that after what happened today?''

''Brenda will get over her crush on Ross.''

''And Mom? You think she'll forget all of this?''

''Mom reacted like a typical mother. If you really care about Ross, I think she'll come around in time.''

''You didn't hear how she spoke to me today.'' The memory was enough to cause Juliet's voice to quiver.

''It was an emotional day for everyone, but here's the way I see it. Our fickle baby sister will get over her wounded pride, and Mom will realize that her daughters are perfectly capable of settling disagreements between themselves.''

"Boy, do you like to wear rose-colored glasses." Juliet's voice was thick with sarcasm.

"I don't lean toward the pessimistic, as certain members of this family have a tendency to do," she said, softening her criticism with a smile.

"And I suppose you think I should just forget about all those awful things Mom said to me?"

"I read somewhere that it's important for daughters to see their mothers as people with faults who make mistakes just like everyone else," Meridee stated in her usual down-to-earth voice.

"Is that sisterly advice?" Juliet asked, a hint of a smile turning up the corners of her mouth.

"No, I'm just sharing thoughts," Meridee answered lightly. Then on a more serious note she added, "I only have one concern when it comes to Ross Stafford."

Juliet wasn't sure she wanted to hear it. Cautiously she asked, "What's that?"

"As charming as he is, he isn't exactly a stay-at-home family man, is he?"

"What you're saying is that you think he's wrong for me, is that it?" The edge was back in Juliet's voice.

Meridee held up her hands defensively. "I'm not trying to interfere, I just want you to think about the reasons why you're attracted to him. Is it because you really like him as a person or is it because you know you shouldn't be attracted to him?"

"Maybe it's a little of both," Juliet quietly acknowledged. "But he's special, Meridee...really special."

"I hope you're right...for everyone's sake." She stood to leave. "I do have one piece of advice."

Juliet groaned and rolled her eyes in mock penance. "I should have known," she mumbled.

Meridee ignored her theatrics. "You're going to have to make the first move with Brenda. You know how she is with reconciliations."

"Don't you think it's time we quit babying her?" Juliet asked a bit impatiently.

"How badly do you want this thing settled?"

Juliet shook her head wearily. "I'll call her tomorrow."

Meridee smiled and gently squeezed her shoulder. "I knew you would. Jules, I am sorry about the way I jumped all over you today at Mom's."

Juliet gave her sister a grateful hug. "I'm glad you came over. I needed to talk to someone."

"I'm glad I did, too. Now I'll be able to sleep tonight."

Juliet knew sleep was the one thing she wouldn't do.

CHAPTER TWELVE

MERIDEE MAY HAVE SLEPT like a baby, but Juliet tossed and turned most of the night. So did Ross. He awoke the following morning feeling irritable and wishing that he had stayed with Juliet. He had wanted to go back to her house late last night, but out of respect for her wishes, he had stayed home. Now he regretted it.

They needed to talk. He needed to hear that she was all right—that her troubles with her mother and her sisters weren't going to mean the end of their relationship. He knew how much her family meant to her, and he hated to think of her suffering because of him.

The thought still troubled him as he quickly showered, shaved and dressed. Normally he didn't leave his apartment without brewing a pot of coffee, but today he didn't even bother to heat a cup of instant in the microwave. He raced down the steps and out to his van, cursing when it wouldn't start.

He raced back up the steps and into his apartment, where he called for a cab. Within minutes, he was seated in the back seat of a taxi heading toward Juliet's house. He only hoped he could catch her before she left for work.

The sun hadn't even poked its tip over the horizon when the taxi dropped him off. It didn't look as though there were any lights on in the two-story home, and he wondered if maybe she had already gone. Again, he cursed silently. What if he rang the doorbell and Brenda was the one who answered?

It was a chance he had to take. "Better wait," he told the cab driver before climbing out of the car. He marched up the veranda steps and pressed his finger to the buzzer. He waited a couple of minutes, then pressed once more, letting his finger linger a bit longer. Just when he thought no one was going to answer, the door slowly opened. It wasn't Juliet or Brenda, but Sara who appeared, shivering as the cold air intruded.

"Hi, Ross." Her greeting was not as enthusiastic as he had expected it to be.

"Good morning, Sara. Can I come in? I need to talk to your mother."

He turned to signal the taxi that it could leave. As soon as he had stepped inside, Sara shoved the door shut with both hands. "Annie made a mess and she's cleaning it up."

"In the kitchen?"

"Uh-uh. In the bathroom." Her eyes looked toward the great staircase leading upstairs.

"Do you suppose it would be all right if I went up?"

She shrugged. "She's awfully crabby this morning."

"Is she getting ready for work?"

"She's not going to work today. It's Christmas vacation."

"Ah," he said in understanding. "What about Brenda? Is it vacation for her, too?"

"She's not here. She slept at Grandma's last night."

"I see," he said, kicking off his shoes. He removed his jacket and hung it on the newel post at the foot of the stairs. "Where's Annie?"

"With Mommy. Will you help me play my keyboard after you talk to Mommy?"

"You can count on it," he said with a grin, then tweaked a blond curl affectionately before going up the steps.

He saw Juliet's feet before he saw her face. They were sticking out of the bathroom as he approached the second-floor landing. A few seconds later he saw the reason why. She was on her hands and knees scrubbing the floor with a scouring cleanser. Annie was sitting in the empty bathtub in a bright red blanket sleeper, her face blotchy from recent tears. When she saw Ross she smiled.

His feet had been silent as they crossed the carpet, and with her back to the door, Juliet wasn't aware that he was standing there watching her. He saw her dip her sponge in the bucket of water, squeeze it mercilessly, sprinkle it with scouring powder, then attack the gelatinous yellow substance on the floor.

Even scrubbing ceramic tile in washed-out flannel pajamas, she looked good to him. When Annie grew restless and attempted to climb out of the bathtub, Juliet snapped, "You sit still."

Annie looked to Ross in supplication. He smiled and made a funny facial gesture that caused the little girl to giggle. Juliet glanced up over her shoulder to see Ross standing in the doorway.

"What are you doing here?" she asked, a look of horror on her face.

He groaned. "I thought we were past that stage."

She covered her face with her pajama sleeve and moaned, "Look at me! I'm a mess! I haven't even combed my hair or washed my face." She stood up and took a peek in the vanity mirror, then moaned even louder. "Oh, good grief! It's worse than I thought."

"You look beautiful to me."

"Oh, pooh!" she said, discrediting his statement with a sound of derision. "I'm wearing the rattiest pair of pajamas I own." She looked as though she wanted to throw the sponge at him.

He eyed the mess on the floor. "What happened?"

"Sara helped Annie out of bed this morning before I was awake and the two of them decided to try out the makeup kit Sara got for Christmas. Only Annie didn't just experiment with the play makeup. She got into my stuff and spilled bath oil and body lotion all over the floor."

"Is Annie in jail?" he asked, amusement lurking in his eyes.

Juliet didn't look as though she found his comment funny. "No. She's covered with bath oil, and I didn't want her tracking it through the house."

"Have you had any coffee yet this morning?" he asked.

"No," she snapped.

"I didn't think so." He smiled then, and said, "Why don't I go downstairs and make us some breakfast?"

"You don't cook."

He slumped against the doorjamb, feigning hurt feelings. "I don't cook often, but I do know how to put breakfast on the table," he assured her.

She sighed. "It's going to take me awhile to get both of us cleaned up after I finish with this." She gestured to the partially scrubbed floor.

"Don't worry about it. It'll take me about half an hour to do breakfast." He straightened, shoving his hands in the pockets of his jeans. "Just come down when you're ready."

Juliet looked a bit uneasy, and he leaned toward her and said in a lower voice, "Now that everyone knows about us, there's no reason for us not to have breakfast together, is there?" Before she could protest, he left.

The first thing he did when he got downstairs was brew a fresh pot of coffee. Then he had Sara run upstairs and ask her mother if he could borrow her car. She came back down with the station wagon's keys jingling in her hand.

"Did she ask you where I wanted to go?" Ross said as Sara handed him the key ring.

"Yup, and I said just what you told me to say—that you were going to go get something to make her sweet."

"And what did she say to that?"

"She said to tell you no way."

Ross shook his head and grinned. "I think you were right. She's definitely crabby this morning. Tell me what your mom likes most for breakfast."

"Are you going to cook?" she asked, a look of surprise on her face.

"I just might, but first I have to know what her very favorite thing is."

"She likes those big caramel sticky buns from the bakery," Sara said.

"No way," Ross drawled, and Sara giggled. "I thought she only ate stuff like grapefruit and bran and granola."

"Most of the time she does, but sometimes she sneaks a sticky bun even though they're bad for her diet."

"And what about you and Annie? What do you like for breakfast?"

"Pancakes are my favorite, and I'll eat oatmeal if I have to."

"Pancakes it is," he told her, then pulled on his jacket, saying, "Can you set the table?"

Sara nodded.

"Good. I'm going to go get some sticky buns, and I'll be right back, okay?"

"And will you bring me some chocolate milk?"

"One carton of chocolate milk coming up." He winked at Sara as he let himself out of the house.

When Juliet came downstairs with Annie, the first thing she noticed was the aroma of coffee. When she entered the kitchen with Annie in her arms, Ross and Sara were playing with the electronic keyboard. In the center of the table sat a plate stacked with caramel rolls, and on the stove were several covered pans.

"Ross made us breakfast," Sara announced cheerfully.

He got up and went over to the stove, where he lifted first one, then a second lid, saying, "Pancakes and sausages for the kids." Then he poured two cups of coffee and brought one to her. "And coffee and sticky buns for the mom."

Juliet blushed as she settled Annie in her high chair, then sat down at the table. She watched as Ross dished up breakfast for everyone. "You did all this by your-self?" she asked.

"Sara helped," Ross told her, which brought a big grin to the six-year-old's face. He was about to sit down when he said, "Oops...I almost forgot the juice and the chocolate milk."

"And the maple syrup," Sara added.

As the four of them ate, Juliet thought about how nice it was to have someone else responsible for breakfast for a change—especially when that some-one was a man. Having a man around the house was something she had missed, and it wasn't until Ross had entered her life that she realized just how much she had missed it.

It gave her a warm fuzzy feeling to see the way he charmed her daughters. Last night after talking to Meridee she had been questioning her relationship with him, worried that he was the wrong kind of man for her. This morning, seeing how easily he fit into her life, those doubts were diminishing.

Then, just as they were finishing breakfast, he said, "We're going to have to reschedule a couple of Sara's piano lessons. I'm going to be playing at a club in Chicago, and I won't be back until the middle of Jan-uary."

"You're leaving?" she squeaked, unaware of the look of panic on her face. She swallowed with diffi-culty. He wasn't supposed to leave—not now, when she needed him more than ever. Maybe her mother was right. Maybe he was all wrong for her and she was simply attracted to him because she knew she shouldn't be.

Her face must have betrayed her inner turmoil, for he said, "Sara, why don't you take Annie into the living room and play while I help your mother clean up the kitchen?''

As soon as the little girls had disappeared through the swinging door, Ross took Juliet in his arms, despite her efforts to evade him. ''You're upset with me, and I don't know if it's because of yesterday or because I've just said I'm going to be gone for a while.''

She finally stopped struggling and relaxed against him, letting her head rest on his shoulder. She wanted to tell him she was feeling insecure about their relationship, that she needed to know where things stood between the two of them. She wanted to know if he was leaving because of the turmoil going on with her family. Only she was afraid that if she did that, she'd get answers she wasn't prepared to hear.

They had agreed from the start that there would be no strings, no serious emotional attachments. She had wanted it that way; he hadn't objected. Now, with the announcement that he was going away for two weeks, she had to face the reality of her situation. She had fallen in love with a man who would never put down roots. There would always be another town, another chance he'd move on.

''Talk to me, Juliet. Tell me what's wrong,'' he pleaded, gently stroking her hair.

She wanted to tell him that it looked to her as though he was cutting out just when the going was getting tough. At the first sign of trouble, when she needed him to be with her, he was going off to play his saxophone. But years of mistrusting Tim had taken its toll, and instead of telling him the truth, she gave him an evasive answer. ''After what happened yesterday, I didn't sleep very well last night. My family's important to me, Ross, and I don't handle stress in that area very well.''

He sighed. ''I'm sorry I ever accepted your mother's invitation.''

She gently pushed out of his arms. ''It really wouldn't have mattered if you hadn't. Sara would have still announced to the whole room that she had seen her mommy kissing Santa Claus, and Brenda would have reacted in the same way.''

''I suppose you're right. Maybe it's a good thing I'm going to be gone for a couple of weeks. It'll probably be easier for you to get things straightened out with them if I'm not around.''

''Maybe,'' she murmured. She had turned her back to him and was clearing the dishes from the table. He came up from behind her and wrapped his arms around her waist.

''I'm going to miss you,'' he said close to her ear.

''I'll miss you, too,'' she admitted, trying not to reveal any emotion. She unhooked his hands from around her waist and carried a stack of plates over to the sink. ''When are you leaving?''

''The day after tomorrow.''

Again, she concentrated on keeping the emotion from her face. ''That soon?''

He moved closer to her. ''We'll have to make the most of our time together. Sara told me you're on vacation.''

''The office is closed because of the holidays,'' she confirmed.

''Can we spend today together?''

She kept her eyes on the dishes, not trusting herself to remain detached if she looked into his eyes. ''I promised Sara I'd take her and Annie sledding and to the Children's Museum.''

''Can't I come, too?''

''You want to come sledding?'' She shot him a look of disbelief.

''I want to be with you.''

This time she met his gaze, and she felt the power he had over her. She didn't try to evade his kiss. She wanted him to be with her. Always. The realization frightened her. She pulled away from his embrace, trembling slightly.

''Fine. You can come sledding.'' She began scraping the leftover food into the garbage disposal. ''You're going to need warm clothes. Why don't you take my car and go get your things? By the time you get back, we'll be ready.''

As long as he was looking at her with his sexy brown eyes, she didn't question the wisdom of what she was doing. As soon as he was gone, however, she started wondering if she was making a mistake getting more involved with him.

There would always be another gig for him to play. She sighed as she finished clearing the table. As she went to throw away the crushed paper napkins, she saw the fast-food containers Ross had stuffed in the garbage. ''Some cook,'' she mumbled to herself.

ROSS AND JULIET SPENT that night together as well. After taking the girls sledding in the park, they stopped for pizza, then headed over to the Children's Museum, where Annie and Sara pulled handles, pushed knobs and climbed steps as they explored the wonders of science through touch-and-feel exhibits.

By the time they returned home, they were exhausted and went straight to bed.

It was while Juliet was making dinner for Ross that Meridee called to inform her that Brenda had temporarily moved in with their mother. Juliet had guessed that her sister had been to the house while they were out, for several of her things were now gone, including the portable television that usually sat on the kitchen counter.

When Ross made it clear that he wanted to spend the night with her, Juliet didn't object. Knowing that she wouldn't be seeing him for two weeks, she didn't want to waste a single moment they could be together.

This time when he stayed with her, he made sure he was up before sunrise and gone before Annie or Sara woke up. When Juliet awoke, she was alone in the bed, with only the faint aroma of his after-shave clinging to the pillowcase to remind her that he had been there.

Even though he had promised to stop by later that afternoon to say goodbye, Juliet already felt as though she had been left behind. She wished she had told him of her anxieties about their relationship, her fears, her doubts. Instead, she had pretended nothing was wrong, remembering the tone they had set for their relationship.

Now she found herself needing a commitment and afraid to ask for one for fear he'd disappear. She couldn't let him leave for his road trip without talking to him about their future—if they even had a future together.

When Sara asked if she could play at a friend's house that afternoon, Juliet was relieved. With Sara gone and Annie down for a nap, she and Ross could have a private conversation without any interruptions.

Only before Ross arrived, Kate showed up on Juliet's doorstep.

"Mother. I wasn't expecting you," she said as she answered the door.

Kate stepped inside and took off her coat, handing it to Juliet. "We need to talk, Juliet. I figured this would be a good time since Annie would probably be napping."

Juliet felt a rush of conflicting emotions. She needed to make peace with her mother yet she also needed to see Ross. Reluctantly, she hung up her mother's coat. "Do you want something to drink?"

Kate shook her head. She wandered into the family room, glancing wistfully around the house. "I was hoping you'd come see me," she said to Juliet when they were both seated.

"I didn't think you wanted me to," Juliet said quietly.

There was compassion on her mother's face as she said, "You're my daughter, Juliet."

"And so is Brenda."

There was a brief silence before Kate said, "Yes, and it saddens me to know that the two of you aren't speaking to each other."

"I've tried calling Brenda, but she refuses to come to the phone. Ask Donovan," Juliet said coolly.

"Donovan's on your side, you know. And so's Meridee. They both told me that just because two sisters are attracted to the same man, it shouldn't make him off limits to either one."

"And whose side are you on, Mom?" Juliet wanted to know.

"Oh, Juliet, you ought to know by now that I'm never on anyone's side," Kate replied with a sigh. "I know I said some things I shouldn't have, and I'm sorry."

"I'm sorry, too, Mom," Juliet said quietly, reflecting on what had happened. "I'd like this to be settled between Brenda and me, but she won't even speak to me."

"She's terribly upset. In fact, she's so upset with what's happened that she's decided to drop out of college."

"Is that what Brenda told you? That's she's dropping out of college because of Ross and me?" Juliet's voice rose in anger.

"I know you think her feelings for Ross were the equivalent of a schoolgirl crush, but she's taking this pretty hard."

"She may be taking it hard, but she certainly isn't dropping out of school because of me." Juliet straightened in her seat, squaring her shoulders. "Mother, she told me weeks ago that she had canceled her registration for winter quarter."

"Then why didn't she tell me?"

"She didn't want you to get upset. She made me promise not to mention it until she had a chance to talk to you herself."

"Didn't you try to talk her into staying in school?" Kate demanded, her tone accusatory.

"Of course I did," Juliet said firmly. "You know my feelings about that."

Just then the doorbell rang, and Juliet knew it was Ross.

"Are you expecting company?" her mother asked.

"I think it's Ross," she admitted, walking toward the door. Her mother followed right behind her. When she reached into the coat closet, Juliet asked, "What are you doing?"

"I don't want to be in the way," Kate answered, shrugging into her coat.

"Don't be silly." She answered the door, and Ross, seeing her mother, said, "I'm sorry. I'll come back later."

"It's all right, Ross. I was just leaving," Kate told him, but Juliet spoke up.

"No, she wasn't."

"I've got a couple of errands to run," Ross said, embarrassed. "Why don't I take care of them and come back later?" Before Kate could protest, he was walking back to his van.

"Why did you do that?" Kate asked when Juliet shut the door.

"Because I thought it was more important to talk to you." She took her mother's coat from her and hung it up again. "Mother, I hate this tension between Brenda and me. How do you suppose it makes me feel to know that my sister refuses to come home because I'm here . . . that she sneaks back in for her stuff when I'm not around?" Her voice cracked with emotion as she attempted to hold back the tears. "But what I hate most of all is that my own mother thinks I deliberately set out to steal her boyfriend." This time she couldn't prevent the tears.

Kate pushed her arm through hers and led her back into the living room, whispering words of comfort. "Come sit down and talk to me about it."

"I don't know what you want me to say." Juliet sniffled. "I can't say I didn't know Brenda was attracted to him, because I did know. I can't say I didn't try to keep it a secret from her, because I did try. I can't say I'll stop seeing him, because I'm in love with him, Mother.''

Kate sighed. "Oh, Juliet.''

"Don't say, 'Oh, Juliet,' as though I'm plagued with some disease. Ross is a wonderful man.''

Kate's deep green eyes mirrored her concern. "I don't doubt that he is, but is he the kind of man who'll make a commitment to a woman who has two children?'' she asked softly.

Juliet stiffened, shrugging away from the arm that had been draped across her shoulders. "Mother, if you're going to start with one of your 'wrong men' speeches, stop right now.''

Kate held up her hands in mock surrender. "All right. No more speeches. I'm not going to say another word about Ross Stafford. But I want you to promise me you'll think about whether he's the kind of man who's worth losing a sister over.''

Juliet sighed in exasperation. "Mother, I shouldn't be losing my sister over him. He was her instructor, not her lover,'' she pleaded. "Why can't Brenda try to see things from my point of view just once in her life?''

"Because she's only nineteen and you're twenty-seven.''

"She has to grow up some time, Mother.''

"I know, darling. I don't want to argue with you.''

"Then maybe it's better if we don't discuss this. As long as you have two daughters who are fighting, you're going to be stuck in the middle.''

Kate nodded gravely. "As long as you understand that that is where I am—in the middle. I came over because I want my daughter back. Is that possible?"

Juliet hugged her mother, but she knew the only way their relationship would return to normal would be for her to resolve her differences with Brenda.

BY THE TIME ROSS returned, Annie was up from her nap, and there was little opportunity for any serious discussions on what the future held for them. With Sara and Annie constantly around, Juliet felt fortunate that they were able to give each other a long, passionate kiss goodbye. When he left, she felt as though he were taking a part of her heart along with him, and she wasn't sure if she was ever going to get it back.

The following week went slowly for Juliet, who tried to keep busy so as not to think about Ross's absence. As she finished up her final week at her job, she felt a bit superfluous sitting next to her replacement, and the more Sara complained about being left at the baby-sitter's during Christmas vacation, the more Juliet regretted not leaving her job a week earlier.

New Year's Eve was spent sponging Annie's forehead with a wet cloth, as a viral infection had her temperature soaring high enough to cause the little girl's skin to flush and her body to go as limp as a dishrag. As Juliet nursed her daughter through her discomfort, she thought about Ross and wondered how he was spending his New Year's Eve.

Despite her mother's attempts to reunite the family, Brenda was still not speaking to her, and Juliet was relieved that she had an excuse not to be a part of the traditional brunch her mother always hosted on New

Year's Day. When Kate questioned whether Annie's illness was serious enough to cause them to miss brunch, Juliet became defensive. She had sat up half the night nursing a sick child, and the last thing she needed was her mother's suspicion. They parted on angry words, and Juliet found herself feeling more frustrated and alone than she ever had before.

She needed to be with Ross, yet when he called to ask her how she was, she didn't mention that Annie had been sick or that she had had another disagreement with her mother or that Brenda was still being impossible. She simply told him she missed him and wished he were home. He told her that his New Year's resolution was to make the upcoming year a good year for the two of them.

She wondered what he meant by a good year. That they'd have lots of good sex? That he'd spend most of his time with her? That there wouldn't be any road gigs?

As she sat watching the Rose Bowl parade on television with the girls, Juliet wondered what the new year would bring for her and her daughters. Would Ross play a part in their future? Would Tim?

The answer to her second question came sooner than she hoped. Because it was her last day at work, her office mates took her out to lunch and sent her home early with a gift they had all chipped in to buy—a leather book bag. After picking the girls up from day care, Juliet drove home and found an unfamiliar car parked in the drive. As she pulled in alongside it, she heard Sara cry out, "Daddy's here."

Daddy wasn't alone. Seated in the car was a blond woman who looked like a Hollywood starlet. In the back seat was a miniature version of the woman in the front. Juliet's heart plummeted. Before Sara could get her seat belt unfastened, she called out, "Wait here."

As she climbed out of the car, Tim opened his door and joined her.

"I called your work number, but they said you were on your way home, so I came straight over."

"Do you want to see the girls?" she managed to say, trying not to stare at his wife and stepdaughter.

"We're here for the weekend, and I thought it would be a good time for Sara and Heather to get to know each other."

"Heather?" She glanced toward the car.

"Gloria's daughter. She's six, and she's been anxious to meet her sister."

"Stepsister," Juliet corrected, resenting how he was forcing this other child into Sara's life. "Do you want her to come with you right now?"

"If she'd like to, she can. Otherwise, we could come back after she's had a chance to get her things together."

"What do you mean get her things together?" Juliet asked suspiciously.

"I thought she might like to spend the night with us at the hotel. She and Heather can swim in the pool and play the video games."

"What about Annie?"

"Maybe it's better if I just take Sara tonight."

In other words, Annie's too much work, Juliet thought bitterly. She looked at the two anxious faces staring at her from the station wagon, and she wanted to tell Tim Harper to take his Hollywood dolls and go back to California. She fought the urge and said, "Why don't you come inside and talk to Sara?"

She opened the front door to unstrap Annie from the car seat and instructed Sara to go inside. The new Mrs. Harper and Heather remained in the luxury rental car with the motor running.

Juliet hoped that once Sara heard Tim's proposition, she'd tell him she didn't want to stay with him overnight. She didn't. She rushed upstairs to pack her bag, leaving Juliet to make conversation with her father.

"I'd like the name and number of the hotel," she said coolly, shoving a piece of paper in his direction.

As he scribbled the information, he said, "We don't have any plans for this evening, but tomorrow we're taking the girls to see *Cinderella* at the Children's Theater."

"What about Annie?"

"She's too young." He dismissed his youngest daughter without any hesitation.

Juliet wanted to point out that the reason it was called the Children's Theater was because it was for children of all ages. She knew, however, that it wouldn't do any good. He probably only had four tickets, and it wouldn't have crossed his mind to call and ask her if Annie would enjoy such a performance.

"*Annie* is your daughter, too," she said pointedly.

"Maybe we'll pick up Annie and take her to get an ice cream after the show," he answered, but Juliet knew it was a token offer.

"Tell me what time and I'll have her ready." When he glanced impatiently at his wristwatch, she added, "I'd better run upstairs and make sure Sara's getting everything she needs." She scooped Annie into her arms and took her along.

To her surprise, Sara had packed all the essential items, for which Juliet praised her efforts. She also told her that if she became lonesome for her mommy during the night, all she had to do was call home and she'd come get her.

Although Sara seemed eager to go with her father, Juliet could see the apprehension in her tightly clenched little fist as she gripped the handle of her suitcase. Juliet had to swallow her tears as she kissed her daughter goodbye and watched her walk out to the big black car.

Juliet expected Sara to call. She didn't. As hour after hour passed with no word from her, Juliet's anxiety grew. When Saturday evening arrived and she still hadn't heard anything, she could only assume that they had decided against picking up Annie and taking her to get ice cream. At around nine o'clock, Juliet finally received a phone call from Sara, telling her she was going to spend another night with her dad.

Although she was relieved to know Sara was safe, Juliet's disappointment at her daughter's announcement was enough to nullify her pleasure at the sound of her daughter's voice. When Sara finally arrived home, it was after ten o'clock on Sunday night, and Juliet was furious.

"You do realize that Sara has school tomorrow, don't you," she said as Sara dragged her weary body into the house. Juliet helped her out of her coat, glaring at Tim when Sara complained of being tired.

"I'm sure the teacher would understand if she slept in tomorrow. After all, it isn't every day that her father visits from California, is it?" Shades of arrogance she remembered so well from the past only increased her annoyance.

"Thank goodness," she murmured, then sent Sara upstairs with a "Mommy will be right up." As soon as Sara had disappeared, Juliet asked, "When are you leaving?"

"Anxious to be rid of me, are you?"

"Just what are your plans?" she asked impatiently.

"We're leaving tomorrow morning. Now, if you'll excuse me, I want to get back to my wife."

Juliet slammed the door on his departing figure. She rushed up the stairs to see Sara, but the six-year-old had already climbed into bed and fallen asleep.

As Sara got ready for school the next morning, Juliet questioned her about her weekend with her father, but she seemed reluctant to talk about it. It was obvious to Juliet that if she were going to learn anything about Tim Harper's plans for his daughters, it wasn't going to be from Sara.

As soon as Sara climbed aboard the big orange school bus, Juliet phoned the hotel where he was staying. She needed to know if Tim would be coming back again or if he still thought he could get the girls to visit him in California.

He had already checked out, but it wasn't much later when she discovered exactly what he was up to. Shortly before noon a processor arrived at her front door and served her with papers. Tim was reopening the custody suit, and she was going to have to go back to court.

CHAPTER THIRTEEN

"I CAN'T BELIEVE I passed up a chance to go to Glam Slam to peel wallpaper," Meridee groaned, flicking a long narrow strip of wallcovering from her fingertips. "This is awful. Whoever put this stuff on must have used Super Glue."

"You didn't have to come over," Juliet retorted, holding the steamer close to the flowered paper lining the bathroom walls. "If you had told me you had a hot date, I would have granted you a reprieve from your offer."

"I didn't have a hot date. One of the girls in the office had free tickets to Glam Slam, and rumor has it that his Purple Highness was supposed to be there tonight."

"You'd give up an evening of peeling wallpaper with your sister just to go see Prince?" Juliet asked in an exaggerated drawl.

"I want you to remember this the next time I need someone to take care of Vanna for me."

"Wait a minute," Juliet said, lowering her arms for a minute. "You never said this was an exchange of favors. I thought you were helping me out of the goodness of your heart."

"I am, although I think you should have hired someone to get this stuff off." Meridee grimaced as she scraped away at the wallpaper with a putty knife.

Juliet gave a sardonic chuckle. "Hire someone? I had to borrow money from you to make ends meet until I start my new job. How would I afford a wallpaper hanger?"

"Mom probably would have paid for one. It is her house," Meridee said logically.

"She's letting us stay here rent-free. I'm not going to ask her to give me money so I can change the wallpaper in the bathroom." Juliet swiped at the perspiration on her forehead with her sleeve. "You didn't tell her I borrowed money from you, did you?"

"No." Meridee tossed the putty knife aside and sat down on the edge of the bathtub. "But I have to tell you, Jules, I don't understand why everything has to be so hush-hush."

"Because if Mom knew I was short of cash, she'd be paying my bills for me, and I can't take any more help from her." Juliet's expression became sober.

"Why? Because of this thing with Brenda? I thought that was all water under the bridge."

"Mom says it is, but there's a strain in our relationship. No matter what she says, I know she wishes I weren't seeing Ross."

"It *would* simplify things," Meridee observed dryly.

Juliet paused to give her sister a wounded look. "I thought you were on my side."

"Why do I have to take a side?" Meridee rested a hand on her hip.

"Now you're sounding like Mom," Juliet chided her.

"I'm going to take that as a compliment. Mom has always been the peacemaker in the family. I wonder why her methods aren't working this time?"

"Maybe you should be asking Brenda that question," Juliet retorted sullenly.

"Did I tell you she wants to move in with me? She says she feels out of place with the honeymooners."

That caught Juliet's attention. "Are you going to let her?"

"Only if she finds a job and agrees to help pay the rent."

"I guess that means she's not coming back to live with me, eh?" She hadn't meant to sound so flip.

Meridee's eyebrows arched. "Do you want her to?"

Juliet shrugged. "That was part of the bargain I struck with Mom. In exchange for free rent, I'm supposed to be looking out for Brenda. I guess I mucked up my end of the deal, huh?"

"There must be a way this can all be straightened out," Meridee insisted, her optimistic nature asserting itself.

"Well, when you find out what it is, let me know, all right?" Juliet sighed and ran her hand through her hair. "I have too many other things on my mind to figure it out right now."

"You're worried about the custody hearing, aren't you."

"With good cause."

"I don't see how any judge in his right mind could even consider granting custody to a man who deserted his children."

"Harvey doesn't think Tim will win, but he may be able to take them to California whether I want him to or not."

Meridee removed her glasses and held them up to the light, inspecting them for smudges. "Does Sara realize what her father's up to?"

Juliet shook her head. "I'm really worried about her. His reappearance has caused her a lot of anxiety."

"Why? What's she been saying?" Meridee replaced her glasses.

"It's what she's not saying. Each time she's been with him she comes home and goes into this sullen state where she hardly talks. I don't know if it's because she's unhappy he's gone or if it's because she didn't enjoy herself when they were together."

"She always gets so excited whenever she talks about him," Meridee remarked.

"I know, but I'm wondering if she really wants to see him or if it's because he brings all sorts of presents every time he comes."

"Sara doesn't strike me as the kind of child who can be bought," Meridee said pragmatically.

"Which means she must still care for the jerk, right?" Juliet shook her head disconsolately. "I don't understand it."

"Jules, he *is* her father," she reminded her.

"There's more to being a father than the transfer of genes," she said bitterly, setting the steamer on the vanity top.

"I'm not defending the guy. All I'm saying is that Sara wants a daddy—we both know that."

Juliet leaned back against the wall and sighed. "I want her to have one, too, only not someone who treats her like an extra piece of baggage. She needs someone who'll read her stories and give her piggyback rides to bed at night. Someone who'll be there when she sings in the school program and has her first piano recital."

"Did you have a particular someone in mind?" Meridee asked suspiciously.

Juliet couldn't prevent the blush that spread across her cheeks. "No, I don't."

"Good. For a minute I was worried you were going to say Ross Stafford."

Juliet paused, her hands on her hips. "What if I had? What's wrong with Ross?"

"Nothing's wrong with him. He's dishy, but he's not exactly a family man, is he?" When Juliet didn't say anything, she added, "You're not thinking he's going to settle down and grow domestic feathers, are you?"

"I have no delusions about Ross's intentions," Juliet stated, wishing she didn't feel like such a liar. "And if you don't mind, I'd rather not talk about him."

"All right, but I hope you know what you're doing." Meridee rose to her feet and began scraping away at the wallpaper again.

"I do."

"Good." At the sound of the doorbell, Meridee glanced at Juliet and said, "It's a little late for company, isn't it?"

"You're closest to the window. Peek out and see if there's a car in the drive."

Meridee spread two laths of the vinyl blind and said, "It looks like Ross's van to me."

Juliet glanced at herself in the mirror. "He wasn't supposed to be back until tomorrow." She groaned at her reflection. "Look at me! I've got the frizzies!"

"Do you want me to entertain him while you freshen up a bit?" Meridee asked, following her from the bathroom.

"Would you?"

"What are sisters for?"

"Thanks." Juliet started up the stairs, then stopped. "Oh, and don't mention the custody suit, all right?"

"Why not? Haven't you told him about it?"

"No, and I'm not going to. It's my problem, not his. Besides, I don't want to make him feel obligated."

Meridee gasped. "Obligated to what?"

"Oh, forget it. You wouldn't understand," she said with a wave of her hand and hurried up the stairs while Meridee went to open the door.

In her room, Juliet exchanged her paint-stained slacks and faded sweatshirt for a cable-knit sweater and a pair of jeans. She pulled her hair, made kinky from steam, into a clip at the nape of her neck, then scrubbed her face and applied a light dusting of powder.

When she went downstairs and saw Ross, she wished she had taken more time with her makeup. She stood staring at him, amazed at how handsome he was, wanting to throw her arms around him, yet shy because of her sister's presence.

Meridee, seeing how the two of them were ogling each other, said, "Well, I guess I'd better get going."

"You don't have to leave on my account," Ross stated.

"I'm sure you two have lots to talk about," Meridee said with a knowing smile as she stepped around him. "I'll call you tomorrow, Jules."

"Good night," Juliet called out to her departing figure. "And thanks."

As soon as she heard the front door close, she was in Ross's arms. "It's good to have you back," she murmured close to his ear. "I didn't think you were going to be home until tomorrow."

"I couldn't make it one more day without this." He kissed her long and hard, his lips taking hers with an urgency that confirmed his words. When he lifted his head, his dark gaze was intent. "I didn't know two weeks could be such a long time."

"Me, either. Tell me about your trip," she urged him as they sank down onto the sofa wrapped in each other's arms. "Did you have good audiences?"

"There was only one thing that would have made them better. My woman being there with me," he growled, nibbling on her ear. "I've missed you."

"I missed you, too," she told him, snuggling closer. She pushed all negative thoughts from her mind and gave in to the pleasure of the moment. It felt so good to be back in his arms, to hear him refer to her as his woman. She didn't want to think about family feuds or child-custody hearings or whether these arms would always be there for her. She simply wanted to cherish this time with him.

She listened as Ross talked about his road trip, her head resting on his shoulder, their hands entwined in her lap. She had forgotten how much she loved to hear his voice, and as he recounted the events of the past two weeks, she felt as though after years and years of waiting, the right man had finally come home to her.

"Can you spend the night?" she asked.

"What about Sara and Annie?"

"They're staying overnight at my mother's."

"And Brenda?"

"She's moved out." She couldn't keep the bitterness from her voice.

"She's still angry about us?"

She shrugged. "I'm not sure what she's feeling. She refuses to talk to me."

He lifted her chin and said, "I'm sorry."

"It's not your fault, Ross. Our problems go back to before you ever met any of us, believe me." A forlorn look passed over her face.

"And your mother?"

"Well, at least we're talking." She tried to sound upbeat. "She hates to see any dissension in the family, and I can't really blame her."

"I was hoping that my being gone might ease the tension a bit."

"Meridee thinks it'll take some time, that's all."

His fingers gently traced her cheeks. "And what do you think?"

"I think that it's time we quit talking about my family and gave our undivided attention to things we have control over." Her fingers toyed with the buttons on his shirt.

"Such as?"

"Such as the fact that we have this house all to ourselves for at least...oh...eight or nine hours." She had worked the buttons loose on his shirt and slid her fingers inside.

Eyes dark with desire gazed into hers. She wanted him in a way she'd never wanted another man. It didn't matter how tentative their relationship might be, how unsure she was about their future together. Right now she needed to spend the night in his arms.

When she hooked her finger inside his belt, Ross sucked in his breath. Instead of undoing the buckle, however, she smiled wickedly and said, "It's cold down here without a fire."

"I take it you have someplace warmer in mind," he murmured as she pulled him up from the sofa. Leaving a trail of clothes scattered behind them, they found their way up the stairs to Juliet's four-poster, where she gave him all the warmth in her body and soul.

"I LOVE YOU," Ross murmured next to Juliet's ear, wondering why the only time he could utter those three words was when she was sound asleep. At four o'clock in the morning, they seemed like the easiest three words in the world. Why was it, then, that he hadn't been able to say them when he had shuddered in her arms in a climax so powerful it had cut deep into his soul?

He was in love with Juliet. There was no point in denying it. His heart ached with the need to tell her, yet when passion had bathed them both in its wonderful warm afterglow, he hadn't confessed that love to her. He justified his omission by telling himself that he had communicated his love through his actions.

He had never craved a woman's touch the way he had yearned for Juliet's. Two weeks away from her had seemed like two years, and despite being up for thirty-six hours straight, he had driven like a crazy man back to Minneapolis just to get back to her. Now he was here, he wished he never had to leave again. But in a couple of hours it would be morning, and it might be a long time before they could sleep together again.

Sleep. He laughed to himself. Here he was dead tired, yet unable to fall asleep because he hadn't told her he loved her. But then, she hadn't said those three little words, either. He had thought she was going to say them. Just before she fell asleep she had pressed her cheek to his chest and softly said his name. He had waited for her declaration, only it hadn't come. Instead, her voice had gone all mushy as she said, "Great sex."

"Great sex," he mumbled aloud, wondering why he was disappointed. Any other time he would have crowed with delight, but not tonight. After being separated from her for two weeks, he wanted to know that her feelings for him went beyond physical satisfaction.

Maybe that's what was keeping him awake. The thought that her feelings might not run as deep as his. It was a sobering thought and one he refused to consider. Why else would they have been able to find such completion in each other's arms?

"Great sex," a nasty little voice answered for him. He looked again at the beautiful woman in his arms. She wasn't the kind to give of herself simply for great sex. She was the mother of two children, a family-oriented woman with a strong sense of values.

That didn't necessarily mean she was in love with him. The more he thought about it, the less sure he became of her feelings. If she did love him, why hadn't she told him? Why did he feel as though she were pulling away emotionally, shutting him out of a part of her life she didn't want to share? He didn't like any of the answers that came to mind.

Tomorrow, he vowed, he'd get to the bottom of it. Before he fell asleep, he whispered in her ear one more time, "I love you, Juliet."

WHEN ROSS AWOKE the next morning, he was alone in the four-poster. Propping himself on one elbow, he looked around the room. He could hear water running in the attached bathroom and guessed that Juliet was washing up.

A few minutes later she emerged, dressed in a two-piece knit dress of royal blue. She was hooking the clasp on her watch and gave Ross a big smile when she saw that he was awake.

"You're finally awake."

"What time is it?"

"Not quite nine."

He grimaced as she twisted the louver on the blinds and a blast of sunshine brightened the room. "Why aren't you here beside me?"

"I have to meet my mother at church. She's taking the girls to Sunday school." She slid her feet into a pair of low heels.

Ross was not happy. He had hoped to have a serious discussion with her this morning—wrapped in each other's arms in a bed scented with memories of their lovemaking. He swung his legs over the edge of the bed and ran a hand around the back of his neck.

"Does this mean I don't get any breakfast?"

She gave him an apologetic look. "I have to leave in five minutes."

He moaned and wrapped the sheet around his middle. "What are you doing after church?"

"It's Sunday. We have to go to my mother's for dinner."

Again he felt her withdrawing from him, slowly squeezing him out of a part of her life. He suspected that even had it not been for Brenda, he wouldn't have been included in the Sunday dinner.

His disappointment must have shown, for she added, "Why don't you come over this evening after the girls are in bed? We could put a World War II movie in the VCR, and I could pop some popcorn.''

There it was again, Ross thought. *After the girls are in bed.* She was deliberately excluding him from spending time with Sara and Annie. ''I thought you hated World War II movies,'' he said a bit gruffly.

A smile lit her eyes. ''I'll pick out one with a love story.'' She glanced at her watch. ''I'd better go or I'm going to be late.'' She reached for her purse and started toward the door.

''Wait!'' Ross called out to her and she stopped. He got up from the bed and walked stark naked toward her. When he was only inches away from her, he pinned her against the door, a hand on either side of her head. ''You didn't tell me what you did with my clothes.''

''They're in the bathroom on the vanity.'' She wet her lips with the tip of her tongue as her body came into contact with his.

''In the bathroom, eh?'' he repeated, trailing kisses across her cheeks and down her jaw until his lips nuzzled the warm smooth column of her throat. ''What time do you want me back tonight?''

She turned her head to allow him better access to the sensitive skin. ''How about eight-thirty?'' she said softly, her breathing becoming shallow as his lips worked their magic.

He lifted his mouth to hers. ''Eight-thirty it is,'' he whispered against her lips, then sealed it with a kiss. He had intended the kiss to be short and sweet, but as usual, the minute he tasted her satiny-smooth lips he couldn't get enough of her, and their embrace became wild, hungry.

It was Juliet who pulled away. "If we don't stop, I'm not going to get to church on time...." she said raggedly.

He groaned and reluctantly released her. "I wish you had woken me earlier."

"I tried to, but you were dead to the world. Must have been all that driving you did yesterday," she said with a cheeky grin.

"I'm awake now," he growled. He pressed up close to her to prove his point.

"Ross, I'm on my way to church!" she protested, slipping out of his arms with a look of mock reproach. "What you need is coffee. I left a fresh pot brewing in the kitchen."

"A cold shower would be more effective."

"You can have both."

"But not you, right?"

"Sorry." She blew him a kiss. "Don't forget to turn the coffeemaker off before you leave." And with a wave of her fingers she was gone.

Ross found the coffee in the kitchen, and a clean bowl and spoon on the table next to a box of bran flakes. He smiled at Juliet's thoughtfulness. But it was only as he turned over the cup she had placed upside down on the saucer that he saw what she had done. In the middle of the off-white plate was a key to the house.

"HOW COME YOU BOUGHT this kind of cereal?" Sara asked her mother several hours later. They had stopped home after church, instead of going directly to her mother's, and the first thing Sara had noticed was the box of bran flakes on the table.

"I thought we should try something different," Juliet answered, noting that Ross had rinsed his breakfast dishes and left them in the sink. Memories of their night together brought a warm flush to her cheeks.

"Are these bran flakes?" Sara asked, wrinkling her nose as she suspiciously handled the box. Upon learning that they were, she said longingly, "I wish you'd buy us Cookie Crunchers. They give toys in their boxes."

"You don't need toys in your cereal. Besides, plain old oatmeal is much better for you than any sugar-coated cereal." Juliet took the box of bran flakes and put it in the cupboard. "Now, why don't you and Annie play for a while. I want to make a fruit salad to take to Grandma's for dinner."

As she watched the two of them skip out of the kitchen, Juliet tried not to think of the difficult afternoon ahead. In the past she had always looked forward to the Sunday family gatherings. Now she avoided them. And all because she knew there was bound to be awkwardness, and she would be the cause.

She was tempted to stay home, but thoughts of her mother made her put aside the temptation. She would never ease the strain in their relationship that way. And once she got through the afternoon, she could spend the evening with Ross.

If it weren't for Brenda, she'd be bringing Ross to dinner with her this afternoon. Instead, they were carrying on as though they were having some sort of clandestine affair, and she wondered if the day would ever come when he would be welcomed by her family.

She had sensed a change in her relationship with Ross last night. She wasn't sure how or why it had happened; all she knew was that something was different. She had wanted to tell him about the problems she was having with her ex-husband, but she wasn't yet confident of his feelings for her. Although she knew she pleased him physically, emotionally he hadn't given her any indication that he was ready to take on the problems of a divorced woman with two small children.

She kept thinking back to when they first met and how she had insisted there be no emotional entanglements. How would a man who had claimed he and domesticity didn't mix react to the domestic battle she was in?

What if their relationship was too fragile, too new, to be burdened with the kind of troubles she was experiencing? It frightened her to think he might be the kind of man who disappeared the minute he heard the words responsibility and commitment.

But they were words she thought about often that afternoon. Being around Donovan and her mother reminded her that love meant sharing and accepting each other's problems. She wanted the kind of relationship her mother had with her stepfather, not some temporary love affair that would fizzle out like a used firecracker. The question was whether Ross wanted the same thing.

Dinner at her mother's proved to be less stressful than Juliet had expected. Brenda had gone skiing with her friends, and because of a business trip, Meridee left shortly after dinner. Kate and Juliet cleaned up while George and Frances played gin rummy with Donovan. Kate took advantage of the circumstances to have a mother-daughter discussion.

"I'm glad you came today," she told Juliet as they worked together in the kitchen.

"It was a good dinner, Mom. Thanks for having us," Juliet said warmly.

Kate gently squeezed her shoulder. "You know I love having all of you around me—especially on Sunday. I miss you when you're not here."

There was a hint of reproach in her voice, and Juliet reacted defensively. "The reason I didn't come the past two weeks wasn't because I was sulking. I knew that if I was here, it would be awkward for everybody."

"Then what made you decide to come today?"

"Because I missed you, too," she said, her voice filled with emotion. "And something else happened this week."

"What was that?"

"Sara didn't get invited to a birthday party."

Her mother shot her a quizzical look.

"There was one little girl at school who invited every other girl in her class to her birthday party except Sara."

"But that's awful! She must have been crushed." Kate's eyes were sympathetic.

"To make matters worse, the little girl who deliberately excluded Sara is the same child I insisted Sara invite to her party—even though she didn't want to. Sara had told me time and again that this little girl was mean, but I made her invite her."

"I know it probably doesn't mean much right now, but you must know you did the right thing?"

"Maybe, but I was so angry, Mom, I called that little girl's mother and gave her a good piece of my mind."

"Did it do any good?"

Juliet chuckled. "It made me feel better. As for Sara...they sent her an invitation, and you know what she said to me? 'I don't want to go to her icky old party, Mom. She's too mean.'"

Kate looked as though she didn't know what to say.

"I mean, here I was, Mom, doing battle for my little baby, and she didn't even want to go." Juliet shook her head reflectively. "It made me realize that I felt her pain more deeply than she did."

"Mothers usually do," Kate said wisely.

"I know that now." Juliet gave her mother a hug and said, "And I know that when I hurt Brenda, I hurt you, too, and I'm sorry."

"Oh, Juliet, I don't like to see you hurting, either." Kate reassured her with an extra squeeze. "I wish I could protect all of my daughters from the hurt that's lurking out there in the real world, but I can't. No mother can."

Juliet sighed as she picked up the dish towel. "Why does it have to be that way? I've never felt so helpless as I have these past few weeks."

"You're doing everything you can to protect Sara and Annie."

"I only hope it's enough," she said grimly. "Tim is financially secure, he's remarried and he's doing everything in his power to make it look as though he and his Hollywood dollies have a healthy family life-style."

"Judges don't award custody to fathers simply because they make more money. You are Sara and Annie's mother. You're the one who's taken complete responsibility for their welfare. After the way Tim's behaved the judge has no right to even consider changing the custodial rights."

Juliet chewed on her lower lip. "Harvey's optimistic. I guess that's a good sign."

"Juliet, you haven't done anything that Tim could use against you, have you?"

"If you're referring to Ross, Mother, the answer is no," she stated unequivocally. "The girls don't even realize that we're dating."

"Are you going to tell Sara?"

"Eventually." Seeing the concern on her mother's face, she added, "It won't be a problem, Mom. She's crazy about him."

"That's what worries me."

"Why? Would you rather have her dislike him?" she asked with a sardonic chuckle.

"No, but I'm not sure it's such a good idea for Sara and Annie to become attached to him, either. Especially not Sara. She's already been abandoned by one man she trusted. I'm not sure she could handle it if it happened again."

Juliet wanted to say that Ross wouldn't do such a thing, that he'd never desert the three of them. But she couldn't make such a statement, for despite wanting to believe it, she didn't know if it was true, or how he really felt about her and the girls.

"What you're saying is, you don't think I should give Sara any reason to believe that Ross could be a father to her."

"I think it would be best if she regarded him as her piano teacher and not as your boyfriend," Kate admitted.

Juliet could tell from their conversation that her mother thought her affair with Ross would be short-lived. She wanted to shout out loud, He loves me and he's good for me and we're going to live happily ever after! Instead she promised her mother that she'd be very discreet in her relationship with Ross and not do anything to jeopardize Sara's emotional state.

Although she was happy that she and her mother had finally reconciled, Juliet was not in a very cheerful frame of mind when she went home. Until her mother had brought up the subject of Sara's perception of Ross, she hadn't given much thought to how her relationship with him might affect her children. He was so good with Sara and Annie, she hadn't considered the possibility they might suffer emotionally if he were to disappear from their lives.

It was just one more thing for her to worry about. As she drove home she decided it was one thing too many. The minute she stepped inside the kitchen, she walked over to the phone and dialed Ross's number.

"Hi. It's me. Look, I'm going to have to cancel our plans. I've got a splitting headache."

CHAPTER FOURTEEN

ROSS WAS NOT HAPPY that Juliet had canceled their date. Once again, the chance to tell her how he felt had eluded him, and it seemed as though circumstances were slipping out of his control. He needed to see her, to find out where things stood between them.

He suspected that her headache was in part due to spending the day with her family. Had they put pressure on her to stop seeing him? And if they had, would she heed it?

On Monday morning he called her to see how she was feeling, but there was no answer. When he did finally reach her, it was late in the afternoon and she had just picked up the girls from the baby-sitter. Upon hearing that she was feeling better, he suggested they have dinner together.

"Why don't I pick up some Chinese takeout and bring it over?"

"That sounds wonderful, but I'm afraid tonight's not a good night. Sara's school is having a carnival, and I promised I'd take her and Annie. We'll probably just have a light supper there."

Ross waited for her to ask him to join them, but she didn't. Instead, she said, "Maybe you could stop over later, after they're in bed."

"I'm doing the late show at the White Wolf," he told her, trying not to sound annoyed.

"What about lunch tomorrow?" she suggested. "I'm going to be on campus. I could meet you at the student union."

Ross was hoping for a more romantic setting in which to declare his love. The only other night he could see her that week was Friday. He hated to wait until then, but at least they would be alone. "What about dinner on Friday?"

She sighed. "Friday's my first day as the new dietary aide at the nursing home. I have to work from four until nine."

"Can't we make it a late dinner?" he asked.

"I guess we could," she answered tentatively.

"Is that a yes or a no?" Ross asked shortly.

"Yes."

"Good. I think we need to talk. What time should I pick you up?"

Again she hesitated. "I'd better check to make sure I can get a baby-sitter first."

He could feel her withdrawing from him again, and it left him feeling anxious. He wondered if it was something her family had said or if she was deliberately trying to keep a distance between them.

"Juliet, do you want to have dinner with me or not?" He hadn't meant for the words to sound so abrupt.

"Yes, I want to have dinner with you," she assured him in a soothing tone that reminded him of the way she would talk to Sara or Annie. "Maybe it would be better if you came over here. That way we won't have to worry about a sitter and we'll be alone—or almost alone."

"I'll bring dinner."

"Great. Look, I've got to go. I think Annie's into something she shouldn't be. I'll talk to you on Friday."

"We definitely will talk," Ross said as he replaced the receiver on the cradle. There was just one person he needed to see first. Someone he should have talked to long, long ago. Brenda Osborne.

JULIET CAME HOME from her first day at work wanting nothing more than to sit down and put her feet up. After seven years in a sedentary office job, she couldn't believe her feet could ache as badly as they did after standing constantly for four hours.

As soon as she had Annie and Sara tucked into bed, she took a hot bath, soaking in the revitalizing crystals her mother had given her for Christmas. Then she hurried to get ready for her dinner with Ross.

Instead of using the dining room, she threw a small tablecloth over the glass-topped coffee table in the living room and shoved it onto the furry rug in front of the fireplace. Then she arranged two place settings, one on either side. With a fire burning in the fireplace and a thick scented candle glowing on the table, it would be the perfect setting for Chinese takeout.

She had been nervously anticipating their meeting all week. Ross had sounded so tense on the phone, she had been imagining all sorts of horrible scenarios.

He'd come over and tell her he had accepted a job in another city. He'd remind her they had said no strings, and now it was time for him to be moving on. He'd tell her there wasn't much of a future for the two of them and that it was over.

It was a sense of foreboding she couldn't shake, and as she looked at the intimate setting in her living room, she knew that the real reason she had decided to eat in front of the fire had nothing to do with sitting on the floor; she wanted to re-create the intimacy they had shared in that room.

The minute she opened the door to him, she knew her apprehension had been warranted. Ross's face was set in a look of grim determination she'd never seen before. She smiled weakly in greeting.

"Brrr. It's cold," she said, rubbing her hands up and down her arms as he closed the door behind him. "I'm glad I started a fire."

"What should I do with this?" he asked, holding up the sacks with their dinner.

"Take it into the living room. I thought we'd eat in there," she told him, stepping gingerly across the hallway.

"What's wrong? Why are you limping?"

"My feet are sore. I don't think I sat down once the whole time I was at the nursing home."

"Apart from that, how was the new job? Do you think you're going to like being a dietary aide?"

"Once I get my feet broken in," she replied with a weary smile.

His features softened a bit. "You don't have to work again tomorrow, do you?"

She shook her head. "Uh-uh. I have a couple of days to get them in proper working order again."

As they ate sweet-and-sour pork, wontons and cheese puffs, their conversation was more like that of two polite friends than of intimate lovers. They talked about her classes at the university and the adjustments she was having to make as a full-time student.

Juliet knew that there was something very wrong. And it was making her nervous.

"You're uncomfortable with me being here tonight, aren't you?" Ross said as soon as they had finished dinner.

"No. Why would you think that?" she replied, hating the way her hands shook as she set her cup in the saucer.

"I thought maybe you had spoken to Brenda and found out that I had gone to see her."

"You went to see Brenda?" Juliet felt the hairs rise on the back of her neck. "Why?"

"Because I thought she was the reason why you wouldn't let me get close to you."

Juliet didn't understand what he was saying. All those times they had made love—hadn't it meant as much to him as it had to her? "Ross, we've been as close as two people can get."

"Physically, maybe. But there's a part of you I can't reach, Juliet. You won't let me in."

"That's not true," she declared.

"Then why haven't you told me about the custody suit your ex-husband has filed against you?"

Juliet didn't like the abruptness in his voice. "Brenda told you about that?"

"Obviously she thought it was a little bit more important for me to know than you did." He looked as though he were holding his anger carefully in check.

"That's not fair!" she cried. "I didn't tell you because I didn't want to burden you with my problems. I didn't think you'd be interested in my custodial battle with my ex-husband."

"Not interested?" He gave her a look of disbelief. "How can you say that?"

"You're a single man who's never been married."

"So that means I can't have any feelings for your children?" His anger poured out unstemmed.

Juliet shivered and lifted a hand to push back a stray wisp of red hair. "Of course not, but I didn't think it would be fair to unload my problems on you."

"Fair? Is that why you didn't want me going with you to the school carnival? And why you're always suggesting I time my visits so that Sara and Annie are in bed? Because you wanted to be fair to me?"

His tone was so harsh, Juliet flinched. "Why are you so angry with me? Just because I didn't want to involve you with the problems I'm having with my ex-husband?"

"What you really mean is you didn't want to involve me with your family. You didn't think I'd fit in. I don't quite measure up to the 'Miss Juliet' standard of a proper father figure," he bit out.

"You're wrong!" she said, frightened by his anger. "I do think you'd fit in with my family."

His answer was a tired laugh. "Brenda told me how you feel about me and your family."

"Brenda? What would Brenda know about how I feel?" she demanded. "She hasn't spoken to me in more than three weeks, and now look what she's done to us." She threw up her hands in frustration. "I don't understand why you went to see her when she's been nothing but trouble between us."

"Brenda isn't the problem here."

He actually sounded sympathetic toward her sister, and Juliet clenched her teeth to keep from shouting at him. She took a deep breath and said, "She certainly hasn't done anything to make life easier for us."

"At least she told me the truth," he said soberly.

"The truth?" Juliet mimicked in disbelief. "What truth?"

"Did you or did you not tell Brenda that I wasn't the right kind of man to fit into your family... that I didn't have a sufficiently respectable job to meet their standards?"

"Ross, you're talking about something I said before I knew you. I—"

"Did you or did you not say it, Juliet?" he interrupted.

"Yes, but I'm sure it wasn't the way Brenda made it sound." She tried to explain about her reservations concerning him as a date for Brenda, but he cut her off.

"I should have known better." He slowly shook his head in remorse. "You told me right from the start that I wasn't the kind of man you wanted in your life. You said no strings, no emotional entanglements. Only I was so captivated by you I wouldn't listen. I let you pull me in close, then push me right back out again like some kind of yo-yo. Every time I got too close to you, you spun me out and left me dangling."

"Ross, you have to let me explain," she pleaded.

"Explain what? That I'm not good enough to be a part of your daughters' lives?"

"I wish you'd quit saying that. It's not true. It's just that I have to put Sara and Annie's best interests first." She tried not to let her tears break loose. "I need to protect them."

"You think I'd hurt them?" His face twisted in disbelief.

"Not intentionally, no. But they're especially vulnerable right now, and as a single mother, I can't take any chances on them getting attached to someone who is only a transitory father figure."

"Is that how you see me? As a transitory father figure?"

His tone made her defensive. "You yourself told me you've lived in ten different cities since you left home. You're a man who's used to coming and going as he pleases with no family ties, no responsibilities. What was I supposed to do? Let my children get attached to a drifter?" She knew the minute the words had left her lips she had made a mistake.

"A drifter, eh?" The words were uttered with an almost deadly calm. Ross reached inside his pocket and pulled out the house key she had given him, tossing it up and down in his hand. "And here I thought you had given me this as a sign of your trust." He tossed the key onto the tablecloth. "I can see now you only wanted me to have it so I could sneak in and out in the middle of the night."

Juliet felt a pain stab her chest. She couldn't let him walk out of her life. "I wanted you to have it because I love you." The tears could no longer be stopped, and they poured down her cheeks unchecked.

Her words had no effect on Ross. He turned and started walking toward the door.

"Ross, where are you going?"

He didn't answer.

She followed after him. "Ross, please don't leave like this."

He pulled on his coat, and Juliet felt her heart tearing in two. "Please listen to me," she begged. "I didn't mean it the way it sounded... I know you're not a drifter." She placed a hand on his sleeve, but he shrugged it away.

"The sad part is, you don't know me at all," he said, then walked out the door.

JULIET HAD HOPED it was all a nightmare, that she'd wake up in the morning and discover it had been nothing but a dream. But the next morning, when she saw the dirty dishes in the living room, she knew it had been all too real.

Yesterday she had awakened to a sense of foreboding. Today it was emptiness. She felt as though she had lost her best friend, a feeling she didn't understand, since she had only known Ross two months. Yet in that time she had connected with him in a way she had never experienced with anyone else.

She tried to blame what had happened on her sister. If Brenda hadn't told Ross about the custody suit, he wouldn't have been angry, they wouldn't have exchanged words and he'd be here right now. But she knew that wasn't true.

She also tried to blame it on her mother. If Kate hadn't planted doubts concerning Sara's fondness for Ross, she would have encouraged him to get to know her children. But she knew that wasn't true, either.

She even tried to blame it on Tim. If he hadn't come back into their lives, she wouldn't have been so overprotective of Sara and Annie and so mistrustful of men in general. But the truth was, she couldn't blame her breakup with Ross on anyone but herself.

She hadn't trusted him enough to tell him how important he was to her. But then, he hadn't told her how important she was to him, either. She still didn't know what he felt for her—other than anger. He had made no declarations of love, no promises for the future.

The more she thought about it, the angrier she became. He had wanted her to commit to him, yet he had withheld the one thing that would have made it possible for her to do so. Not once had he told her he loved her and that he wanted to be a father to her children.

She wouldn't let it end this way. She couldn't! When he came for Sara's piano lesson, she'd make sure he understood exactly how she was feeling.

But he never came for Sara's lesson. Nor did he call to say he wasn't coming, which only fueled Juliet's growing frustration. Did he really care for her or was he relieved that they were breaking up and happy he could put the blame on her?

When another day passed and she didn't hear from him, she decided to pay a visit to the White Wolf, only to find that Ross wasn't expected for several days. The only information she could glean from one of the employees was that he was gone. Period.

Gone? Juliet didn't understand how he could up and leave in the middle of a school term. She went to the theater arts department at the university, hoping to get more information. Unfortunately, no one seemed able—or willing—to tell her anything about his sudden departure.

To make matters worse, the following morning her attorney phoned with the news that the court date for the custody hearing had been moved forward. As Harvey went over the possible outcomes, Juliet became even more nervous. Although her mother was supportive, what she needed more than anything was to talk to Ross. Being unable to reach him only reinforced her doubts about his reliability. Would he ever be there for her when she needed him or would there always be another audition, another gig? Maybe she was only fooling herself by thinking he would want to settle down and give up his life on the road.

That didn't stop her from wishing it was him every time the phone rang. However, by the time he finally called, her anger outweighed her anxiety.

"Why are you calling, Ross?" she demanded when she heard his voice.

He immediately became defensive. "You sound as though you don't want me to call."

"Where are you?"

"I'm at my apartment. I just got back from the West Coast, and I think we should have a talk." There was a brief silence, then he said, "It's important."

Normally it was not in her nature to be stubborn or unreasonable. But he had missed Sara's piano lesson, and he had left without telling her where or why he was going. So instead of telling him she missed him and she wanted to see him, too, she said, "I don't think that's a good idea." She was perversely pleased to hear his sigh of frustration.

"Juliet, I need to talk to you," he pleaded.

"I'm not interested in anything you have to say, and I really don't want you calling me," she told him childishly. Then she did something she hadn't done since she was a child. She hung up the receiver without so much as a word of warning.

She sat and stared at the phone, waiting for it to ring. But Ross didn't call back.

When someone pounded on the back door a half hour later, she swallowed hard at the thought that it was probably him. It was Brenda. Juliet's frustration poured out before she could think about the effect of her words. "Oh, good. Just the person I wanted to see."

Brenda's face twisted into a pout, and she spun around to leave again.

"Brenda, wait!" Juliet called out. Brenda paused, giving Juliet a petulant look over one shoulder. "Look, I'm sorry. Why don't you come in as long as you came all the way over here?"

"Do I have to do penance first?" Brenda asked dryly.

Juliet waved her inside. "It's supposed to be your home, too."

Brenda walked into the kitchen, looking as uncomfortable as Juliet was feeling. She pulled out a chair and sat down at the table, not bothering to take off her jacket. With her face looking as humble as Juliet had ever seen it, she said, "I came to apologize."

"Finally caving in to Mom's pressure, are you?" Juliet said cynically, standing with her arms folded across her chest as she leaned up against the counter.

Brenda rolled her eyes impatiently. "I'm not here because Mom made me come."

"Then you must have heard that Ross and I aren't seeing each other anymore and you're here to gloat."

"You and Ross broke up?" Brenda looked taken aback.

"As if you didn't know," Juliet said dryly.

"I didn't," Brenda insisted, her expressive face mirroring the truth of her words. There was no glimmer of satisfaction in her wide eyes. "When did this happen?"

"Right after you had your little chat with him."

"But that doesn't make any sense." She looked totally confused now.

"Why not? Everyone said he was wrong for me."

"I never said that."

"No, you haven't said anything to me for three weeks, but you were thinking it."

"Okay, so I've behaved badly, but you're wrong about that. I may have been green with envy, but I never thought Ross was wrong for you. I think you're lucky to have a guy like him fall in love with you."

"Yeah, real lucky," Juliet muttered sarcastically.

"What's with you?" Brenda shook her head and gave an ironic chuckle. "Boy, was Mom wrong about you. She said you knew how to accept an apology graciously." She gave Juliet a look that could have wrung remorse from the heart of a hardened criminal.

Feeling rightfully chastised, Juliet wearily dropped down onto a chair, her head in her hands. "This isn't the best of times for me, Brenda."

"I know it isn't and I'm sorry," her sister said, her voice softening with compassion. "That's why I wanted to get things straightened out between us. Jules, *I'm* worried about Sara and Annie, too."

Juliet looked up to see Brenda's troubled eyes staring into hers, and she felt her anger slowly fade. Brenda had always been close to Annie and Sara, and it was a relationship she treasured for her daughters.

She also knew that of the three Osborne sisters, Brenda had always been the one who had the most difficulty reconciling differences. It couldn't have been easy for her to come over this evening, especially when she was rarely the one to make the first overture.

Juliet reached across the table and covered her sister's hands with her own. "I never meant to hurt you, Brenda," she said, her voice breaking with emotion.

"A man was the last thing I ever wanted to come between us."

Brenda squeezed Juliet's hands. "I know that, Jules." She kept her eyes downcast as she talked. "But he doesn't have to be between us. That's why I came over. I realized that it doesn't matter whether or not you're involved with Ross. He still isn't going to be interested in me."

Juliet could see how hard it was for her to make that admission. "I'm sorry, Brenda."

She shrugged. "Ross was never interested in me the way I wanted him to be. I was a student of his, that's all, and it took me a while to realize that."

"If Ross had told me there was the slightest chance of the two of you getting together, I never would have gone out with him at all," Juliet said earnestly.

"I know that, too," Brenda told her. She pushed herself away from the table and walked over to get a glass of water. "He's too old for me, anyway. I don't need someone who's going to treat me like a father would," she said before taking a long sip.

"Why? What did he say?"

"When he found out I had dropped out of college, he gave me a lecture that sounded like what Dad would have said to me if he were alive." She dumped the remainder of her water out and set the glass on the counter.

"Brenda, just why did Ross come to see you?" Juliet asked, curious.

"Don't you know?"

Juliet shook her head.

"He was trying to patch things up between you and me. I thought you sent him," Brenda told her, leaning against the counter. "He told me he knew how important it was for you to have close ties with your sisters and that he'd do whatever was necessary to preserve that bond, including breaking up with you."

"He said he'd break up with me?"

Brenda nodded. "He told me nothing's more important than family. That's when I realized how foolishly I'd been behaving these past few weeks. I told him I didn't want him to break up with you because of me and that I was going to come see you and get things straightened out." She grinned sheepishly. "I guess it took me a few days to get up my courage."

Suddenly the conversation she had had with Ross made sense.

"Jules, the reason you and Ross broke up...it didn't have anything to do with me, did it?"

Juliet waved her hand distractedly. "It doesn't matter now."

"What do you mean it doesn't matter?"

Juliet sighed and shoved the hair back off her forehead. "I told you. We're not seeing each other anymore. Maybe Mom was right about Ross."

"Mom likes him," Brenda told her.

Juliet shook her head and laughed out loud. "No, I don't think so."

"Oh, yes, she does. She told me so," Brenda insisted. "She said there's something about him that reminds her of Dad. I think she's right."

Juliet cocked her head. "That's funny, because I felt that way, too, but I'm not sure why."

"Maybe it's his high energy level. He juggles an awful lot of stuff in his life—the theater, his music." Brenda came back over to the table and sat down again. "Jules, I think Dad would have liked him."

"You could be right," Juliet conceded with a wistful expression.

"It's not really over between the two of you, is it?"

Juliet shrugged. "I'm not sure. There are so many complications."

"One's been eliminated...me." Brenda grinned impishly. "Do you think we could maybe pretend these past few weeks didn't happen between us?"

For what seemed to be the zillionth time, Juliet conceded defeat to that grin. "Consider it done." She held out her hand for a handshake, but Brenda insisted on a hug. "There's nothing as important as family," Juliet said as they embraced.

"That's what Ross said," Brenda told her as they separated.

"Yes, but does he want to be a part of our family?"

"The only way you're going to find out is if you ask him."

"Ask him?"

"Golly, Jules, you're only eight years older than I am, but you'd think you were from another generation." Brenda rolled her eyes. "If you want the guy, go after him."

"I'll think about it," Juliet said evasively.

Brenda gave her a look of exasperation. "Don't be such a coward. The guy's probably dying for you to make the first move."

Juliet didn't believe it for a minute.

"Now that we've successfully erased three weeks of bad history, does this mean you're moving back in with me?" she wanted to know.

"Uh-uh. Once you patch things up with Ross, you'll be like a couple of lovebirds cooing around this place. But I will baby-sit for you whenever you need me."

"Thanks." Juliet gave her another grateful hug. "It's good to have my sister back."

GO AFTER HIM. Brenda's words haunted Juliet for most of the following day. Could she go after Ross? What if Brenda was wrong? What if he didn't want to be part of her family? Going after him could be risky business. If only he had given her some indication that he was planning for the two of them to share a future.

She had never been any good at going after what she wanted. As a child she had always been the one to wait to be invited to a friend's house, to wait to be asked to play. And now, the thought of going after a man was about as appealing as going to the dentist.

If only Ross would come after her, she thought miserably. After her treatment of him the last time he telephoned, she knew the chances were next to none that that would happen.

Besides a carpet-cleaning solicitor and her mother, the only other person to call that day was Harvey. Upon hearing his voice, Juliet felt her nerves tense in preparation for a new twist in the proceedings.

But Harvey surprised her by saying, "Are you ready for some good news?"

"Is the hearing being postponed?"

"Better than that, Juliet. Tim withdrew his petition. You've won."

"Tim withdrew? But why? I don't understand."

"Apparently he's changed his mind about seeking custody. From what I understand, he never really wanted custodial rights. He was only filing the petition because it seems your former in-laws set up a couple of trust funds Sara and Annie will inherit when they reach the age of twenty-five.''

"I know about that. They sent me copies of the documents.''

"Then you probably know that as long as you have custody of the girls, the trusts remain under the guardianship of the senior Harpers. However, if Tim were to become their legal guardian, he would gain access to the money. My guess is that it was a way for the Harpers to pressure Tim into seeking custody of the girls.''

"Are you saying he only wanted to get custody of them so he could get his hands on their money?'' The thought made Juliet cringe in distaste.

"That about sums it up.''

"So why did he withdraw the petition?''

"Your friend Mr. Stafford persuaded him it would be in his best interest.''

"Ross did what?''

"Mr. Stafford went to see Tim in California, didn't you know?''

"No, I didn't.''

"Well, at any rate, the subject's closed. I don't think you'll be hearing much from Tim in the future. You give those two little girls a kiss and hug for me, and I'll see that you get a copy of the formal papers.''

Juliet hung up the receiver, still stunned by Harvey's revelation. Ross had gone to California to see Tim. No wonder he had wanted to talk to her when he came back. And she had hung up on him!

She picked up the phone and quickly punched in the digits. "Mom, it's Juliet. Could you come over right away? I've got something important to tell you.''

CHAPTER FIFTEEN

JULIET STOOD IN A DARK, smoky section of the White Wolf, listening to the jazz combo adroitly segue from bebop to pop. Instead of sitting at a table, she chose to lean against a small ledge that ran the length of the wall. In the standing-room-only crowd, no one seemed to notice or care that she was by herself, and with the exception of a couple of interested glances in her direction, she drew little attention.

Anxiety clawed at her stomach as she waited for Ross to appear on stage. In the hour she had been there, she had heard Bubba announce twice that the saxophonist would be coming out shortly. She wondered what shortly meant to a jazz musician. Five minutes? Fifteen? An hour?

She glanced at her wrist and smiled to herself as she remembered Ross telling her she looked at her watch more than anyone he knew. That wasn't too difficult to believe. He moved in a crowd where time didn't mean the same thing as it did to people working nine-to-five.

The thought caused a few lingering doubts to surface. Maybe she had made a mistake in coming. She and Ross were so different. He was impulsive; she rarely did anything without a detailed outline. She had even sat down and planned what she would say to him tonight.

The longer she waited for him, the less confidence she had in her decision to go after him. Maybe if she had gone backstage as soon as she had arrived, she wouldn't be filled with such apprehension. She shook her head in self-recrimination. This was no time for second-guessing her plan. It would be easier just watching him for a while before confronting him face-to-face.

When Ross finally emerged from behind the dark velvet curtain, Juliet felt her confidence reassert itself. Dressed in black leather with several days' growth of beard darkening his jaw, he looked much the same as he had the first night she had seen him.

As he walked onto the stage, the crowd started to cheer and whistle. With good reason, Juliet thought as the mellifluous sounds of his sax filled the air. Briefly she closed her eyes, wanting the music to carry her away to that magical place where time didn't matter. As it had so many times before, his music seemed to float around her, enchanting her, touching her in a way nothing else ever could. When she opened her eyes and saw him on stage, she knew that she had been right to come.

Juliet's eyes never left his face as he performed. There was something almost wickedly delightful about being able to watch him when he had no idea that she was even in the room. Still, as exciting as it was to hear him play, she couldn't wait for the jazz combo to take a break so she could talk to him.

She decided she wouldn't wait. Grabbing a pen from her purse, she scribbled a message on a paper napkin, then handed it to one of the waitresses with instructions that it be given to Ross, and Ross alone. Surprised by her impulsive behavior, she stood back and watched the waitress work her way up to the stage.

The audience frequently sent up requests, but it was usually Bubba who fielded them. However, Ross could see by the expression on the waitress's face that the note in her hand was intended for him. Probably another request to hear "Songbird," he thought. A night seldom went by without someone asking to hear the song made popular by the saxophonist Kenny G.

Ross took the paper napkin from the waitress and flipped it open with a flick of his thumb. Written in red ink were the words, "If I promise to color outside the lines, will you play a little Beethoven for me?"

Ross felt as though a bird were fluttering inside his chest. He looked toward the exit behind the stage, but Juliet wasn't there. He looked out at the crowd, but the glare from the spotlights made faces indistinguishable. Shading his eyes with his hands, he took a second look, but he could only see a small portion of the crowd. None of the faces was Juliet's.

"You ready to do the Wainwright composition?" Bubba asked in his gravelly voice.

"Maybe we should try a little Beethoven instead," Ross suggested.

"Beethoven?" Bubba laughed and scratched his jaw. "What do you think this is? The symphony?"

Ross ignored his reaction. "Someone in the audience wants to hear Beethoven."

"Then he'd better truck on over to Orchestra Hall 'cuz there ain't no Beethoven in here," Bubba drawled good-humoredly. "Charlie Parker maybe, or Herbie Hancock, but no Beethoven."

Ross turned instead to the man at the piano. "Kenny, we've played Beethoven before, haven't we?"

The wiry man sitting at the piano answered with several bars of a concerto. Ross looked at Bubba. "See. Beethoven." Kenny proceeded to jazz up the classical piece, and one by one the other musicians joined in, improvising on the classical theme. When it was over, the crowd showed its approval with a thunderous round of applause.

"And that was Beethoven at the White Wolf," Bubba announced into the mike, then added in a lower voice, "By special request."

Ross looked again to the exit sign behind the stage, and this time Juliet was standing there. He knew how much she hated the nightclub scene, yet she was there waiting for him, looking totally out of her element. He wondered how he could have ever fallen in love with her. She needed order and schedules; he avoided looking at clocks or calendars. She was sentimental and steeped in traditions; he was a pro at cutting ties and moving on.

Then she smiled, the kind of smile that made him feel as though she had reached out with her delicate fingers and gently caressed his heart. It was the kind of smile that made him want to believe all the differences between them didn't matter.

"I need a break," he told Bubba. Not waiting for a response, he leaped off the stage and rushed to Juliet's side. He wanted to tell her how good she looked and how happy he was she was there, but a sudden nervousness made him say, "What are you doing here?"

"Gee, now I know how you feel," she answered with a shaky laugh.

Without even the hint of a smile, he silently ushered her backstage where the sounds of the nightclub became muted. He stared at her for several seconds, wishing he could read her expression. He couldn't, and he finally asked, "Why *are* you here?"

She moistened her lips with her tongue, then said, "Harvey told me you're the reason why Tim withdrew his petition. I'd like to say thank you, but somehow the words seem inadequate. I don't know how I'll ever be able to repay you for what you've done."

To Ross, the words sounded formal and rehearsed, and he was surprised she didn't offer her hand in gratitude. Disappointment robbed him of any hope he had harbored about salvaging their relationship. She hadn't come because she was in love with him. She had come out of gratitude.

He dropped his hands to his sides and looked away, feeling a bit foolish. She was the daughter of a congressman, brought up to say all of the proper things at the proper time. She had already told him he didn't fit in with her family, yet here he was expecting her to tell him the reason she had come to the club was because she couldn't bear to spend another night without him. So much for fantasies, he chided himself. Aloud, he said, "I didn't do it expecting to be thanked, Juliet."

"Why did you do it?" she asked, looking directly into his eyes.

He wanted to tell her that it had killed him to think of her suffering because of another man. That he'd do anything in his power to make her happy because he loved her. However, when he opened his mouth, none of the right words came out.

"I had to go to California to make a demo tape for some friends of mine. I figured as long as I was there it wouldn't hurt to look up my old college roommate. He's a private investigator."

"So you had him check up on Tim?"

Ross shrugged self-consciously. "I didn't like him from the moment I laid eyes on him. He looked like the type who'd sell his own mother for a swimming pool in the backyard and membership at the country club."

"Or take his daughters away from their mother to get his hands on their trust funds," she added.

He shoved his hands into his jacket pockets to keep from pulling her into his arms. "Yes, well, that's no longer a threat."

She looked up at him then, her eyes glossy with emotion. "How will I ever thank you?"

He turned away from her. "I told you, I didn't expect anything in return."

His voice was unusually rough, and Juliet thought she had made a mistake in coming to see him after all. He didn't want her there; he could barely stand to look at her.

Suddenly she needed to get away before she broke down in front of him. "I'd better go. You need to get back on stage," she managed to say despite the tears threatening to overwhelm her.

Ross turned around. For just a second Juliet thought she saw a flicker of desire in his eyes. It was brief and quickly hidden, but it was enough to remind her of what they had shared.

It also made her remember something her mother had said earlier that evening. There could only be one reason why a man like Ross would care whether or not Tim Harper had custody of Sara and Annie. Love . . . for her and her children.

Juliet couldn't walk away from him—not without a fight. What they had together had been too good to let slip away.

"Ross, I . . . I didn't just come to say thank-you tonight."

He looked at her expectantly, and the sparkle of interest in his eyes gave her the courage to go on. "I wanted to apologize for hanging up on you the other evening when you phoned. I'm sorry."

He shrugged. "You didn't want to talk to me."

"You're wrong. I did want to talk to you—badly. It's just that I was afraid."

"Afraid?"

She lowered her eyes and took a deep breath. "I was afraid that I'd tell you how I felt about you, that I'd scare you away."

"Scare me away?"

She lifted her eyes and met his curious gaze. "I thought if you knew how much I loved you, you'd take the next bus out of town." He didn't speak right away, and Juliet thought her heart would quit beating.

"I hate riding the bus," he said as he moved closer to her. "And I've grown rather fond of this town." He had hoped to make her smile, but apprehension still clouded her eyes. "And usually when two people love each other they make plans for the future—together."

"Do you love me, Ross?" she asked, her eyes full of hope.

He put his arms around her and kissed her tenderly. "Yes, I do love you, Juliet," he said huskily. "I thought I told you that every time we made love." He gently caressed her cheek. "They say actions speak louder than words."

"In that case..." She ended her sentence with a kiss that told him everything he wanted to know. They stood wrapped in each other's arms, foreheads gently pressed together.

"Oh, Ross, I've missed you."

"I've missed you, too, Juliet."

She tilted her head back and ignored the tiny flutter of nerves in her stomach. "Now, what about the future?" she asked boldly.

"I'll always love you, Juliet, but I'm not sure there's room in your future for me." For just a moment, he let his guard down and she saw the vulnerability there.

"My future includes a husband." She held her breath as she waited for his reaction.

"That's not what you were saying a couple of months ago," he reminded her with a wry grin.

"That's because a couple of months ago I didn't know I was going to fall in love with a man who would fill my soul with such very special things." She smiled at him, her blue eyes full of love and hope. "A man who is strong, yet capable of feeling gentle emotions. The kind of man I'd want as a father for my children."

"I want to be that man, but when it comes to family life, I'm a little short on experience."

"Why is that, Ross? Other than the fact that you don't have much family, you haven't told me anything about them."

"There's not much to tell. I'm an only child. When I was eleven, my parents divorced and I was sent to live with my grandparents."

"Why was that?" she probed gently.

"I couldn't go with my father because he was in the military. He still is."

"And your mother?"

"I guess she thought she'd have a better chance to make it big as a singer if she didn't have the responsibility of a child." There was no bitterness in his tone, just sadness. "It wasn't that she was a bad mother. She did what she thought would be best for me, too. Living out of a suitcase, moving from town to town, wouldn't have been any kind of a life for a kid."

To Juliet, it sounded as though he was still trying to convince himself that what he said was true.

"She never did make the big time, but she's still singing. She does opening numbers for several of the performers in Las Vegas." A small grin played at the corners of his mouth. "She's really quite good."

"Does she know you play the sax?"

"We're not estranged, Juliet," he said, sounding oddly defensive.

"I'm glad to hear that. Family is important, Ross," she said quietly.

"I never realized how important it was until I met yours." He lifted her chin with his fingertip and stared into her eyes. "I'm not a drifter, Juliet."

"Oh, Ross, I know you're not. I'm sorry I ever used that word. I know you thought I was deliberately trying to keep you from getting close to Sara and Annie, but the truth is, I was afraid to let you be a part of their lives, even though I wanted that more than anything. I didn't want them to be hurt, and circumstances seemed to be working against us."

She sighed and slowly shook her head. "First it was trying to keep our relationship secret. Then Tim showed up and announced that he wanted to change the custody agreement. That's when I realized that it wasn't just me I had to consider when I fantasized about a future with you. Sara was devastated when Tim walked out on us. I couldn't let her become emotionally bonded to another father figure who might one day decide he didn't want to be her father anymore."

"Why didn't you tell me this?"

"I wanted to, but maybe I just wasn't ready to trust any man after what I went through with Tim," she said thoughtfully. "And then, I really didn't know how you felt about me. You never told me." When he would have protested, she placed a finger over his lips. "You may have *shown* me, but you didn't *tell* me. We had both agreed there would be no strings."

"I want strings, Juliet," Ross said with conviction. "I want a wedding ring. I want to be a part of a family." He lifted her fingertips and kissed them. "I've wanted that ever since that day I came late for Sara's piano lesson and you were so angry with me."

"Why didn't you let me know?"

He shrugged. "Maybe I was a little afraid, too. Until I met you, I hadn't even considered getting married, having children. Maybe because I've never experienced being a part of a traditional family."

"Ross, I want you to be a part of my family."

"I want that, too, but I don't have a lot to offer, Juliet. I still have another year of school left before I get my doctorate, which means I'll probably have to continue doing some nightclub work until then."

"I thought you liked performing?"

"I do, but I have no great ambition to make it big in the music business. Being an entertainer means long, crazy hours and traveling on the road when I'd rather be at home with the woman I love. I'd rather work in the theater, and rumor has it there's a good chance I'll be offered a permanent position on staff at the university."

She tenderly brushed her lips across his. "Musician or set designer—it makes no difference as long as you share your life with me."

He studied her intently. "It's not going to be easy. We'll both be in school."

"You'll have an instant family."

"A family any man would be proud to call his." He gently tucked a strand of hair behind her ear. "When I discovered what kind of man Tim Harper was, I was filled with so much anger. I thought, here was a man who had had everything I wanted, yet he had thrown it all away." He looked into her eyes and declared, "I'm going to do everything in my power to protect you from him."

"He's always going to be Sara and Annie's natural father," she cautioned.

"I realize that, and I won't get in the way if they want him to be a part of their lives. But I won't let him hurt any of you, either. Did you know he has a gambling habit?"

Juliet looked surprised. "No. When we were married he had his weekly poker night with the guys, but that was only penny-ante stuff."

"He's in a little deeper than pennies now, I'm afraid. Apparently he's a regular visitor in Las Vegas."

"You're kidding!"

"Between roulette and the race track, he spends money faster than he can make it, according to my ex-roommate."

"That would explain why the child-support payments were so erratic."

He took her hands in his and gazed into her eyes lovingly. "You don't need to worry about that anymore. I'm going to take good care of all three of you."

She kissed him again. "When I'm with you, I feel as though there's not a single problem we can't solve together."

"That's because there isn't."

Bubba's raspy voice called out to them. "Hey, Stafford! Are you going to make some music or are you going to stand back here making time with your woman?"

"That depends. Want to try a little more classical music?"

"Not more Beethoven." Bubba wrinkled his nose.

"Get used to it, Bubba. It's here to stay." Ross gave Juliet a smile that warmed her from head to toe. Then, for her ears only, he added, "Forever."

EPILOGUE

"GRANDMA, DO YOU THINK my mom's gonna cry?" Sara asked Kate, who was adjusting the bow on her granddaughter's pink taffeta dress.

"Weddings are happy occasions, Sara," Kate said softly. "Let's hope your mom's all smiles." She gave both of her granddaughters one final appraisal and declared, "There. You two look perfect."

They were in the back of the church waiting for the ushers to seat them. Juliet and Meridee were only a few feet away, but behind the closed door of the dressing room.

"I hope I'm doing the right thing," Juliet said as she stood in front of the mirror, her fingers nervously tugging at the shirred bodice of her wedding dress.

"You're not having second thoughts about getting married, are you?" Meridee asked cautiously, running a critical eye up and down her sister's slim silk-and-taffeta dress. "If you are, you have about ten minutes to call it off."

"I don't want to call it off!" Juliet said, alarmed. "I'm a little uneasy about the way we're doing it, that's all. It's become such a big production. Look at me." She spread her hands expressively. "I look like I'm off to a New Year's Eve party."

"You look the way the bride of a jazz saxophonist should look," Meridee told her. "Trust me, your dress is perfect." Her fingers poufed out the hip-hugging ruffle circling her sister's trim figure. "It's glamorous, it's sophisticated..."

"It's not me," Juliet interrupted with a tiny moan. "I should have gone with the ivory chiffon."

"Chiffon is for mothers of the bride, and if you had chosen that dreary ivory dress, no one would notice your legs," Meridee answered, enviously eyeing the shapely legs protruding from the knee-length skirt.

"It's not my legs I'm worried about. It's all of *this.*" She gestured to the exposed skin on her shoulders and once more tugged at the shirred taffeta.

Meridee lightly brushed at her fingers. "If you keep doing that, the only place you're going to have that body highlighter is on the inside of your dress."

Juliet sighed impatiently and dropped her hands. "I feel funny in white."

Meridee exhaled a sigh of frustration. "Will you stop it? You're worrying about nothing. You heard what that woman in the bridal shop said. Just because this isn't your first marriage doesn't mean you can't wear white, and you, my dear sister, look drop-dead gorgeous in white."

Juliet forced a grateful smile to her face. "Is my hair all right?"

Meridee examined the cascade of red curls spilling out from under the satin headpiece. "Every inch of you looks perfect," she declared firmly.

The door to the dressing room opened and Brenda entered, an astonished look on her face. "Hey, Jules, you look like you could have stepped out of the pages of *Bride* magazine. That dress is perfect!"

"See." Meridee gave Juliet an "I told you so" glance as their eyes met once more in the full-length mirror.

"You are a lovely sight," her grandmother agreed, entering the room on Brenda's heels. "All of you look picture-perfect." Her gaze swept across her three granddaughters affectionately. "This is such a happy day for me." She dabbed at her eyes with her handkerchief.

"You were right about Ross, Gran. He really is a prince of a guy." Juliet put her arm around the fragile old lady and gave her a gentle hug.

"He's going to be a good father to Sara and Annie and a good husband to you," Gran continued on. "You're a lucky girl, Juliet."

"I know, Gran," Juliet said soothingly. "I'm happy, too."

"At least now I can stop worrying about *one* of my granddaughters," Gran said with a sigh.

Meridee muffled an automatic protest. "You don't need to worry about me, either, Gran."

The old lady's eyes brightened. "Does this mean you and Richard are going to be making an announcement?"

"No!" The word came quickly and emphatically. "Gran, I'm never going to marry Richard."

"Oh? I thought maybe he was the man for you."

"He wasn't even close, Gran." Seeing the concern in her grandmother's eyes, Meridee said in a lighter tone, "I think the fairy godmother's already set a limit of one Prince Charming per family."

"I hope not," Brenda piped up. "I'm counting on Gran finding one for me."

"You be patient," Gran replied, patting her hand. "Your time will come soon enough. But first, we have to get Meridee settled."

"I don't want to get married, Gran," Meridee answered in an exasperated tone.

"But Juliet does, and if we don't get moving, everyone's going to wonder where she is," Brenda interjected, reaching for one of the floral bouquets resting on the table. "Is everyone ready?"

Juliet took a deep breath. "I'm ready. Where's my bouquet?"

Meridee reached for the garland of pink roses and baby's breath and handed it to her. "Just make sure you don't toss this thing anywhere near me," she said in an aside her grandmother couldn't hear.

Juliet ignored her sister's comment and looked in the mirror one last time."

"Okay?" Brenda asked.

"Okay," Juliet replied.

"Then let the wedding begin," Brenda proclaimed, holding the door open for her sister.

Meridee was the last one out of the dressing room. As she passed, Brenda said in a low voice, "What's with you, Meridee? It would serve you right if you did catch the bouquet."

Meridee laughed. "I'm going to have my hands behind my back."

Brenda could only shake her head. "Someday you're going to be the one saying the wedding vows and I'm going to be the one laughing."

"In your dreams, little sister," Meridee answered smugly.

Kate stood to one side and smiled. She held out her arms to Juliet and enfolded her in a warm embrace, then followed her daughters into the church.

*　*　*　*　*

Look for Meridee's story,
SWINGING ON A STAR, in February.
There are more surprises in store
for the Osborne family
in the last book of the trilogy.

Harlequin Superromance®
Family ties...

SEVENTH HEAVEN
In the introduction to the Osborne family trilogy,
Kate Osborne finds her destiny with Police
Commissioner Donovan Cade.

Available in December

ON CLOUD NINE
Juliet Osborne's old-fashioned values are tested when
she meets jazz musician Ross Stafford, the object of
her younger sister's affections. Can Juliet only achieve
her heart's desire at the cost of her integrity?

Available in January

SWINGING ON A STAR
Meridee is Kate's oldest daughter, but very much her
own person. Determined to climb the corporate
ladder, she has never had time for love. But her life is
turned upside down when Zeb Farrell storms into
town determined to eliminate jobs in her company—
her sister's among them! Meridee is prepared to do
battle, but for once she's met her match.

Coming in February